These days, he removed his gun for no man and no woman.

Mal watched Frannie sleep. She'd finally dozed off about an hour ago, giving him one last glance from those big blue eyes. How was it that this woman he'd known less than thirty-six hours had given him two of the most frightening moments of his life?

Dammit, all he'd been looking for with Frannie was one night. One night of pleasure and comfort and release. Sex. An interlude. One night. It hadn't happened, and right now he wondered if he'd rest easy again until it did.

Her eyes snapped open, and her body jerked slightly, as if she'd awakened from a bad dream. Blue eyes settled on him, she smiled, and then her eyes fluttered closed again.

Damn.

Dear Reader,

Once again, we're back to offer you six fabulous romantic novels, the kind of book you'll just long to curl up with on a warm spring day. Leading off the month is award-winner Marie Ferrarella, whose *This Heart for Hire* is a reunion romance filled with the sharply drawn characters and witty banter you've come to expect from this talented writer.

Then check out Margaret Watson's *The Fugitive Bride,* the latest installment in her CAMERON, UTAH, miniseries. This FBI agent hero is about to learn all about love at the hands of his prime suspect. *Midnight Cinderella* is Eileen Wilks' second book for the line, and it's our WAY OUT WEST title. After all, there's just nothing like a cowboy! Our FAMILIES ARE FOREVER flash graces Kayla Daniels' *The Daddy Trap,* about a resolutely single hero faced with fatherhood—and love. *The Cop and Calamity Jane* is a suspenseful romp from the pen of talented Elane Osborn; you'll be laughing out loud as you read this one. Finally, welcome Linda Winstead Jones to the line. Already known for her historical romances, this author is about to make a name for herself in contemporary circles with *Bridger's Last Stand.*

Don't miss a single one—and then rejoin us next month, when we bring you six more examples of the best romantic writing around.

Yours,

Leslie J. Wainger
Executive Senior Editor

Please address questions and book requests to:
Silhouette Reader Service
U.S.: 3010 Walden Ave., P.O. Box 1325, Buffalo, NY 14269
Canadian: P.O. Box 609, Fort Erie, Ont. L2A 5X3

BRIDGER'S LAST STAND

LINDA WINSTEAD JONES

Silhouette®
INTIMATE™MOMENTS®

Published by Silhouette Books

America's Publisher of Contemporary Romance

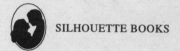

SILHOUETTE BOOKS

ISBN 0-373-07924-9

BRIDGER'S LAST STAND

Copyright © 1999 by Linda Winstead Jones

This edition published by arrangement with Harlequin Books S.A.

® and TM are trademarks of Harlequin Books S.A., used under license. Trademarks indicated with ® are registered in the United States Patent and Trademark Office, the Canadian Trade Marks Office and in other countries.

Printed in U.S.A.

LINDA WINSTEAD JONES

has loved books of all kinds for as long as she can remember, spending her leisure hours with Nancy Drew and Miss Marple, or lost in worlds created by writers like Margaret Mitchell and Robert Heinlein. After years as an avid reader she decided to try her hand at writing her own story. Since 1994 she's been publishing historical and fantasy romance, winning the Colorado Romance Writers' Award of Excellence for her 1996 time-travel story *Desperado's Gold*. With the publication of *Bridger's Last Stand* she steps into the exciting arena of contemporary romance.

At home in Alabama, she divides her time between her husband, three sons, two dogs, reading whatever she can get her hands on and writing romance.

A special thanks to
Homicide Detective Nadis Carlisle
of the Decatur Police Department,
for his time and invaluable insight.

Chapter 1

Someone had punched up a disgustingly cheerful seventies tune, and Mal considered, just for a moment, taking his revolver from the holster on his belt and putting an end to the high-pitched voice that was wailing gleefully about an all-night party. He stared into his glass, at what was left of his Jack Daniel's and Coke, and stifled the urge. Good cops didn't shoot jukeboxes.

From a booth in the far corner, a woman laughed loudly. Without turning to look, Mal knew it was the skinny redhead who'd arrived shortly after him to meet two other ladies for a girls' night out. Gigglers all, but the redhead had a particularly irritating laugh. She sounded remarkably like Wilma Flintstone.

The bar was all but deserted on this miserable Tuesday night. That's why he was here, after all, instead of at a bar where he knew friends—other cops—would be. He didn't want to talk to anyone, didn't want to answer another question or endure another pat on the back. He'd been in this place a few times, so he'd come here. It was usually packed on the weekends, but on weeknights after ten o'clock it was quiet, a good place to be alone.

Usually the weeknight patrons left the damned jukebox alone. The three giggling women in the corner, however, had been feeding quarters into it as if it were a slot machine.

At least the bar wasn't crowded. Besides the three women, there was a couple seated at one of the round tables in the middle of the room, and an old man who was a regular at Rick's Retro Bar 'n' Grill. And him.

He tensed as the door opened. Because this wasn't his usual hangout, where all the other cops went to unwind, he was alone and there was no one to watch his back. He might be off duty, but that didn't make him stupid. He was always aware of who was around, especially after a day like today. His nerves were raw, jumpy, and the Jack Daniel's hadn't even begun to settle them down. If this was a newspaper reporter, or another blasted airhead television "investigator," he was likely to lose it, here and now. He relaxed, though, when a lone woman came in, her eyes on the bartender and *not* on him. He watched with his peripheral vision as she slid onto a bar stool, leaving two empty stools between them.

"I'll give you five bucks to unplug that infernal machine," she said grumpily, waving a crumpled five-dollar bill at pretty boy Benny, who gave her a brilliant smile and shook his head.

Mal watched the woman, without appearing to, as she ordered her drink, a strawberry daiquiri, and slipped out of a dark all-weather coat that was still sparkling with raindrops. Her hair was wet, not soaked through but damp with dewlike moisture. It was raining. He wasn't surprised. It was a fitting end to a lousy day. He looked away as the woman tossed her coat over an empty barstool.

She didn't say anything else but placed her elbows on the bar and leaned forward, waiting patiently while Benny fixed her drink. The bartender was, as usual, efficient. She didn't have long to wait.

"Well." Behind the safety of the bar, Benny grinned brightly and planted himself between Mal and the woman. His face was tanned, his teeth were white, and his dark hair was moussed into a stupor. Though born and raised in Decatur, Alabama, he managed to talk without a trace of a Southern accent. It was damned unnatural. "I don't think I've ever seen two more miserable people in all my years as a bartender."

All his years? The kid was no more than twenty-five. Mal was not impressed.

The newest patron was concentrating on her frothy, fruity drink, leaning forward slightly so that her light blue sweater fell away from her body, giving Mal a glimpse of pale shoulder to the beginning swell of her breasts. There was only a small amount of skin exposed, but it was a powerfully tempting sight. Too tempting to linger on. A navy blue skirt came just to her knees, barely covering nice, long legs. His eyes really shouldn't have lingered there, either, but they had. She sipped her frozen drink through a straw but paused long enough to respond to Benny's comment.

"I've had a really bad day."

"Me, too," Mal mumbled.

The woman shot him a furtive glance between sips, her bright blue eyes set in a classically pretty face drilling right through him. Looking at him and into him. The effect was immediate and powerful and unexpected. At another time, in another place, on a better day, a man could get lost in eyes like those.

She had the look of the girl next-door —wholesome and healthy, a bright, clean-cut, all-American girl who was much too pretty to be sitting all alone in a bar on a Tuesday night. Surely she was waiting for someone, some lucky man whose day hadn't turned to crap before eight in the morning.

His wandering eyes lit on a damp strand of blond hair that brushed her cheek. Soft, barely curling hair, it was cut too short and in one of those ragged styles that was trendy and definitely beyond him.

When women found out he was a cop, their reactions almost always fell into one of two categories. They were abnormally fascinated or they were repulsed. He didn't care for either response, but he was used to them. Usually he could look at a woman and know which category she'd fall into, but he couldn't tell about this one.

"Really bad," he added, as if he had to defend himself.

She stared into her rapidly disappearing rose-colored drink. "I was fired," she said as she attacked the straw again.

Fired. That was nothing. People were fired every day.

She played with her strawberry daiquiri, swirling the straw through the frozen mix, lifting icy clumps on the end of the straw and watching them plop back into the glass. Finally she released the straw and swiveled to face him. "If I couldn't do my job I would understand, but to be fired because the boss's new fiancée needs a job, well, that hurts. He said I was late one time too many, but I don't buy it. I always make up my time when I come in late."

Mal answered with a noncommittal hum.

"My car's making a funny noise," she added.

He wouldn't touch that one with a ten-foot pole. Once you got involved with a woman's automotive troubles you were in too deep. He wasn't going to say a word. Hell, he didn't want to know, and he surely didn't *need* to know. "What kind of funny noise?" he asked, the male instinct within him unable to resist.

She made a harsh gurgling noise that made no sense, mechanically speaking, and Mal just shook his head.

"I got home," she continued, "to find five messages on my machine. All from my mother. She wants her only daughter—that would be me—to get married. She wants grandchildren before she's too old to bounce a baby on her frail old knee." Her sweet voice was laced with sarcasm. "I get this every time one of her friends has another grandchild," she said, before grasping the straw with restless fingers.

"She still doesn't understand why I broke up with my last boyfriend. Even though it's been over a year, she somehow thinks it's all a cruel joke Reese and I perpetuate just to distress her." She looked at him, a sidelong and somewhat suspicious glance, as if she were wondering whether she could trust him with her deepest secrets. "Reese, the guy I dated for almost two years and was engaged to for six months, and the boss who fired me today. That toad," she muttered under her breath.

Mal shook his head knowingly. "Messy."

She nodded in agreement and sucked down a good portion of her daiquiri. "And then," she said as she took her mouth from the straw, "some demon within suggested that I get a new haircut to cheer myself up." With both hands she framed her shaggy hair. "And I get this. Brutal, don't you think?"

"It looks nice," Mal said evenly, even though it was pretty bad. It was hard to tell exactly how bad, since she'd been out in the rain, but that didn't make any difference. He was old enough and savvy enough to know there were some questions a man never answered truthfully. *Does this dress make me look fat? Am I getting old? Isn't this a horrid haircut?*

She leaned toward him, and the wide neck of her lightweight sweater shifted again, just a little, to expose a generous portion of the gentle curve of her shoulder. His mouth went dry. Ah, God, he didn't need this now. On the other hand, maybe this was exactly what he needed. He stilled the urge to reach out and lay his fingers on that warm, soft-looking skin.

"Nice?" she asked incredulously, running her fingers through the short, jagged strands. "It looks like she used a weed-whacker instead of scissors."

He laughed. A few minutes ago he'd thought it impossible to ever laugh again, and now here he was...

"So," she said as she resumed the position above her drink. "What about you?"

Mal shook his head.

"Come on," she crooned. "I shared."

Mal grimaced. "I don't *share*. Ever."

She sighed and drew away from him, distancing herself physically and mentally. "Sorry," she mumbled. "Now don't I feel like a complete fool. I unburden myself to a perfect stranger—"

"Detective Bridger's not perfect," Benny interrupted.

Hell, he had that right.

Mal hesitated before looking up. She knew he was a cop, now. And he'd look into those big blue eyes and know what she felt, whether she was fascinated or disgusted. He didn't really want to see either.

But Benny moved down the bar, and Mal swung his stool around so he was facing this woman who'd had such a bad day. "I shot a man," he said softly. The truth, all of the ugly truth out in the open for the world to see. Funny, but he didn't see the too-bright light of obsession in her eyes, or the sudden distance of loathing. So he went on. "Jeff Thrasher, who already had an impressive record of burglaries and drug possession, tried to rob a convenience store. There were people in the store—a woman and her little boy on their way to school, a young girl picking up a quart of

milk, and a cop on his way to work, gassing up and grabbing that first cup of coffee.'' And a Twinkie, though he
wouldn't mention it. Sounded too much like the proverbial
doughnut.

''I take it you're the cop in question?''

Mal nodded. What, the woman didn't watch television
or listen to the radio? It had been all over the news. Every
time he'd turned his car radio on or caught a glimpse of
TV, the story had been there. He was sick of it, tired of
hearing the details again and again.

But for some reason he didn't mind telling it now. For
her. ''Thrasher was unhappy to find that there was only
twenty-four bucks in the cash register. Very unhappy. He
grabbed the clerk across the counter and started waving a
gun in his face. The woman screamed, and he spun around
and fired a shot that barely missed her.'' Mal had known
when he saw those eyes that Thrasher would kill everybody
in that store without a second thought.

''You killed him?''

''I killed him.'' It was the first time he'd said the words
aloud, and they came with a catch in his heart he couldn't
ignore. A thousand times in this long, hellish day, he'd
relived the moment when he'd pulled the trigger. A bullet
to the chest and one to the head, a textbook shooting. If he
hadn't stopped Thrasher when he had, someone else would
be dead. The woman or her little boy, the clerk or the girl
who'd dropped her milk when the shooter had spun around.
Maybe all of them.

He'd seen a lot in his years on the force, but he'd never
had to kill anyone before today.

''Oh.'' She nodded as if she understood perfectly. ''You
win,'' she said as she lifted her half empty glass in salute.
Bless her, he didn't see anything in her eyes but sympathy.
There was no pity there, no revulsion, none of the sick thrill
of someone else's tragedy.

''What's the prize?'' As soon as the flippant question was out of his mouth, he regretted it. She was an attractive woman, they were both drowning their sorrows; she was bound to take it the wrong way.

She didn't. She waved an elegant hand to Benny, indicating that this round was on her.

Mal scooted over one stool. So did she. His knee brushed against hers, and they both adjusted themselves quickly. ''Frannie Vaughn,'' she said when she was comfortably seated on her new perch, and she offered her hand as any man would do.

''Malcolm Bridger.'' He touched her, slid his fingers over her palm and wrapped them around her hand. Her fingers were delicate, her skin warm. ''But everybody calls me Mal.'' It felt so good to hold her hand, so satisfying, that he was reluctant to let it go. He had to, though. As his fingers slipped past hers the jukebox started up again.

''I thought disco was dead,'' Frannie said with a forlorn sigh.

It was a little late for second thoughts, but Frannie knew she really shouldn't drink at all. She'd never been able to handle more than a single glass of wine.

She did feel better now than she had when she'd come in, but she had a sneaking suspicion that the daiquiris had nothing to do with her improved mood. What was it about shared misery that could make even the worst day of her life seem tolerable?

So she had no job, no man in her life, no prospects for either. Decisions, important decisions, would have to be made, and soon. She had a mortgage to think of, and there was insurance, food, the last few car payments. Right now none of that mattered. She and Bridger had dismissed their problems, for a while, to come up with a few inventive and destructive ways to disable the jukebox.

She would have pegged him for a cop even if Benny hadn't called him "Detective Bridger," even if she hadn't spotted the weapon that peeked out from under his suit jacket when he moved just so, the badge that was hooked to his belt close to the gun. Cops held themselves differently, taller, cockier, even when sitting on a barstool. Add to that posture the no-nonsense haircut, the rock-hard jaw, the wary eyes that were never still, and you had a cop for sure.

The mere presence of the gun had scared her at first. God, she hated them! But after a while she'd managed to almost forget it was there. Bridger wasn't the type of man who would abuse the power a weapon gave him.

In spite of the fact that he'd had a day even worse than hers, in spite of the fact that he wore a gun so casually at his waist, there was a comforting air about Bridger, and somehow she was encompassed by it. That air was masculine and sheltering, so sheltering she knew nothing bad would touch her tonight.

The ladies in the corner booth left, talking about how in a few hours they'd have to get up to see kids off to school and husbands off to work. How mundane, how boring.

How wonderful.

The jukebox was still playing as they left. Just her luck. They'd fed so many quarters into the machine it might very well play all night. But as she was silently cursing the return of music from the seventies and eighties, a new song came up on the jukebox. This was one she could live with. "Loverboy," she whispered.

"What?" Bridger leaned in close.

She glanced at him and smiled. "On the jukebox." "This Could Be The Night" played softly. "Do you dance, Detective Bridger?"

He shook his head slowly. "Never."

Frannie slid from the bar stool, taking Bridger's hand as her feet hit the floor. "Never say never."

He followed her, hand in hand, to the small dance floor. His arm slipped around her waist and he eased her against him as they fell into an easy and graceful motion, as if they'd danced to this song a thousand times. It was nice, she thought. She liked the feel of his hard, warm fingers wrapped so carefully around her own, liked the feel of the strong arm around her. Heavens, the man smelled *good*. Not artificially sweet or tangy, like a cologne or aftershave might, but real. Malcolm Bridger smelled like a man, of warmth and musk and salty sweat. Under her hand, the muscles of his shoulder flexed as he moved, and she was so distracted by the sensation that she almost forgot to move with him.

They swayed easily, rhythmically and without conscious thought, and Frannie placed her head on Bridger's shoulder. His thighs slid against hers. "I love this song," she whispered. "When I was a kid I practically wore my cassette player out playing Loverboy over and over."

"Considering what we've been listening to all night, it's an improvement," he muttered, his mouth close to her ear.

She felt good here, sheltered from the rain and the reality outside these walls. It was Bridger more than the old familiar song, she realized, companionship rather than the daiquiris. Had she come to Rick's with the intention of hiding?

"I've never seen you here before," Bridger said softly.

Maybe the silence and the easy dance were too much for him, and he had to break the mood somehow. She understood. Heaven help her, it was quickly proving too much for her. She didn't want this song, or this night, to end.

"I'm usually in here for lunch a couple times a week. Benny makes a mean salad and a wicked cup of coffee." With every move, every gentle sway, she was somehow closer to Bridger. Heavens, too close. She lifted her head to look at him and backed up so there was a little more distance between her body and his. "The office is just a few blocks up the street."

The office. Just like that her troubles came rushing back. For more than three years she'd been a key player at Haywood's Southern Candies. She wrote software to accommodate the mail-order business, and she'd recently been working on an on-line catalog. Since it was a small company, she also answered phones on occasion, and played troubleshooter with clients as well as with her computers. Reese had no right to fire her. It wasn't fair, what was she going to do now?

Bridger swayed close, just a little bit too close, so that his scent teased her nostrils again. So Reese wasn't fair, right now it didn't matter.

The music came to an end, and they stopped moving. Bridger didn't let her go right away, but held her hand and kept a steadying arm around her. "Maybe we shouldn't blow up the jukebox after all," he whispered.

Another selection soon took the place of the slow love song, and the spell was broken. Harsh sounds filled the bar, and Frannie jerked her head around to look at the jukebox. "That's it," she said, forgetting Reese and her lost job.

Bridger's arms fell away. "What?" He faced the jukebox with her, his entire body alert as he faced an unseen threat.

"That's the noise my car's making." A man with a reverberating deep voice was repeating a short phrase, quick, choppy and harsh, the sound vibrating through tinny speakers. It sounded just like the engine of her Buick.

Bridger relaxed visibly and led her back to the bar. "I don't know a lot about cars, but I'd say that's at least a five-hundred-dollar noise."

"That's what I was afraid of."

They reclaimed their stools, side by side. The place was uncomfortably empty without the chattering women they'd listened to all evening. Frannie played with what was left of her drink. It was melted, unappetizing, and she'd had her limit, anyway. But she didn't want to leave. What did she have waiting for her at home? She loved her little house, but there was nothing—no one—waiting for her there. There were just messages from her mother and a little harsh reality, and she was in no mood to face either at the moment.

An old man, the last of the night's crowd but for Bridger and Frannie, tossed a bill onto the table and weaved his way to the door, waving over his shoulder to Benny.

"He's not going to drive, is he?" Frannie asked as she watched the man stumble, check the floor for a nonexistent hazard, and move on.

"No," Bridger answered. "He lives around the corner in that old department store they converted into apartments a couple years back."

"Last call," Benny called cheerfully, and they twirled around to face him as he placed two fresh drinks on the bar. "This round's on me."

The jukebox was silent at last. Benny was turning the chairs up on the tables that were scattered throughout the room, preparing to sweep up and close for the night.

Frannie didn't want to go home. She played with the drink before her, stabbing at the frozen concoction with her straw and drinking nothing, delaying the inevitable. Bridger was gloomy again, as miserable as he had been when she'd first arrived and seen him sitting there staring into his drink. Maybe he didn't want to go home, either.

They hadn't talked about the shooting since he'd told her what happened, but it had to be on his mind. He'd saved lives today, but he'd also taken one. That couldn't be easy. She glanced again at the gun he wore.

She liked Bridger too much. It wasn't just that he was pleasant to talk to, or that he was a great dancer. He had a kind soul, and she'd known it after talking to him for five minutes. She sat beside a kind soul in a six-foot-plus body, a guardian angel with a gun strapped to his belt, a man who could love a woman and protect her from anything.

Two drinks and she was hallucinating. "Good night, Detective Bridger," she said, a false brightness in her voice as she slid from the bar stool and put those ideas out of her mind. "Thanks for commiserating with me."

He mumbled something that sounded like "any time," but she couldn't be sure.

"Good night, Benny," she said without looking back. "I'm going to make one stop and then I'm headed for home."

She really didn't want to go home, back to the house that was small and yet too big for one person, back to the messages from her mother that she would eventually have to answer, back to the reality that she didn't have a job anymore. She was at a crossroads, and she didn't know where to go from here.

When she came out of the rest room, she was surprised to find Bridger waiting for her. He was leaning against the wall by the pay phone with his head down and his hands in his pockets. As the ladies' room door swung closed, he lifted his head.

When his eyes latched on to hers her heart skipped a beat. Malcolm Bridger had cop's eyes: eyes that had seen too much and never missed anything. How could eyes like that be anything but lonely?

"I can't let you drive home," he said softly.

"I walked," she said quickly. "I wanted to show that good-for-nothing car of mine that I didn't need it. My house isn't too far, I don't think it took me twenty minutes to get here." Of course, it had started raining on her when she'd been halfway to Rick's. Maybe walking hadn't been such a good idea after all.

"I'll drive you," he said, never moving from the spot where he'd planted his feet. She had the impression it was a statement, not an offer.

She was treading on very dangerous ground, and she knew it. She should play it safe, brush him off, call a cab, maybe laugh at him for good measure. Frannie Vaughn did not make a habit of picking up strangers in bars. She was a good girl, a cautious woman. Her mother had taught her well, by bad example if not design.

So why did she have the overwhelming desire to walk into Detective Bridger's arms and ask him to hold her tight? Why did she want to bury her face against his chest and breathe deeply once again? Loneliness, certainly. Lust, maybe. She wasn't particularly well acquainted with the latter.

"I need some fresh air," she said, and tearing her eyes away from Bridger, she headed for the door. He fell into step behind her, reaching past to open the door before she could do it herself. His arm almost encircled her and Frannie held her breath. When he stood this close something inside her changed, tightened and whirled and hinted at something more. This time, she was certain the daiquiris had nothing to do with her reaction. As she stepped through the door, Benny yelled a cheerful good-night.

The spring air had turned muggy and too warm, but the rain had stopped. Frannie stepped onto a wet sidewalk that was sporadically lit by streetlamps down the deserted avenue.

"I should just walk," she said, looking away from Bridger and down the long street. She jammed her hands into the pockets of her raincoat, and found the beginnings of a small hole in the left one. She worried it nervously with her middle finger.

It really wasn't all that far from Bank Street to her little house on Oak, and the walk would do her good. A wave and a smile and a cheerful good-night, and this was over. But she hesitated. She didn't want to be alone. Not tonight.

"I'll walk with you," Bridger offered.

Frannie had only known him a few hours, but she didn't imagine he was accustomed to anyone refusing his commands.

"I shouldn't be driving until my head clears a little, and besides, it's really not safe for you to walk home by yourself this time of night."

He was right, of course, though she hadn't given it much thought. And to be honest, she wasn't quite ready to tell Detective Bridger good-night. Against all her better judgment, she wanted him to lean close to her again. Just once. "This way," she said, pointing in the proper direction.

Downtown Decatur was deserted at this hour. After the music and chatter of Rick's, the silence was overwhelming. There was just the sound of their footsteps against the wet pavement, her sensible heels and Mal's shiny polished black shoes loud in the night, and the distant wail of a siren. Their images were reflected in the windows they passed, two figures together and yet separate, silent and lonely and dark. Why was she shivering?

As they passed one window, Frannie stopped without warning. Bridger stepped on, beyond her, and then did an abrupt turnabout.

"Are you all right?" he asked softly. She couldn't see his face nearly well enough. A colorless light from a streetlamp illuminated one half of his face, but she couldn't see his eyes clearly enough to suit her.

She took a step forward, toward him, and cocked her head to one side for a better angle of vision. "No," she confessed. "I'm not all right. This has been the worst day of my life. The very worst, and I don't want to..." She stopped suddenly. Bridger would think she was insane if she said what she was thinking aloud. What if he didn't feel it? The connection, the comfort.

Impossibly, he smiled, and the smile did good things to that hard face. Two long strides and he stood before her. The smile faded, and with a steady finger he lifted her chin so she was looking straight into dark, lonely eyes.

Thank God, he was going to kiss her. Relief shuddered through her, and Frannie closed her eyes as his mouth descended toward hers. She expected the contact but still, when Bridger laid his lips over hers, it was a shock. His mouth was warm and firm, and the kiss was perfectly innocent—for a moment.

As the kiss changed, his arms stole around her, hard, comforting arms that encircled and protected her. Her lips parted, his tongue tested and teased, and her insides turned to liquid fire. Just like that. Amazing.

She heard the rain before she felt it, fat drops that splattered on the sidewalk and her coat and Bridger's shoulders. A single drop found her face before he led her under the awning of the store they'd just passed.

His lips never left hers as he all but danced her to the window. The contact was light as his lips grazed across hers, then harder as he fastened his mouth to hers hungrily. The glass behind her and Bridger's arms around her provided all the support she would ever need. The rain came faster and harder all around them, but together they were safe here. Safe and warm.

Without warning, Bridger's mouth left hers. Frannie gasped, and fought the urge to grab him and bring his lips back to hers. His body leaned against hers, heavy and solid, and his arms held her tight.

"I think we'd better stop right now," he whispered huskily. "Before you get more than you bargained for."

Frannie slipped her hands beneath his jacket, placing her

palms against his waist. Beneath her hands he was solid, warm and hard and comforting, and the touch grounded her. *More than she bargained for.*

Heaven help her, she didn't want to spend the night alone. She'd joked all evening about this being the worst day of her life, but it was a fact. It was more than a lost job or a bad haircut or a funny noise in her engine. In truth, her mother's messages disturbed her more than all the rest.

Thirty-one years old, and she hadn't made a ripple in the sea of life, much less a splash. If she died on the spot she wouldn't be truly missed by anyone but her mother. Darlene, her hairdresser and her friend, might shed a tear or two, and Reese might feel a twinge of guilt for the way he'd treated her, but in a week or two it would be business as usual for the world around her. She was so tired of always being alone.

And in the middle of this crisis, along came Bridger. She was drawn to him in the strongest, strangest way, a way she couldn't begin to explain. She needed to touch him, to hold him awhile longer. With a bravery she didn't normally possess, Frannie rocked forward and kissed him. She surprised him, but his lips quickly molded to hers. Maybe, after the day he'd had, he didn't want to be alone, either.

Mal took Frannie's hand and they ran through the rain, back the way they'd come, to the nearest cross street. Raindrops fell, soft and plenty, over and around them as they ran. They turned the corner and there it was, its red neon light flashing garishly in the night and reflecting on the wet street and sidewalk. Riverwatch Hotel. The hotel had been in downtown Decatur for a hundred years, and perhaps it had once had a view of the river—from the roof. It had been elegant, perhaps even as little as thirty years ago; today it was just two steps up from a flophouse.

But it was close, and the rain was coming down harder. In the distance, thunder rumbled.

He pushed the door open and pulled Frannie into the lobby. The lights were too bright, showing off the faded and worn spots on the mismatched chairs and the wrinkles on the clerk who stood behind the counter. To his credit, the old man didn't even look surprised to have two late-night customers come in sopping wet.

The smile faded as his eyes lit on the gun on Mal's belt, turned to obvious suspicion when he noted the badge.

"I don't know anythin' about nothin'," the old man said as Mal stepped to the desk.

"Fine," Mal said, unable to resist wondering what went on in this old hotel. "I want a room."

The clerk narrowed his eyes and pushed the old-fashioned leather guest book slightly forward. Mal actually considered, for a moment, signing something clichéd like Mr. and Mrs. Smith. He took a quick glimpse at the names in the register, some scrawled and some neat, and noted several Smiths already among them, along with a Jane Doe and a number of Joneses.

Something was going on here. His reliable gut instinct told him there were probably any number of illegal activities taking place above his head at this very moment.

But for tonight, he wasn't a cop. It was rare that he found himself able to put who he was and what he did aside, even for a few hours, but tonight was different. Frannie made it different. He'd been wounded when he'd walked into Rick's tonight, and Frannie—with her big blue eyes and crooked smile and lazy dance—had made everything better. He wasn't ready to let her go, not just yet.

Whatever was going on here would still be going on tomorrow night, and the next, and the next.

He ended up writing his own name in the Riverwatch Hotel's guest book.

Chapter 2

The elevator was old and creaking and incredibly slow, and Frannie was sure that even in her slightly impaired condition she could have walked up the stairs to the fourth floor as quickly as this old elevator carried her.

Bridger hadn't said much since they'd left the lobby. He held her hand, though, and she found the gesture wonderfully sweet and intimate. His hand engulfed hers, but large and hard as that hand was, it was also tender and comforting. When his fingers twined through hers her heart jumped a little. She held on to him for dear life, and he held on to her just as surely. No kiss had ever been as intimate as this warm, tight connection.

As if Bridger knew what she was thinking, he pulled her into his arms and kissed her quickly. The light brush of his mouth across hers took her breath away, swept her up in a whirlwind of sensations so immediately intense and overwhelming they startled her. Her knees literally went weak.

"Second thoughts?" he whispered against her mouth.

She knew, without a doubt, that if she did have second thoughts Malcolm Bridger would let her go without so much as a single angry word. Tough as he was, Bridger was a gentleman in a world where gentlemen were rare. That certainty whisked away any fear she might have felt on this impulsive night.

"No," she said as the elevator lurched to a stop. "No second thoughts."

They were stationary for what seemed like forever, and Frannie thought for a moment that the elevator was broken and they were stuck here for the night. She positively hated contrary elevators. Good heavens, she hated *efficient* elevators. The very idea of being stuck in this tiny, airless box all night caused a flash of panic. The panic didn't last, though. Bridger was here, with his wide shoulders and his warm hands. With his gentle voice and tender lips. If she had to be trapped...the doors finally groaned and opened slowly.

"Tomorrow," she said softly, as much to herself as to Bridger, "I take the stairs."

Still holding her hand, Bridger guided her down a hallway covered by carpet that looked to be at least fifty years old. It was thin and faded so that the vines and flowers against the dark background were almost unidentifiable. Perhaps the carpet had once been a rich burgundy, but it was impossible to tell now. Randomly placed lamps in the walls lit their path with low-wattage bulbs behind milky glass, casting a dim yellow light over everything.

At intervals, delicate armchairs with faded padded seats and tiny tables sat, sporting vases of dusty silk flowers. They were sad attempts to make the old hotel more than it was—more what it had once been.

This entire night was like a dream, where nothing was as it should be. Bridger, the rain, this old hotel, they were somehow unreal. What was she doing here? she asked herself. But she asked only once.

Their room was at the end of the hall, and Frannie felt her first real burst of apprehension as Bridger placed the key in the lock, turned it and pushed the door open. The door creaked as it swung in, and Frannie held her breath. Then he reached in and flipped on a light, and her fears fell away.

The room was faded and old and out-of-date, like the rest of the Riverwatch Hotel, but it was also clean and bright and utterly charming. The air was a little musty, smelling like old books and mothballs, but she liked even that. She stepped inside with a smile on her face. It was like stepping into a dream.

"This is a wonderful room," she said. "Very shabbily chic." There was a single queen-size bed covered in a white chenille spread, a scarred desk and chair, a matching dresser, odds and ends—a ceramic cat, a lace doily, a small clock—scattered about the room as if this were a maiden aunt's guest room rather than a seedy hotel.

Bridger closed the door behind him, reminding Frannie of exactly why she was in this shabbily chic room at nearly two in the morning. The thud of the door was an ominous and promising sound.

If her brain was functioning properly she would slip out of this room, run down the stairs and have the little man at the front desk call her a cab. She should run away, run for home with whatever dignity she had left. It wasn't too late.

Who was she kidding? If her brain was functioning at all she wouldn't be here.

Bridger placed his hand on her shoulder and brushed the side of her neck with his thumb, and a bolt of warmth shot through her, reminding her clearly that her brain had nothing to do with her decision to be here. Nothing at all. Tonight she was listening to her soul, to her body, even to her heart. Not her brain.

"Chic?" he said softly. There was a comforting trace of humor in his voice.

"I like battered old things," she said, turning to face him. "They're warmer and much more interesting than anything new. You should see my house."

Malcolm Bridger had such a disarming smile, it made her heart skip a beat. That smile transformed his entire face, taking away the harshness but not the strength.

"Then you're gonna love me," he said as he lowered his mouth to kiss her again. Her dripping raincoat and his soaking wet clothes came between them as his mouth moved over hers in a softer caress than the one they'd shared in the rain, a sweeter, almost romantic kiss. He parted her lips with his tongue, teased and stroked and promised. A kiss like this could make a girl forget where she was, who she was. And tonight, Frannie wanted to forget.

Bridger's fingers slipped under the collar of her coat, pushed it gently aside, and then he placed his mouth against her skin, sucking gently there where neck became shoulder. A wave of pure sensation shot through Frannie at the moment of contact, a ripple that shook her to her toes. Hot lips lingered there for a long, wonderful moment, then traveled slowly to her shoulder.

When Bridger lifted his head he had an almost contented smile on his face. "I've wanted to do that all night," he whispered.

She raised a hand and placed her palm flat on his shirt. The contact steadied her, somehow. Through the wet fabric she could feel the heat and the hardness of his skin, the steady pounding of his heart.

"You're soaking wet."

"I know."

"You really should…"

He kissed her again, quickly this time. "I will."

Bridger broke away and headed for the bathroom, shrugging off his jacket as he went and draping it over the back of the wonderfully wretched chair at the desk. When the bathroom door closed behind him, Frannie took off her raincoat. She found a few hangers in the closet and hung the damp coat there.

Her stockings, shoes and purse were soaked, and she shed them quickly, laying them on a small, bare table that rocked on one short leg when she touched it. Her sweater was relatively dry, and so was her skirt. While Bridger was in the bathroom she took them off, slowly, carefully, not allowing herself to think too much about what she was doing. She folded each piece neatly and placed the small stack on the dresser.

Standing before the mirror above the dresser, wearing only a plain white slip and her sensible underwear, she had her first moment of panic. What in hell was she doing here? Yes, Bridger made her feel safe and warm and secure following a day when she'd felt only cold and uncertain. Yes, there was a connection between them she couldn't explain or deny. She wanted someone to hold her tonight, and she wanted that someone to be Malcolm Bridger.

Her hair was damp and standing out at all angles, and she straightened it as best she could. Darlene's styling spray and the rain had not been overly kind to her hair. When she discovered it couldn't be straightened, she ruffled it energetically.

Which was truly worse, a one-night stand with a perfectly agreeable stranger or yet another miserably lonely evening? Her nights were all the same—a little supper, a little television, maybe a book and off to bed by ten. It was becoming a comfortable routine, and she could see herself heading down the old-maid path.

Even her house fit the spinster stereotype, complete with rocking chairs and afghans and plenty of knickknacks of her own. All she needed to complete the picture was a cat or two.

There was something about Malcolm Bridger that touched her, that made her want to rebel against the routine she'd fallen into. Was he really so special, or had she sunk to a level of pure desperation? Maybe what she felt wasn't even lust. Maybe it was plain old fear.

She turned away from the mirror, not really anxious to study her life or her image at the moment.

The muffled roar of the shower told her Bridger would be a few minutes, and she went to the window to part the heavy drapes and look down on a peaceful, quiet town. She wanted peaceful and quiet, right? That's why she was here in Decatur instead of Birmingham or Atlanta or Nashville. She liked knowing her neighbors, being able to walk to the store or down the street to Darlene's to get her hair cut at a moment's notice. In this day and age crime was everywhere, but in this small town it didn't dominate the news or the minds of the residents. There were men like Bridger out there, watching the streets, keeping the town and its residents safe.

In the distance, a flash of lightning split the night sky. The rain came down harder than before, and at that moment Frannie put aside all her fears and doubts, dismissed the questions she would never be able to answer. For now, all that mattered was that she felt wonderfully comfortable in this shabby room.

She let the drapes fall closed and threw back the chenille cover on the queen-size bed. The white sheets looked clean and crisp and inviting, and she slipped into the enticing cocoon.

This had been the longest, most horrible day of her life, but tonight had been sweet and wonderful. As she settled herself into the lumpy mattress it became the most decadently cozy place in the world. What a wonderful place to hide.

Under the covers she curled into a ball. Rain pattered against the window, Bridger's shower roared, a boom of far-off thunder shook the night. Frannie smiled against the pillow. She was sheltered here. Safe. Nothing ugly would touch her tonight.

Mal cleared the mist from the mirror with the palm of his hand. He felt better—warm, almost dry, completely sober. Sober enough to wonder what the hell he was doing here.

He was getting too old for this. Hell, there wasn't a single condom in his wallet, and in this day and age of safe sex you didn't pick up pretty and willing women in bars without one. Or two. Not that he'd so much as entertained the notion of a one-night stand in the past few years.

But Frannie Vaughn was more than pretty and willing. She was irresistible. Maybe it was the legs, or the big blue eyes. And then again maybe it was that slightly crooked smile of hers, a mesmerizing smile she'd flashed a few times tonight.

"You *have* had a bad day," he mumbled to the man in the mirror. He needed a shave. He needed coffee. He needed to sleep for about three days.

But the truth of the matter was he needed Frannie. Here, now, and then again. Consequences be damned.

He needed Frannie to wash away the memories of this day. Needed her to make him forget that life was so fragile it could be taken away in a split second.

She'd done that all night, with her smile and her dance, with her laugh. With a kiss that wiped away the image that had been planted foremost in his mind all day—a man dead, a woman screaming, a kid crying as he held on to his mother's skirt. That little boy had been as scared of Mal, when it was all over and done, as he'd been of the man who had taken a shot at his mother. Mal remembered, all too vividly, looking at the kid and seeing pure terror in his wide, tear-filled eyes.

But for tonight, Frannie would help him forget. He wrapped a towel around his waist, turned away from the condemning face in the mirror and opened the bathroom door.

Frannie was a lump in the bed, and all he could see was her shock of blond hair. The lights were still on, each and every one of them. So she wasn't shy. Good. If he was going to make a mistake it might as well be a big one. If he was going to have sex with the perfect stranger he was going to do it right. All night and into the morning. Hard and fast the first time, slow and easy the next. With lights burning all around them, in the dark, in the sunlight. Laughing one minute, crying the next.

His earlier doubts were gone, swept away in the moment it took these images to become crystal clear in his head.

And then she snored.

It was a very small, quite feminine noise, but it was definitely a snore.

"Frannie?" he whispered as he stepped to the side of the bed. She was lying on her side, curled into a little ball of pale skin and white sheets. Her pink lips were parted, just barely, and her eyelashes lay dark and still on creamy cheeks. He could reach out and touch her, easy fingers against her face or her shoulder, in her hair, and she'd wake.

But he wouldn't. Frannie wasn't just dozing, she was out like a light.

He was frustrated, and at the same time a small part of him was relieved. With the effects of the Jack Daniel's fading, he knew very well what had happened here. Neither of them had wanted to be alone tonight, and so they'd found and clung to each other in the storm.

"Misery loves company," he whispered.

Rain beat against the windows, and thunder rumbled close by. Hell, he wasn't going anywhere tonight. He grabbed a blanket from the high shelf in the closet, turned off all the lights but the one in the bathroom, and, wearing only a Riverwatch Hotel towel, he very carefully lay down beside Frannie. The bed dipped and creaked, and a sleeping Frannie rolled toward him. Her body heat seeped quickly through the covers to warm his body, the softness of her breasts pressed against his arm, and he considered, again, reaching out to wake her. He needed her, needed another kiss, her body beneath and around his, warmth, passion. He needed to get lost in her tonight.

For some reason she trusted him. Enough to come to this place, enough to sleep beside him without so much as stirring. That naive trust made him think twice about reaching out to her. She must need this sleep she'd fallen into so quickly and completely.

He wouldn't get what he needed, not tonight. He knew that and accepted the fact grudgingly. So what should he do now?

Nothing, nothing at all. It was a big bed, Frannie was under the covers and he was on top, and dammit he was too old and too tired and not nearly noble enough to even consider sleeping on the floor.

Frannie didn't dream at all. She slept a deep and complete sleep that was exactly what her body and her mind had demanded. When she woke she didn't open her eyes, not right away. She was warm, and her body had burrowed into a comfy place in the soft mattress, and the arms around her were snug and secure.

Arms. She opened one eye and found herself staring at

a broad, muscled, only slightly hairy chest. Bits and pieces of the previous night came back to her, enough for her to know who he was, at least. Detective Malcolm Bridger, fellow hater of disco and a really good kisser.

She'd made a lot of mistakes in her life, but this one was a doozy. Exactly what had happened last night? She didn't remember a thing after climbing between the covers and closing her eyes for a moment of rest while she waited for Bridger to finish his shower.

He was still sound asleep, and she watched him for a few long minutes. When he was sleeping, he looked years younger. The tension was gone, though his features were still rock hard and somehow unyielding. It wasn't a pretty face, not by a long shot, but it was very, very nice.

He'd broken his nose, she realized as she studied him further, but it had healed nicely. A tiny scar jagged above his right eyebrow, white and thin and old. His mouth was relaxed, not grim and determined as it had been on occasion last night.

A blanket bunched at the end of the bed, tangled around his big feet, hanging over the side and to the floor. Long, muscular legs, dusted with dark hair, stretched up and up and up to his hips, where he wore a towel and nothing else. In the night the stark white towel had unknotted and twisted, and now it covered only the bare essentials.

She'd said something last night about liking old, battered things, and he'd said, "You're going to love me," in a wry voice. He did look a little battered, but this morning he didn't look old at all. He looked oddly beautiful.

Two daiquiris wouldn't make her forget anything, she was certain. She wore her slip and panties, and Bridger slept on top of the covers, she noticed. Maybe she hadn't forgotten anything about last night after all. Maybe nothing had happened.

She had to get out of here. Very carefully, Frannie ex-

tricated herself from Bridger's hold. She lifted the heavy
arm that encircled her waist, scooted toward the edge of
the bed and, with deliberate ease, placed his hand on the
mattress. The long fingers flexed, just once. His other arm
was beneath her, and all she had to do was roll carefully
away. She was terrified that she'd wake him. What would
she say if he opened his eyes and whispered a gruff good-
morning? If he took her hand and pulled her back into his
arms with the intention of finishing what they'd started last
night? She worried for nothing. Bridger was dead to the
world.

She sat up carefully, trying not to rock the mattress any
more than was necessary. Her head pounded and ached,
just a little, a gift from the daiquiris she was unaccustomed
to. She would never drink again, she swore to herself as
she rolled easily from the bed. She wouldn't ingest so much
as one of Darlene's rum balls at Christmas.

In the dim light cast through the half-closed bathroom
door, she dressed quickly, stepping into her skirt and pulling the sweater over her head, watching Bridger the entire
time for signs of life. His chest rose and fell with regularity,
his eyes remained closed, he didn't so much as stir. She
stuffed the panty hose into her purse and stepped quietly
into her shoes, listening for a telltale squeak that might
wake the man who was sleeping so soundly.

When she went to the closet for her raincoat, she hesitated only half a second before grabbing a thin blanket from
the top shelf and returning to the bed. For a moment she
stood over Bridger with the blanket clutched in her hands.
Without someone to hold on to, he was likely to catch a
chill.

Very carefully, she covered his wonderfully male body
with the blanket.

"Thank you," she whispered. She didn't know exactly
what she was thanking him for. For spending the night

talking to her and helping her forget her bad day, maybe. For not taking advantage of her last night, as he very well could have. For understanding.

She walked backward most of the way to the door, watching his face as she retreated. If only she'd met him somewhere other than Rick's. If only they hadn't been drowning their sorrows and ended up in a hotel. They might have dated a few times and taken it slowly, and then, maybe…she spun around and unlocked the door, and walked out on Malcolm Bridger and her stupid *what if*s.

"You're welcome," Mal murmured, opening his eyes as the door closed. If Frannie hadn't covered him with the blanket he never would have heard her leave, so he thought it only fair to allow her to make a clean getaway.

He reached for the clock on the bedside table, turning it and blinking until he could read the numbers. Almost seven. On a normal day he'd be getting ready for work, but this was not a normal day. He'd be on desk duty until the investigation into the shooting was done, and Harry was pressing him to make an appointment with the psychiatrist who was available to the department. Just what he needed—a visit with a shrink who would ask him about his childhood and his *feelings* and why he was thirty-seven years old and had never been married. He decided then and there that if Harry did bully him into a session, he wouldn't tell the shrink about Frannie. It seemed only right that he keep her to himself.

It was too bad things hadn't worked out differently last night. He liked Frannie Vaughn, a lot. He liked her goofy haircut and her crooked smile and her legs. She had great legs. Ah, it would have been great to spend the entire night making love to the perfect stranger.

He closed his eyes and drifted off to sleep, and dreamed of jukeboxes and blondes and great legs.

The dream, disjointed as it was, didn't last nearly long enough. The disco pulse became irregular, punctuated by beats as intrusive and annoying as the familiar voice calling his name.

Mal opened his eyes and rocked into a sitting position, checking the clock to see that nearly two hours had passed since Frannie had left the room. The drumbeat, a furious pounding on his door that echoed in his aching head, continued, as did the grating voice that called his name.

"Just a minute!" he shouted, realizing too late that shouting was *not* the way to go this morning.

He made his way to the door, the blanket Frannie had covered him with wrapped around his waist and trailing on the floor. One hand grasped the blanket, the other protected his pounding head.

He wanted to throw the door open and scowl at the man on the other side, but he had to satisfy himself with opening it slowly and glaring with one eye opened and the other firmly closed. "What the hell do you want?"

He expected Harry to flash his aggravating superior smile and make a joke, but his weathered face was serious. Too serious.

"What's up?" Mal backed away from the door and let Harry, the second-best cop in Decatur, in his opinion, into the room. Harry was built like a bulldog, short and solid, and when he went after something he was just as tenacious as one. "How did you find me?" Mal glanced toward the bathroom, wondering if his pager was vibrating and beeping as they spoke. Then he remembered that he'd turned it off before going into the bar last night.

"I didn't expect to see your name in the guest book of this rattrap, Mal," Harry said accusingly. "You want to explain to me what you're doing here?"

Mal tried to think of a simple way to explain the night that had passed. *I met a woman in a bar*…he couldn't say that. *It was raining…* also no good, since his car was just a few blocks away. ''No.'' He headed toward the bathroom and his clothes.

Harry waited while Mal stepped into his now-dry pants and shirt and strapped on the belt with his revolver and badge. He even grabbed the ruined tie from where it hung over the shower curtain, and slipped it around his neck. A glance in the mirror told him he was in bad need of a shave and a few more hours of sleep—and maybe a real vacation.

He sat on the side of the bed to put on his socks and shoes, grateful that the socks were completely dry.

''I called you a dozen times last night,'' Harry said accusingly. ''I went to three bars, all the usual places, looking for you, and no one had seen you since you left the station. You turned your cell phone off.''

Mal remembered very well turning the cellular off and slamming it into the glove compartment as he'd parked on Bank Street.

''I paged you, I went by your apartment. Darn it, Mal, Paula was worried sick.''

Mal actually smiled. Harry's new wife had him wrapped around her little finger. Poor Harry couldn't drink, curse or smoke anymore, thanks to Paula. She even had him on a diet, for all the good it was doing. Harry ate his salad and fruit at home like an obedient husband, but on the job he loved burgers and Twinkies as much as Mal did. The sergeant's little potbelly was there to stay.

''I'm a big boy, Harry. I don't need to check in with you and Paula on an hourly basis just because I've had a bad day.'' The facts of that *bad day* came back, and his smile faded away. ''I can take care of myself.''

Harry studied the hotel room with critical eyes. It was hell to be happily single, Mal thought not for the first time, and have a friend who was happily married. Paula, wife number three who at thirty-nine was ten years younger than

Harry, was always fixing Mal up with a cousin or a friend she thought was perfect for him. She wouldn't approve of this. Harry couldn't keep his mouth shut, not where Paula was concerned, so she was sure to get all the ugly details. Mal knew he was in for lectures, finger shakings, and at least three blind dates with some of Paula's *nice* girlfriends. He shuddered at the memory of the last of those disastrous excursions. Last night hadn't ended as he'd wanted, and he was still going to have to pay.

"Tell me about the woman you were with last night," Harry said in a soft voice Mal recognized too well. Harry used that voice to cajole confessions out of the toughest customers, and every warning bell and whistle in Mal's brain went off.

"What do you want to know about her?" he asked calmly.

Harry walked to the window and threw back the drapes, letting horridly bright sunlight into the room. Mal closed his eyes hard, then opened them slowly. The light turned Harry's gray hair a silvery white, and Mal had to squint against the unnatural brightness.

"I don't know how to tell you this." Harry slumped slightly, rounding his shoulders as he stared out the window. "Shoot, Mal, I didn't even know you were seeing anybody."

Mal didn't jump in to tell his old friend that he hadn't been, and still wasn't, seeing anyone.

Harry took a deep breath and jammed his hands into his pockets. "The handyman found a body in the stairwell an hour ago. A woman in her late twenties, early thirties maybe. Blond hair, no ID."

The shock pounded into Mal's chest and his brain, and for a minute he couldn't breathe, much less move or speak. Finally he stood slowly. His hands shook so slightly Harry surely wouldn't notice, and his knees wobbled uncertainly.

Blond hair. As clearly as if Frannie stood before him, he saw the way she had dragged her fingers through those pale, ragged strands. There was bound to be a number of blondes in this hotel, he reasoned. It could be anyone. Still his heart thudded much too fast.

"There's no handbag, so we figure maybe it was a mugging that went bad," Harry continued. "The killer got her throat clean and deep with a very sharp knife. Sam says whoever cut her got the carotid artery, so she lost consciousness just a few seconds later. She was dead within minutes." Harry's voice was gentle, almost consoling, as if to assure Mal that she hadn't suffered.

"Mal," he continued softly. "The desk clerk thinks she might be the woman who came in with you last night. I hate to ask you to do this…"

Mal knew what was coming, even as deep inside he prayed to be wrong. This happened to *other* people. He delivered the bad news, he didn't endure it himself.

"We need you to take a look."

Chapter 3

All Mal could think about, as he followed Harry down the long hall past the elevator, were Frannie's words as she'd stepped into this hallway last night. *Tomorrow, I take the stairs.*

He'd seen a lot of dead bodies in his lifetime, more than anyone should ever have to see. Strangers, mostly. A friend, once. It was never easy but he was tough, a cop for fifteen years, a homicide detective for the past five of those years. The prospect of viewing a dead body never unnerved him.

Until now.

He didn't know Frannie Vaughn, not really. A few hours of shared misery, a kiss or two or three, a promise of something wonderful that never came together...but as he approached the metal door with the word *stairs* stamped at eye level, his heart nearly stopped.

Mal tried to prepare himself for the worst as he followed Harry down a flight and a half of stairs. The stairwell was narrow and steep, the walls sported crude graffiti and ancient stains, and the concrete steps were cracked and crumbling. The air was stale, with an underlying, unidentifiable stench wafting from the dark corners. It was a lousy place to die, and he'd brought her here.

Mal's steps slowed as he and Harry neared the crime scene. His feet were like lead, his heart like a block of ice in his chest, and with every step it became harder to breathe. It couldn't be her. Frannie was alive and bright and beautiful, color in a black-and-white world, peace amidst turmoil. The desk clerk had to be wrong. Dear God, just this once…

They passed a uniformed officer who had been posted at the third-floor exit to keep the crime scene clear. Voices grew louder, gruff, lowered voices that echoed in the stairwell. Mal saw the blood first, a splash pattern that shot across a step at the bottom of this flight. He couldn't breathe, but he descended behind Harry. *I'm sorry, Frannie,* he thought as his momentum carried him down the stairs. *God help me, I never should have brought you here.*

He saw Sam Wingate, a member of the crime scene division, leaning over the body, silently and efficiently doing his job. There was more blood here. Too damn much blood.

He caught a glimpse of blond hair curving across the concrete, lying so obscenely close to a pool of blood his vision swam slightly. As his vision cleared he noticed that the hair was too long and a shade too dark. It wasn't Frannie. The relief that rushed through him would have brought him to his knees if he hadn't prepared himself for whatever might have been waiting.

"It's not her," he said. And then softer, as Sam moved aside and the distorted features of the victim came into view. "It's not her."

With that done he did his best to turn his mind to the case, asking questions, keeping cool. The anxiety hadn't completely gone, and he kept seeing Frannie's face and hearing her soft thank-you, but no one would ever know it. No one. Every now and then his fingers would twitch without warning. No one seemed to notice. Harry kept trying to remind him that he was on desk duty this week, and Mal kept ignoring him.

Eventually Harry gave up and filled him in on what little they had. He already knew that the body had been discovered by the handyman, Stanley Loudermilk, just over an hour ago. Loudermilk was not too bright, and had apparently become hysterical when he found the victim. He'd then checked to make sure she was dead, covering himself with her blood in the process. The guy was a ready-made suspect, but there was no murder weapon at the scene and none on Stanley, and the time lapse was so short he would have had to stash it nearby. Their lone suspect was currently at the hospital being treated for shock. He'd been escorted by two uniformed officers.

The desk clerk Clarence Doyle, the same old man who had signed Mal in and taken his money last night, hadn't seen anything. Big surprise. He'd taken a glimpse of the body and declared absently that it might be the blonde who'd come in with Bridger, though he hadn't paid close attention and couldn't be sure.

Mal followed Harry through the lobby and into the sunlight, trying to blink away the morning and dismiss the headache that was threatening to take his head off, trying to wipe away the fear that had consumed him when he'd thought it was Frannie lying dead in the stairwell. He'd never been that scared before. Never. He didn't like it.

"Go home," Harry said, turning to confront Mal before he reached his car. "You definitely need a day off, pal. Get some sleep. I'll keep you posted, I promise."

"You'll keep me posted?" Mal leaned forward, one eye practically closed as he tried to glare at his friend. "I don't like the idea. Somebody killed that woman right under my nose, and I don't like it. I don't like it at all. Then some half-blind old man says it might be a...a friend of mine, and scares ten years off my life.''

"I didn't know you were seeing anybody."

"I'm not," Mal snapped. "And don't try to change the subject. I'm going to be a boil on your butt until this case is solved."

"In other words," Harry deadpanned, "your usual self. A pain in the ass."

Mal grinned, even though he didn't feel like smiling at all. He was tired, he hurt all over, and he had a curious and insistent urge to see Frannie Vaughn to make sure for himself that she was still breathing. He wanted to touch her and prove to himself that her skin was as warm and soft as it had been last night. He wanted to lay his mouth over her neck, to feel for himself that the blood pumped strongly through her veins.

This was business. "Frannie Vaughn left the hotel during the estimated time frame for the death. Last night she said she was going to take the stairs instead of that ancient elevator, which means she either stepped over the body, or there's a good chance she saw something. I think we ought to talk to her."

"I think *I* ought to talk to her," Harry countered.

This time Mal's smile was a real one. Painful but real. "She knows me. She'll talk to me."

Under his breath Harry said, "Dagnabit," and turned away. "Well, come on then."

Mal followed obediently. His head hurt, and it was an abominably bright morning. "You got a pair of sunglasses in your car?"

Harry laughed at his distress, but then what were friends for? "In the glove compartment. Where does this Frannie Vaughn live, anyway?" he asked as he opened the driver's side door.

Mal collapsed onto the passenger seat and reached for the glove compartment. "I don't have any idea."

Frannie felt almost human again. Two cups of coffee and a long hot bath had almost done the trick. She'd happily discarded her sweater and skirt for a comfortable pair of pale green shorts and a matching T-shirt. There would be no heels for her today, even though it was a Wednesday. A pair of thick white socks covered her feet.

Three latherings of her hair had removed the styling spray Darlene had been more than generous with, and her hair was drying in soft curls rather than stiff spikes. She might be able to live with this haircut after all.

Focusing on her hair and getting her third cup of coffee just right almost took her mind off the man she'd left sleeping soundly in the Riverwatch Hotel. It even almost helped her to accept the fact that she no longer had a job, even though she was good at what she did.

She was usually unfailingly sensible, and she had enough money in her bank account to see her through a few months with no problem, longer if she was frugal. With her experience as a computer programmer she should be able to find a good job quickly—if she was willing to relocate to a bigger city.

But she loved this old house. It was small and always in need of one repair or another, but she'd put so much of herself into the place she couldn't let it go. Just last year she'd painted it a creamy yellow with white trim, and planted azaleas around the small front porch. The garden in the fenced backyard was bigger and more productive every year. She'd painted her bedroom a very pale pink, and was planning to paint the bathroom next. The claw-foot bathtub in the single large bathroom was decadently deep and comfortable. It was home. How could she give all this up?

Maybe this time off would give her the chance to do something with the second bedroom. Right now it was home to her computer…and every piece of junk she owned, as well as several storage boxes. With a little work, it would make a nice home office.

She hadn't really had a home growing up, not a haven like this house had become. Her mother had gone from husband to husband, from town to town, from man to man. Every time Frannie felt she was making a place for herself in a new home, whether it was a nice house or a trailer or a small apartment, there would be a fight or a tearful scene, and she and her mother would be on their own again. For a while, anyway. Lois Vaughn loved men, and she was never long without one. Unfortunately, she also had terrible taste where husbands were concerned.

Frannie's mind drifted again and again to Malcolm Bridger. Going to that hotel room with him had been reckless and stupid and downright dangerous, but she'd never felt anything other than safe in his company. She could close her eyes and remember how his body felt against hers. Dancing. Kissing. Just holding on. She could close her eyes and see him sleeping peacefully atop the chenille bedspread, his brown hair on a white pillow, his face rough with dark stubble and his chest rising and falling rhythmically. Looking downright adorable.

When someone knocked on her front door, she was glad of the interruption.

She opened the door and froze at the sight before her. Malcolm Bridger stood there, hiding behind dark glasses, conjured up by her senseless daydream. Don't panic, she told herself. It's just Bridger. In spite of her resolve to remain calm, her heart lurched in her chest.

Bridger looked bigger in the sunlight. Taller, broader, meaner. He wore the same suit he'd worn last night, only now it was wrinkled and limp. His jaw was rough with stubble that had been attractive on a sleeping man but just appeared slovenly on a man in a rumpled suit. He didn't look adorable at all. He looked like pure hell.

"Frannie…"

She slammed the door in his face.

A muffled and harsh bark of laughter came from the other side of the door. A bright, joyful laugh that wasn't Malcolm Bridger's, she knew.

Frannie rested her forehead against the closed door. The thought came, too late, that she shouldn't have slammed it in Bridger's face. He probably thought she was a basket case, a lunatic. She really should open the door again, she supposed. She didn't move.

The knock came again, softer than before. Frannie took a deep breath and opened the door slowly, and this time she saw that Bridger was not alone. An older man, another cop, she knew without bothering to look for the badge on his belt, stood just behind him. He was, no doubt, the man who'd laughed when she'd slammed the door.

This time Bridger stuck his foot in the doorway so she couldn't shut him out again.

"Frannie." Exasperation came through in the way he said her name, exasperation and more than a touch of weariness. "We need to ask you a few questions."

For a moment she was confused, but her confusion quickly turned to anger. Last night had obviously been some sort of setup. A sting gone wrong, a misdirected scam. Was she a suspect of some sort? When he'd spoken to her at the bar had he thought she was—her heart constricted in another wave of panic—a prostitute?

It was the story of her life, wasn't it? All her Prince Charmings eventually turned into slimy, disgusting toads.

"I haven't done anything wrong."

"Miss Vaughn," the older man said as he nudged

Bridger aside and took his place before her. "You're in no trouble, no trouble at all."

The officer had a soothing voice, a nice smile, and kind eyes. Frannie immediately relaxed.

"I'm Sergeant Harry Dixon. We hate to disturb you, but there was an incident this morning at the Riverwatch Hotel, and we're questioning everyone who was there."

"Oh." She opened the door wider and stepped back, relieved. "I thought..." Her eyes cut to Bridger. "Never mind. Come on in. I've got coffee."

They stepped into her house, right into the living room. "None for me," Sergeant Dixon said with a smile.

Frannie looked at Bridger, narrowing her eyes slightly as she studied his face. She hadn't expected to see him ever again, and here he was standing in her living room just a few hours after she'd slunk from the hotel bed they'd shared. She felt so guilty. For sneaking out while he slept— for being there with him in the first place.

"I'd kill for a cup," he mumbled. "Black." He didn't remove his sunglasses, but continued to hide behind them even though the light in her house was dimmed by barely opened venetian blinds.

Grateful for the excuse to leave Bridger and his sergeant behind for a few minutes, she fled to the kitchen to gather her composure while she poured a mug of coffee. There was no reason for alarm, she told herself as she chose a large white mug with a hand-painted sunflower on one side. They'd ask her a few questions about their *incident,* she'd tell them she didn't know anything, and then they'd be on their way.

There was no reason to be so embarrassed, either, even though Bridger probably thought she made a habit of getting sloshed and picking up strange men in bars. That couldn't be further from the truth, but she didn't need to explain herself to him. She didn't care what he thought.

What a lie that was, she admitted to herself as she slowly made her way to the living room. She cared very much. When she handed Bridger the mug of coffee she couldn't make herself look squarely at him, sunglasses or no sunglasses.

He took the cup without touching her. They engaged in a ballet of cautious movements, the way she offered the mug, the way he took it—first balancing the bottom of the mug on his palm and then taking the handle just as she released it. She didn't want to touch him at all, not even an innocent brush of fingers. Ha! Nothing about Bridger was innocent.

"Have a seat," she said, motioning to the white sofa. Dixon smiled and sat, withdrawing a small notepad from the pocket of his suit and snapping it open. Bridger lowered himself slowly, cradling the warm mug with both hands. She could almost feel sorry for him. She didn't feel so great herself. His head probably ached the way hers did, and he was probably hungry.

"What time did you leave the Riverwatch Hotel this morning, Miss Vaughn?" Dixon asked, pencil poised above the notepad.

Frannie opened her mouth to answer, but Bridger was quicker. "A little before seven," he growled.

She shot him an accusing glance. Had he been lying there pretending to sleep while she quietly dressed and slipped from the room? While she covered him with the blanket? While she whispered, "Thank you"? She could feel the blush rising in her cheeks, hot and unwanted. She couldn't very well deny her embarrassment now.

"Let the lady answer for herself," Dixon said with a hint of impatience.

"He's right," Frannie said as she sat in the rocking chair by the window. "I think it was ten till seven, to be exact."

Dixon made note of her answer.

"Did you take the stairs?" Bridger asked gruffly.

Dixon glanced sideways at Bridger, annoyance on his sturdy, pleasant face.

"Yes," she said, directing her answer and her attention to the man she'd spent the night with. She couldn't see his eyes behind the dark glasses, and it was just as well. Everything she'd seen and felt last night was obviously a lie. The connection, the security. If Bridger could play it cool, so could she.

"Did you see anyone?"

Dixon leaned back, evidently resigned to Bridger's interference. Eyes down, the sergeant gave his attention to his notepad.

Frannie took a deep breath. Her mind hadn't exactly been clear as she made her getaway, and she had to think for a moment. "A man in the hall, changing a lightbulb." Mentally she took the trip again, down the shabby hallway, past the elevator to the stairs. The stairwell hadn't been any more enjoyable than the elevator, and by the time she'd descended one flight she was wishing she'd endured another jolting and slow ride in that contraption.

"A woman on her way up, between the first and second floor," she added after thinking for a long moment. "I ran into her, literally. She was running up with her head down, and I wasn't exactly paying attention, and we collided. We spoke for a minute then moved on."

On the couch, Dixon's head popped up and Bridger leaned forward, tense and tight. "Describe her."

"Like I said, I wasn't paying a lot of attention." As she'd made her way down the stairs her only thought had been to get out of the place, but she couldn't say that, could she?

"It's important, Frannie," Bridger said softly.

She closed her eyes and tried to remember. "She was pretty. Tall and skinny, like a model. She was wearing a tight royal blue dress and matching high heels, like maybe she was just coming in after a long night out.'' Frannie opened her eyes and stared at Bridger. While she'd been sitting here with her eyes closed he'd removed his dark glasses, and she found herself looking into his all-knowing deep brown eyes.

"Hair," he prompted curtly.

"Medium," she said, doing her best to remember. "Light brown or dark blond, maybe shoulder length, maybe longer."

Dixon and Bridger exchanged a cryptic glance.

"You guys want to tell me what's going on here?" A hint of hysteria rose within her. She had a sudden feeling that something very wrong had taken place in that old hotel. "What kind of incident was this?"

"When you collided," Bridger said, ignoring her question, "what did she say?"

"She apologized and so did I, and then she asked me who did my hair."

"And you told her?"

"Sure. Why not?" Frannie took a deep breath and continued. "She said it was 'very cool,' and then she asked for my name so she could tell Darlene what kind of cut she wanted."

Dixon furiously scribbled notes, and Bridger stared at her, an odd expression on his stern face. "Anything else?"

Mal watched Frannie's face as she remembered what had happened. She was the perfect witness—clearheaded, specific, thoughtful. And all he could think of was how close she'd come to the killer. How she'd put herself in danger by taking the stairs. He wanted to cross the room and put his arms around her. Dammit, she'd given him the scare of his life, and she didn't even know it.

"No."

"Was she carrying anything? A handbag, a suitcase, anything at all."

"No...oh, wait. She had a small purse that matched her dress. A blue shoulder bag." Frannie grew more and more intrigued as the moments and the questions passed. He could see the curiosity in eyes that were boring into him. "What happened? Did she do something?"

"She was—"

"Hold on, Mal," Harry said, a hint of warning in his voice. Then he turned to Frannie. "Miss Vaughn, we'd like you to take a look at—"

"No." Mal placed his half-empty mug on the cluttered table by the sofa, amidst a number of ceramic angels. One or two of the figurines were perfect, but most were damaged. One had a chipped wing, and another had only half a halo. "It's not necessary." He didn't want Frannie to be forced to view what was left of the leggy blonde she'd passed on the stairs. It was hard enough for him, but for her it would be a moment she'd never forget, the kind of memory nightmares were made of. He could spare her that.

"The heck it's not," Harry seethed.

"A photograph," Mal conceded.

"Would someone please—" Frannie stood.

"It would be best if she came down to the—" Harry began.

"No," Mal said forcefully.

"We can't mollycoddle a witness just because you..."

Suddenly the room was filled with bright sunlight, and Mal covered his eyes instinctively, protectively. The headache he'd forgotten about came roaring back with a vengeance. When he peeked between two fingers he saw Frannie standing before the picture window, blinds raised to let the sunlight come blazing through. If not for the shade tree in her front yard, he'd probably be prostrate on Frannie Vaughn's floor right now.

"Would someone please tell me what's going on?" she demanded, hands on hips and eyes narrowed so that he knew she didn't like the bright light any more than he did. He hadn't seen her really angry before, not even last night as she'd talked about her lost job and her lousy ex-fiancé. But she was angry now.

"Sure." He kept his voice low, as soothing as he could manage, given the circumstances. "A woman was murdered this morning in the stairwell of the Riverwatch Hotel. From what we can tell, she was killed about the time you left. The woman you ran into on your way down matches her description."

It obviously wasn't what she was expecting to hear. Her eyes grew impossibly wide, and her knees shook slightly as she made her way back to the rocking chair.

He was already sure it was the same woman, though Frannie would have to make a positive ID. When it came to murder, nothing, not a single detail, was taken for granted.

Frannie had passed the handyman on the fourth floor, placing him close to the scene at the right time, but a case was rarely that simple. He had to ask. "Was there anyone in the lobby as you left? The clerk, maybe a customer checking out...anyone at all?"

She nodded slowly. "The desk clerk wasn't there, but there was a man standing by the elevator."

Her memory of the victim had been clear, her description perfect. Could they be so lucky? He pressed for more. "Describe him for me, Frannie."

She bit her lower lip while she contemplated. "He was kind of young, I think. I mean, not too old. His hair was dark. Brown, not black. Medium build...that's all I can remember."

It wasn't enough. "What was he wearing?"

"I don't remember," she whispered.

"Can you recall anything memorable about his face?"

She shook her head. "His back was to me, and I really didn't take a good look. If he'd run into me like she did, I'd remember, I swear I would."

Big blue eyes lifted to him, and Mal saw something there he didn't like. Fear. Uncertainty. Even worse, there was a plea in her eyes, and it was directed to him and him alone. It went deeper than last night's shared need, much too deep for his comfort.

"He scratched his neck," she said softly, raising her own hand to the back of her neck. "I don't guess that's any help."

Frannie had come very close to a killer and she knew it. How long after she'd left the stairwell had he struck? Minutes? Seconds? How close had he been? Whether it was Loudermilk on the fourth floor, or the man by the elevator, or someone else, she'd been too damn close. Right now she was scared and, dammit, he was scared for her.

As much as he wanted to, he couldn't comfort her, couldn't take away the fear. All he could do was his job, and his job was to find the person or persons who'd taken that leggy blonde's life in the stairwell of the Riverwatch Hotel.

Offering solace for a single night was one thing. That he could do. He'd wanted Frannie last night and he wanted her now just as badly. One way or another they were going to have their one-night stand.

But taking this woman—or any woman—under his wing and into his life and keeping her there was out of the question.

Chapter 4

Mal wrote his home phone number on the back of his business card, and handed it to Frannie as she showed him to the door. Her fingers fluttered, as if she were thinking of refusing, but after a moment's hesitation she took the card from him, pinching it between two pale fingers as if she'd really rather not so much as touch it.

Harry thanked Frannie for her cooperation and left with a promise to return the following day with the distressing but necessary photographs.

He knew that he should follow Harry with a curt and professional thanks of his own. But Mal found himself lagging behind as Harry made his way down the sidewalk to the car that was parked at the curb. Frannie looked so distraught, and rightly so, that he had the urge to reassure her, maybe take her hand and comfort her. Dangerous thoughts.

"I'm sorry you're a part of this," he said gruffly. "You never should've been there."

"Don't you dare lecture me—" she began.

"I'm not," he interrupted before she could go any further. "How could I? It was my fault. I never should have taken you to that place."

She relaxed but didn't look directly at him. The light that shone through the open door behind him turned her hair and her face golden. He wanted to see her eyes in the sunlight, to see if they were truly as clear a blue as he remembered.

"It's not your fault, Bridger." Her voice was soft, not quite a whisper. "It, uh, seemed like a good idea at the time."

"It did, didn't it." He couldn't help himself. His hand lifted to touch her neck, his fingers light there where the sun shone on creamy skin. Frannie stepped back almost immediately, but he got his wish. She looked straight at him. Yes, her eyes were every bit as blue as he remembered.

"It was a mistake," she insisted, though he didn't quite believe her. "Let's just forget it ever happened."

Forget? Not likely. "Sure."

There wasn't any reason for him to stay here any longer. Harry was waiting, Frannie had dismissed him, and he had work to do. Still he lingered. "Call me," he said, motioning to the card in her hand. "If you have any questions or if you remember anything else, just give me a call. I'll be in the office this week, during business hours, and in the evening you can call me at home. Or page me," he added quickly. "Or try me on my cell phone. Those numbers are on the front."

"I will," she said, but he had a feeling his business card was going to end up in the kitchen garbage on a nest of coffee grounds.

Mal backed out of the doorway and Frannie very quickly and firmly closed the door in his face. She couldn't be rid of him fast enough, apparently. He spun around to see

Harry leaning against the car, his pose casual, his gray hair silver in the sunlight.

"So," Harry said softly as Mal approached the car. "You think she did it?"

"No," he said, shocked that Harry could even consider Frannie a suspect. "No way."

Harry rounded the car slowly. "Why *no way?* Because she has a pretty face? Because she collects broken angels? Or maybe because you obviously have the hots for her?"

Mal stood by the passenger door and stared at Harry across the top of the tan Oldsmobile. "She's not the type."

With a despairing sigh, Harry leaned against his door. "There is no such thing as *the type,* and you know it. Remember that nice old lady who killed her son-in-law because he criticized her Thanksgiving turkey? The fifteen-year-old girl who killed her parents and then tried to make it look like a home invasion? How about that baby-faced kid last year—"

"Enough." Mal threw open the door and slid into Harry's car. "I get your point."

Harry was much calmer as he took his seat. "If it makes you feel any better I don't think she did it, either," he said casually. "Maybe Loudermilk's smarter than we think, and he's got us fooled. Then again, we could be looking at a simple robbery that went ugly. All that aside, odds are there's an angry husband or boyfriend or ex somewhere, and he's our man." Harry slammed his keys into the ignition.

"I just threw Miss Vaughn out there as a suspect to confirm a little suspicion of mine. A disturbing notion I have." His voice was soft, almost as if he were talking to himself. Still Mal had no doubt that the statement to come was for his benefit. "Detective Malcolm Bridger, thinking with his johnson."

"Leave my johnson out of this," Mal grumbled, his eyes

on the road as Harry started the car. He remembered the slam of Frannie's front door in his face…twice. "I am."

She'd checked every door and window twice, making sure the house was locked up tight and the blinds were tightly closed. It didn't make sense that she would be so nervous, but she was, and she had been all day.

The woman she'd passed in the stairwell that morning had been so alive, so pretty, and now…now she was gone. Frannie didn't want to see the pictures Sergeant Dixon insisted on bringing by tomorrow, but she would look at them and confirm that this was the woman she'd spoken to.

She pulled on her oversize football jersey and puttered around the house by the faint illumination of the bathroom light. One last sip of water, another check of the front door, and one more peek through the blinds in the living room. The driveway was empty, since Darlene's cousin Newton had carried her rebellious car off late that afternoon. He'd promised to have a look at it tomorrow and see if he couldn't figure out exactly what that noise in the engine was.

But the sight of the empty driveway made her feel even more alone than before. Why was she so nervous? This was her home, her haven, and she was safe here.

For tonight the bathroom light was staying on. A soft glow spilled down the hallway as she made her way to her room, lighting her footsteps on the hardwood floor. The distant glow made her room appear gray and shadowy, the pinks and greens drained of their color, the white no longer quite white.

The sleigh bed against the far wall was her pride and joy, a dusty bargain she'd picked up at a flea market and polished until the dark wood gleamed. This was the most elegant room in the house, with its rich polished wood grains and lace and ruffles. It was a small bedroom, but she had made it her own and she loved it.

She sat on the edge of her bed and glanced at the business card by the phone. She'd almost thrown it away. How long had she stood over the garbage can and tried to toss it out? She wasn't going to call Bridger, not for any reason. She wasn't going to remember anything else, and there was no other reason for her to call him. As she slipped her legs beneath the comforter, she took the card and looked at the numbers he'd scrawled on the back.

What an idiot she was! How many times today had she looked at those numbers? A dozen, surely, probably more. The prefix was the same as hers, and a simple arrangement of two numbers made up the rest. It was almost midnight. What would he do if she called him right now?

Frannie tossed the card onto the table where it landed by the phone. She could never call Bridger, no matter how much she wanted to do just that. Oh, she'd see him a time or two, maybe, as he investigated the murder at the Riverwatch Hotel, but it wouldn't be the same. It wouldn't be what she wanted.

The last thing she needed in her life was a man whose life was filled with violence. Her second stepfather, Phil Stone, had been a vicious man. They hadn't seen it in him at first, but after a few months with his new family he'd changed. He liked to hit, mostly. The back of a hand, his belt if it was handy, and on one occasion a fist. It was Frannie's mother who was on the receiving end of the abuse, most of the time, though Phil had managed to get his stepdaughter good one time. Just once.

Then one night he'd pulled a gun and threatened to kill them both. They'd been sitting on the couch watching television, and he'd come home drunk and waving a gun around.

Frannie had been eleven at the time, and she could still

remember looking down the barrel of the gun. She could still *see* it, the way the dark metal had reflected the light, and the little raised sight at the end of the barrel that seemed to be trained right on her.

It had been hours later, while Phil slept off his drunk, that Frannie and her mother had packed a single bag and left, catching the next bus and riding off in the middle of the night, afraid, until the bus was well out of town, that Phil was right behind them.

Frannie had never told her mother, but for years afterward she'd occasionally come awake in the night, startled out of a nightmare. Her eyes would fly open and she'd search the dark room, expecting Phil to be standing in a corner or in the closet with his gun pointed at her.

Her mother had married or almost married losers after Phil, but none of them had been that bad. None of them had made Frannie fear for her life.

As she lay safe in her bed she couldn't help but wonder if the woman in the stairwell had had time to fear for her life, or if she'd just…died.

Frannie pulled the covers over her head. What thoughts to be having at bedtime! She'd give herself nightmares, bad dreams of the doomed woman and Phil, of guns and knives.

But she surprised herself. When she did dream it was of Bridger, and it was most definitely *not* a nightmare.

Why was there never anything decent on television at two in the morning? Mal channel-surfed, searching for something even remotely entertaining. A bad movie, an old sitcom, anything. All he found was a bunch of infomercials and an old romantic comedy. He was definitely not in the mood for a romance of any kind, so he ended up vacillating between a show about car wax and another about spray-on hair.

His jacket had been tossed over the back of a chair, his

shoes kicked off, his tie loosened. He had been home more than two hours, but he hadn't even begun to unwind. In spite of the fact that Mal was on desk duty, Harry had allowed him to look at what little information they had about Decatur's latest murder victim, and he couldn't get the case off his mind.

There hadn't been a single defensive wound on the blonde's body, not so much as a scratch. Either the killer had taken her completely by surprise, or she knew him and thought she was safe up to the moment he cut her throat. Maybe she never saw it coming.

Loudermilk wasn't much of a suspect, in Mal's mind or in Harry's. Harry had always relied on his gut instincts, and that substantial gut of his was almost always accurate. Mal relied more on his brain. The guy just wasn't right. There was no history of violence, and he'd been clearly shaken by his encounter with the body. Still they couldn't eliminate anyone at this point.

Until they identified the blonde they wouldn't get far in the investigation. Fortunately, the victim had a small tattoo, a heart, on her ankle. That would help in identification, if nothing came up on the fingerprints.

They still had no murder weapon, and the closest thing they had to a witness was Frannie.

Frannie. Maybe she was the real reason he couldn't sleep. They were unfinished, a song half played, an unsolved mystery.

With a flick of his finger Mal switched back to the car wax. He really was hard up if he was sitting here in the middle of the night fantasizing about a woman who'd slammed her door in his face *twice* in the past twenty-four hours.

She wasn't sure what woke her. Still disoriented and more asleep than awake, Frannie rolled onto her stomach and grasped her pillow tight. What was that dream? Oh yes. She smiled against the pillow and tried to recapture her dream. Bridger.

She was almost asleep again when she heard the noise, probably the same noise that had awakened her. It was not much more than a scrape—a shoe across the hardwood floor, a drawer being opened and closed, perhaps—but it didn't belong, not here, not now. She lifted her head and listened. All was silent for a moment, and then she heard the distinct sound of a drawer in the kitchen being closed.

Her heart lurched and every muscle in her body tensed. Someone was in the house.

For a few very long seconds she was frozen. What should she do? If she headed for the door she might run into the intruder, if she stayed here he might make his way to the bedroom and she'd be trapped. She looked at the window in one wall. Standing in front of that window she'd be fully exposed to the hallway, and since that particular window was painted shut it wouldn't be an easy—or silent—task to open it.

She slid quietly from the bed to the floor, hiding in the shadows and bringing her bedside phone and Bridger's business card with her. Curled up with her back against the bed, she very carefully lifted the receiver from the cradle. The dial tone sounded incredibly loud. Frannie pressed the phone tightly to her ear and prayed silently that the intruder wouldn't hear it.

She glanced at the card by the glow of the lighted dial, and without hesitation dialed Bridger's number. Surely he was home, surely he wasn't such a sound sleeper that the phone wouldn't wake him up. He picked up the phone on the second ring, and his hello was clear and alert.

"Bridger," she whispered. "There's somebody in my house."

"What?"

She didn't dare talk much louder, but she raised her voice a little bit. "There's somebody in my house!"

"Frannie?" He didn't sound so cool now. "Have you called 9-1-1?"

"No," she breathed.

"I'm calling right now from my cell phone," he snapped. She could hear him dialing and speaking in the background, his words clipped and commanding. She listened to the distant words, which were almost as loud as the pounding of her heart. When he was finished, he came back to her, his voice comforting in her ear. "I'm on my way."

"No!" she said, a whole new panic welling up. "Stay on the line, please. Don't leave me."

"Frannie…"

"Don't leave me," she whispered again, hating the desperation she heard in her own voice, unable to deny it. The only thing worse than waiting in the dark for the intruder to find her would be waiting alone. She clutched the phone the way she wanted to clutch Bridger; she held on for dear life.

"The patrol cars will be there soon," he assured her, his voice tight but calm. The very sound of his voice made her heart rate slow, and she was able to take a deep breath. "And as soon as they arrive and you're safe, I'm going to hang up the phone and come over there, all right?"

"Yes," she whispered, leaning against the mattress and closing her eyes. She'd been right all along. She wasn't delusional, after all. Bridger really was a six-foot-plus guardian angel.

She waited to hear the wail of sirens; all was silent but for Bridger's soft voice in her ear. He reassured her, telling her the patrol cars would be there soon, advising her to breathe deep and easy. Amazingly the sound of his voice, the fact that he was *here,* comforted her, and she was able to do as he instructed. She could breathe again.

She didn't hear the intruder again, and she thought—she hoped—that maybe he'd left, sneaking out of her house as silently as he'd sneaked in.

And then she heard the shuffle again, a shoe against her hardwood floor. Only this time it was closer. This time it was in the hallway outside her room. She was afraid even to whisper into the phone.

If he would step into the spare bedroom, maybe she'd have a chance to pass him, to run down the hall and make it to the front door before he came into this room. She wasn't very brave, and the idea of running past the open door while he searched that room full of junk terrified her. But if that was her only way out of here she'd do it. She listened carefully, waiting for her cue.

She saw the shadow first, a long shadow blocking the light from the bathroom, a shadow that moved and danced across her wall and floor. He wasn't going into the spare bedroom after all, but was stepping into this room. Hiding here beside the bed, she was trapped.

The figure of a man came into view, and somehow he knew right where to look for her. His face was hidden behind a stocking cap with crudely cut holes for his eyes and mouth. With a gun in one hand pointed steadily at her, he stooped to take the phone cable in the other.

"No," she whispered, and he yanked forcefully at the cord, ripping it from the wall jack. The phone went dead.

"No." The single word was not much louder than the breath he'd been listening to, but it sent a shiver down his spine.

Then there was a sharp click, a moment of dead silence, and a dial tone.

Mal was ready to go, since he had slipped on his shoes

and grabbed his car keys while he'd been whispering to Frannie. Now he dropped his phone, grabbed the cellular and rushed out the door. He was dialing as he ran down the steps outside his apartment.

"Where the hell are they?" he shouted into the phone when the dispatcher picked up. "There's someone in her house, did you not understand that? He's *in her house!*"

"The officers are on their way, Detective Bridger," the dispatcher said, insanely calm.

"If anything happens to her I'm going to get some badges and some butts, you hear me?"

He punched the end button before she could respond, and jumped into his car. As he peeled out of the parking lot, the dead body he'd seen that morning flashed into his mind.

Bridger wasn't there anymore, but Frannie continued to grasp the phone as if it were her lifeline.

The light from the hallway fell on the gun the intruder held—a steady, dangerous, threatening gun that was pointing right at her. She couldn't see anything else.

"Where is it?" he whispered.

Something in her brain wasn't functioning. She felt detached, disoriented. "What?"

"Where is it?" he asked again, louder this time, punctuating each word with a jab of his gun. Just like Phil, she thought distantly. A bully, a menace, an unpredictable bomb waiting to go off.

Frannie took a deep breath. If she panicked, he would kill her. He wanted her fear, maybe he even needed it. Just like Phil. "Where is *what?*" she asked, trying to stay calm. Her voice shook, and she continued to grasp the dead phone.

"Make this easy for both of us," he whispered hoarsely. "Just give me what I want and nobody gets hurt."

Frannie huddled on the floor, trying to make herself small, trying to disappear. "This is a mistake," she breathed. "I don't know what you want."

He took a single step forward, and then his head snapped to one side. As he was looking down the hallway Frannie heard what he'd no doubt heard first. Sirens, growing closer with every heartbeat.

While he was distracted, she gathered every bit of courage she had. Tossing the phone aside, she jumped to her feet and ran. She didn't look at the intruder, sure that if she did the sight would paralyze her. She had to pass close, too close, to get past him and into the hallway.

He reached out to grab her, his fingers brushing against her jersey as she passed. His grip slowed her for a split second, and then she was free.

The sirens were louder now, they were on this street. She didn't look back, but she wondered, with every step, if the intruder would simply point the gun and pull the trigger. Her back made a clear target in this narrow hallway, the orange number seven on the jersey a bright bull's-eye.

She heard a sharp *crack,* and waited for the pain and impact of a bullet in her back, but there was no pain, no impact.

Until she stepped out of the hallway and into the living room, she didn't breathe. Her heart was pumping too hard, her lungs ached, as she headed for the front door. The sirens were right outside now, and blue and red lights flashed mutely through the closed venetian blinds.

She threw the door open seconds before the responding officers would have reached it. They ran, weapons in hands, up the sidewalk from the street to her front porch.

"He's in my bedroom," she said, but she was so panicked the words didn't come out quite right. She couldn't catch her breath and what came out of her mouth was utter nonsense, so she stepped aside and pointed, and the officers ran past her.

Her legs wouldn't work right, either, so she sank to the top step and placed her head in her hands. One of the officers who had remained with the patrol cars came forward cautiously.

"Ma'am?" he said in a surprisingly soft voice. "Maybe you'd better step over this way. Why don't you tell me what happened here tonight?"

She glanced up at the young officer as he offered her his hand, and after a moment's hesitation she reached up and took it, and he helped her to her feet.

The officers who had rushed into the house came out, guns holstered. "Nobody's in there," one of them said, sounding more disappointed than relieved.

"He was in my room," Frannie insisted.

The officers looked at one another.

"He had a gun," she said, and the shakes started all over again.

"The bedroom window was open," one of them said, and the two of them took off again, circling the house in opposite directions.

That was the crack she'd heard, Frannie thought with a shudder. Not a gunshot, but the sound of her window, painted shut, being forced open.

The strength went out of her legs, and she sat down again. She glanced to the side, seeing the intruder in every shadow. There were lots of shadows at night, she realized. Dark, deep shadows where anyone could be waiting. Even with the flash of those eerie red and blue lights, there were plenty of places to hide. At the moment, Frannie saw them all.

The officer who remained with her was trying to ask questions, but Frannie had a hard time concentrating. She heard maybe half his words, and even then...

A screech of tires on the street in front of her house made Frannie lift her head. A gray sedan had come to a halt beside the two patrol cars, and Malcolm Bridger slid out of the car while the echo of the squeal was still reverberating in the air.

His eyes were on her as he crossed the yard, and all of a sudden Frannie found the strength to stand.

The frustrated officer who had been trying to take her statement said, rather softly, "We didn't call for homicide." Bridger passed him without so much as a glance.

He stopped directly in front of her and looked her up and down quickly. "You're all right," he said, as if he didn't believe it any more than she did.

With trembling fingers, Frannie reached out and grabbed the narrow tie that hung limply from his neck. "There was a man in my house, Bridger." She held on tight. "He had a gun."

Bridger placed a warm and stilling hand on her shoulder, and another on her cheek, and Frannie allowed her eyes to drift closed. Her panic subsided slowly but surely.

Just as slowly and surely, Bridger's arms stole around her. Some part of her brain knew she should protest, but she didn't. She found herself melting against him, hiding her face against his chest, and with every Bridger-filled breath she took, she felt more herself. There was nothing to fear, here, no reason to be afraid.

"I was so scared," she whispered.

"I know."

"Don't leave me." The words were so low she didn't know if he would hear her or not. Maybe it would be best if he didn't. But after the span of a heartbeat or two, no more, he answered just as softly.

"I won't."

He remained silent for a long moment, and then she felt

a subtle shift of his body. He continued to hold her, but now he was tense, rigid.

"What the hell took you so long?" he hissed.

Frannie didn't move as the officer who'd been questioning her answered. This probably looked very strange, but she didn't care.

"We had another call on the other side of the district," the officer said defensively. "We got here as soon as—"

"When you get a call that there's an intruder in someone's house, you drop everything, do you hear me? *Everything!*" Bridger delivered this instruction in a commanding voice that was full of controlled rage and unbending authority. It was the kind of voice Frannie usually shied away from, but tonight...tonight that voice soothed her.

Chapter 5

How was it that this woman he'd known less than thirty-six hours had given him the two most frightening moments of his life?

Mal was kicked back in an overstuffed chair, his eyes fastened on the sleeping woman on the couch. Frannie had finally dozed off about an hour ago, her head on the arm of the couch, her legs drawn up and hidden beneath a crocheted afghan he'd bet money she had made herself. He was surprised she could sleep at all, after the scare she'd had, but she'd taken one last glance at him awhile back, and then she'd closed her blue eyes and drifted off.

The intruder had been looking for something, and that worried him. The contents of Frannie's purse had been dumped out on the kitchen table, but nothing was missing, she said. Credit cards, cash, and an expensive watch with a broken band were left in a jumble on the small oak table.

Drawers were opened, closets rearranged, but nothing was missing. Frannie said she had no idea what the man had meant when he'd asked, "Where is it?" and Mal believed her. The confusion that accompanied her fear and anger was evident.

He had a sneaking suspicion, one he didn't like at all, that this break-in was somehow related to the murder in the Riverwatch Hotel, that the man who'd held a gun on Frannie was the murderer. She thought maybe the man had the wrong house, that the break-in was a simple case of mistaken identity, a wrong turn on a dark street, but Mal didn't quite buy it.

The dead blonde had slipped something to Frannie, perhaps, and she didn't even know it. When he thought it through it made sense. Two women running in opposite directions collided on the stairs, the blonde slipped something to Frannie, and the man who'd broken into this house tonight had been looking for it. That's what the blonde's inquiry about Frannie's haircut and the request for her name had been about. A way to find her after the danger had passed.

Only the danger to the blonde hadn't passed. The killer had caught up with her in the stairwell. Thinking, maybe, that he wouldn't kill her if she told him what he wanted to hear, the woman had told him everything.

It all fell together so easily. There was only one problem—the woman hadn't given Frannie anything. There was nothing in her purse, nothing in the pockets of her raincoat, and there were no pockets on the skirt or the sweater she'd been wearing. So, they were exactly nowhere.

It occurred to Mal that the blonde in the stairwell might have told the murderer a lie, something to appease him so he'd let her go. If that was true, they had nothing and Frannie was still in danger.

He should have Frannie call a friend and arrange for a place to stay, or maybe call her mother and get out of town for a while. She wasn't safe in Decatur, not until they caught the killer and the man who had broken into her house.

Yes, he should advise her to do just that, but he knew that he wouldn't. She was going to stay right here, and he would be right beside her, like it or not. Keeping an eye on Frannie, knowing that she slept peacefully only because she knew he was here watching over her, Mal knew he was already in way too deep.

He shouldn't have to remind himself of the reason this was a bad idea, but he found himself doing just that.

Frannie Vaughn was not his type. She was open and honest, too naive, the girl next door who was no doubt looking for the boy next door and happily ever after. He knew all about her breed; he'd been engaged to one, years ago.

Daphne had been every bit as trusting and squeaky clean as Frannie Vaughn: wide-eyed and innocent, full of hope and plans for an ideal future of white picket fences and babies. She was a kindergarten teacher, for God's sake, a baker of pies and cookies and a really sweet girl. She'd also been terrified of marriage to a cop.

Mal had known it was falling apart when Daphne asked him to stop wearing his gun in her house. She didn't want to be reminded, she said, of what he did every day, and in order to keep peace he'd done as she asked. When she'd asked how his day was she wanted a generic "fine," and nothing more. No ugly details for Daphne, thank you very much, no tales of death over supper.

And then one night he'd been late for a special home-cooked dinner she'd planned. An hour or two, if he remembered correctly, no more. Daphne had met him at the door in tears, and she'd offered her ultimatum before he even had a chance to remove his offensive weapon. It all boiled down to this—her or the job. He couldn't have both.

It had been an easy choice for Mal to make. A relief, if

he was to be honest. These days, he removed his gun at the door for no man and no woman. It was too much a part of who he was, a symbol of his profession and his independence. Being caught without his weapon would be like being caught with his pants down.

Dammit, all he'd been looking for with Frannie was one night. One night of coming together for pleasure and comfort and release. Sex. An interlude. One night. It hadn't happened, and right now he wondered if he'd rest easy again until it did.

Her eyes snapped opened and her body jerked slightly, as if she'd awakened from a bad dream. Blue eyes settled on him instantly, she smiled, and her eyes fluttered closed again.

Damn.

Frannie knew by the faint light through the blinds that it was early morning. She couldn't have gotten more than a couple hours of sleep on the couch, but she felt oddly well rested.

Her eyes lit on Bridger, who slept pretty deeply himself. His head was back, his eyes were closed, his long arms had fallen over the fat arms of the chair. The posture left him looking unusually vulnerable.

She sat up slowly, and that was all it took. At the small creak of the couch, Bridger's eyes flew open. In an instant he was vulnerable no more, but instead was wary, on guard.

"I'm so sorry," she said as she stood. She was tempted to bring the afghan with her, to wrap it around her shoulders and let it hang over her jersey. Even though the blue and orange football jersey fell to her knees, and was thick enough to offer some modesty, she felt exposed at the moment, with her bare legs and bare feet. It hadn't bothered her last night, but it bothered her now.

Bridger frowned. He was obviously one of those people

who took a few minutes to get oriented in the morning, not one who came instantly awake as she did. "Sorry for what?" he grumbled.

"I shouldn't have called you, and I shouldn't have asked you to stay." Everything looked different by the light of day. She'd panicked, when clearly the intruder had broken into the wrong house. She had nothing anyone would be searching for. By now the nasty gun-wielding burglar had surely realized his mistake.

Bridger sat up, shaking off the sleep, stretching and rolling one shoulder, running his fingers through dark hair too short to be mussed much by sleeping in her easy chair. "You did just right. Well, except that you should've called 9-1-1 first and then me, but it worked out fine."

How could she explain picking up the phone and dialing his number almost automatically? She couldn't. "Coffee," she said in a no-nonsense and very awake voice, heading for the kitchen. Oh, she was still a coward, wasn't she? Only this time she was escaping from the good guy instead of the bad one.

"How do you like your eggs?" she called brightly, once she'd made a clean getaway.

"Scrambled." She heard the faint answer. "And *done*. I hate runny eggs."

"Duly noted," she muttered as she reached for the coffee.

Before she even had a chance to pour the water into the coffee decanter, Bridger was standing in the doorway of her kitchen. So much for escape. He watched her with dark, all-seeing eyes, squinting slightly as if he were calling upon all his investigative powers. Frannie wished, silent and deep, that she'd had the sense to get dressed before starting the coffee.

She took a deep breath and smiled. It was a friendly, distant and reserved smile—she hoped. "The coffee will be ready soon,'' she said brightly. "I'm just going to get dressed real quick and then I'll make you bacon and eggs before you have to leave.''

She waited for him to move aside, to clear the doorway so she could pass. He didn't move.

"Before I leave?''

"It's the least I can do to thank you.'' She took a single step closer to the door and Bridger, who blocked her exit quite effectively.

He was solid as a rock, and showed no inclination that he planned to move anytime soon. And the way he looked at her! If she hadn't actually seen him laugh in Rick's, she'd think that hard face was incapable of so much as forming a smile.

She didn't back down. He hesitated a moment longer, and then like a wary sentinel he stepped back to allow her to pass. She didn't look directly at him as she scooted by, but out of the corner of her eye she watched the steady rise and fall of his chest, and she noted with interest the stubble on his chin.

"We'll talk about it after you dress,'' Bridger said lowly.

Safely past, she turned around to look at him. He was lounging in the doorway once again, facing her. "We'll talk about what?''

"My leaving.''

Frannie's heart did a flip-flop in her chest. It sounded as if he didn't plan to leave at all. What on earth had she done? Malcolm Bridger was everything in a man she'd shied away from. He was hard, demanding, and way too testosterone laden for her tastes. She wanted a man who would be sensitive and gentle, one who knew how to take no for an answer.

She had a sinking feeling Bridger had *never* taken no for an answer.

It would be best, she decided, to argue with him after

she was dressed. Maybe after the first cup of coffee. Or two. She'd feel stronger, then, and maybe the caffeine would help her shed this feeling that she'd *like* him to stay.

She took her time dressing, pulling on a pair of jeans and a pale pink sweater, and then spending several minutes in the bathroom.

Frannie loved her old bathroom. Her house wasn't large, but the single brightly lit bathroom was large enough to be called luxurious—in an old-fashioned way. The claw-foot bathtub was decadently long and deep, and there was lots of counter space around the sink. A huge, gilt-framed mirror with a slightly distorted image on one side hung over the sink. She had a big linen closet, a pink clothes hamper near the almost new toilet, and in the middle of the floor there was a pastel braided rug.

She washed her face, hoping it would help her clear her mind, and then she brushed her teeth and combed her hair, ruffling the strands that were so much softer without Darlene's styling spray. A little lipstick wouldn't hurt, she decided, putting on a dab of pink lip gloss. She was reaching for the mascara when she realized what she was doing. There was an attractive man in the kitchen, so she prettied herself up. Just like her mother.

Before she left the bathroom she vigorously wiped the lip gloss off her mouth with a tissue.

She was annoyed enough with herself to be *really* annoyed with Bridger when she stepped into the kitchen and found he'd made himself at home. He sat at her oak table, a cup of coffee in one hand and the receiver from her wall phone in the other, the long cord stretched almost tight behind him.

"If I haven't taken a sick day in years—" she was just in time to hear him say "—then I'm due. Hell, I might even take two."

A sick day. So he really wasn't planning to leave. Frannie was relieved and angered at the same time. With her back to him she fixed her own cup of coffee.

"Call me when you get the report from Birmingham," he said softly. Then he recited her phone number, and added, "If I'm not here try me on the cell phone."

Now she was more angry than relieved. Bridger planned to stay, and he hadn't even had the courtesy to discuss it with her.

The chair scooted across the floor, and a moment later Bridger muttered a goodbye and slapped the receiver into the hook. Frannie kept her back to him, taking deep breaths alternated with long swigs of coffee to prepare herself for the unavoidable confrontation.

She gathered the bacon and eggs from the refrigerator without so much as glancing in the direction of the kitchen table. Her mind was made up. She'd feed him, thank him for coming by last night, and then she'd see him to the door and send him home.

Her first clue that Bridger was directly behind her was the warm brush of fingers across her neck. She was so unprepared for the contact that her whole body jerked in response. The egg in her hand went flying, and an arm shot past her to catch it in the air. The egg landed, unbroken, in Bridger's palm.

"You're still a little jumpy," he said softly as he returned the egg to the carton.

A little jumpy. That was the understatement of the century. She was terrified, nervous, and her heart was beating a mile a minute. And last night's intruder had nothing to do with her anxiety.

"Forget about breakfast," he said, taking her hand and leading her away from the counter. "You need to sit down and drink your coffee."

"No, I said I'd feed you and then you have to go," Frannie said as Bridger led her to the round oak table.

"I can't leave you here alone, not in this condition."

"What condition?" Frannie took her hand from Bridger's and turned to face him. "I'm fine, thank you. I can take care of myself. You are not responsible for..."

He kissed her. She should have seen it coming, should have seen the subtle change in his eyes and the tilt of his head and the parting of his lips. At first she was so surprised she couldn't move. And then a shifting of his mouth over hers elicited a response she couldn't deny, and she kissed him back.

All her fears melted away, bit by bit, inch by inch, and Frannie was overcome by the same sensation that had overwhelmed her the night they'd met. She was safe here.

She wrapped her arms around Bridger's waist and held on tight as he teased her lower lip with his tongue and her knees went weak. This was the kind of kiss to get lost in, a kiss that went on and on until there was nothing else in the world but this.

Bridger buried a hand in her hair and held her close, deepening the kiss. Everything inside her clenched and unclenched, and a small moan formed deep in her throat.

It would be so easy to finish what they'd started at the Riverwatch Hotel, so very, very easy.

She slowly pulled her mouth from Bridger's. "Why did you do that?" she whispered.

"I don't know."

Mal watched Frannie's back as she whipped eggs and turned bacon. Her long neck with its soft curl of pale blond hair cried out to be caressed. Her backside in those tight jeans needed to be touched. Heaven help him, the harder he watched her the harder he got. This was getting very, very dangerous.

If he had any sense at all he'd put a patrol car outside her front door and he'd walk away. Hell, he'd *run* away.

Not likely. If he'd had any sense left that last kiss had destroyed every lick.

He couldn't remember the last time he'd wanted a woman this much. Maybe he never had. There was some kind of cosmic joke going on here, wasn't there? Thirty-seven years old, and he was smitten.

Malcolm Bridger didn't *get* smitten.

It wasn't Frannie, he decided, wasn't some freak of chemistry. It was the memory of an unfinished one-night stand that haunted him, he supposed. They'd come too close to back away. He'd wanted her too much, too hard, and he'd thrown his chance away. He wished with everything he had that he'd reached out and awakened her, when he'd come out of the bathroom and found her asleep. If he had, he wouldn't be suffering this way.

If you waved a lollipop under a kid's nose and never let him taste it, he'd be forever obsessed with what he couldn't have. Frannie was his lollipop. Lord knows, he wanted to lick her.

She put a full plate of scrambled eggs and bacon and toast before him, and refilled his coffee before bringing her own plate and coffee mug to the table and sitting down across from him.

"Thanks," he said, unable to look her square in the eye at the moment, afraid he'd lose what little control he had left and say exactly what was on his mind. "This is good." He wondered what she'd say if he told her he'd much rather have a lollipop?

Frannie picked at her own plate, and finally pushed it away. She cradled a white mug that had pink hearts around the rim, and when he worked up the nerve to look at her he saw that she was staring at him. She wasn't afraid now.

"It won't work, you know," she said softly.

"What won't work?"

"You and me."

He knew he should grin and tell her there was no *you and me,* nothing to make work, no future, no past. Too bad he couldn't manage to work up a grin, at the moment.

"Why not?"

She tried a smile, a weak, rather sad smile. "You're not my type."

"You're not exactly my type, either," he muttered, and Frannie's reluctant smile blossomed to a real one.

"I didn't think so."

The awkwardness that hung between them faded away rather than disappearing suddenly. He could look at her, she could smile. "Mind telling me exactly what you think my type is?"

Frannie placed her elbows on the table and leaned slightly forward. "Big hair, small brain." Ah, what a wicked smile she had. "A woman who doesn't mind being told what to do and when and how to do it. She won't mind if you don't call for a couple of weeks, and when you do call she'll be thrilled to hear from you." Pale eyebrows raised slightly. "And if you never call, well that's all right, too."

"You make me sound like a real jerk."

She took a sip of coffee and shrugged as though to say "If the shoe fits..."

Anxious to turn the subject around, Mal pushed his plate away. "I imagine your type of man is sensitive and considerate and *always* politically correct. No hair, big brain."

She flashed a huge grin at that.

"A man who doesn't mind being told what to do and when and how to do it," he continued. "Whether you admit it or not, you like being in control. Did your—" he snapped his fingers as he searched for the name "—the toad, what's his name?"

"Reese," Frannie said softly. She wasn't smiling anymore.

"I'll bet Reese let you call the shots, didn't he, Frannie?" Somehow, he knew he had this one right. "When you said jump, he asked how high. Did he ever refuse you anything? Did he ever tell you *no?*"

She stared into her coffee, unsmiling and tense. It wouldn't work? Damn straight it wouldn't.

"I hope you don't expect an answer to those ridiculous personal questions," she said frostily.

"Not really."

No, an answer wouldn't help him now. Like it or not, he was responsible for Frannie. She was in this mess because he'd taken her to the Riverwatch Hotel. Her life and peace of mind had been endangered, and it was his fault. Until things were set straight, he was going to be a part of her life—no matter what she said.

Frannie lifted her gaze to him again, and he had a feeling it was a brave move on her part. She stared him down, getting ready for battle.

"Thank you for coming when I called last night, Detective Bridger," she said with a formal distance in her soft voice. "If you've finished your breakfast, I think you'd better go now."

Mal glanced at his empty plate, and then he lifted his eyes and stared at Frannie. "No," he said softly.

His response took her by surprise. Blue eyes widened, pink lips parted slightly, and there was a crack in the tough veneer she'd tried to hide her fear and anxiety behind. "What do you mean, *no?*"

She was right. This would never, never work. "I mean that until I'm satisfied that this is over, you're not getting rid of me."

"But you can't..." She placed her mug on the table. Hard. "If I *ask* you to leave, you *have* to leave." Her eyes narrowed. "Don't you?"

"I see I was right. Nobody ever tells Frannie Vaughn no."

She tried for a stern expression again. "You really, really have to leave now."

Mal smiled. "No."

Chapter 6

Frannie watched Bridger out of the corner of her eye. What exactly was she to do when she had a cop camping out in her kitchen? She supposed she could call Sergeant Dixon and demand that he take this watchdog away, but she didn't want to get Bridger in trouble.

As she pretended not to watch him, she admitted to herself that maybe she didn't want him to leave.

Bridger had spent most of the morning on the phone, and he'd been doing more listening than talking. He took notes, a scribbled mess she had no hope of deciphering when she glanced over his shoulder to study the page. He sat at her table, propped his feet up on a kitchen chair, leaned back and made himself at home.

Silently, and against her will and better judgment, she liked it. She washed and dried dishes while he carried on with his business, and she listened to every word he said. He had a soothing voice, deep and smooth, that was pleasant to listen to. The clatter of dishes didn't seem to bother him, any more than her presence in the room seemed to bother him. It was all very comfortable, even warmly domestic.

She frowned at the last of the dishes, her own coffee mug. There was *nothing* domestic about Detective Malcolm Bridger.

As she put away the mug, he stood and hung up the phone. "We'll have the guy before you know it, I promise."

"And then you'll get out of my kitchen?" she asked lightly.

He smiled, and her insides did an unexpected little flip-flop. Oh, he should smile more often.

"Maybe."

The doorbell saved her from coming up with a suitable response. True to his character, Bridger headed for the front door as if he lived here. With a sigh, Frannie followed.

Sergeant Dixon didn't appear to be at all surprised that it was Bridger who opened the door. "I've got those photos," he said, waving a short stack of stiff polaroids. He had a warm smile for Frannie. "I understand you had a little excitement here last night."

Bridger filled him in as they headed for the kitchen. Frannie tried to interject a couple of times, tried to get Dixon to see that this intruder had nothing to do with the murder in the Riverwatch Hotel. She tried to point out that all kinds of unsavory characters lived just around the corner, and the gun-wielding man who'd broken into her home last night was surely looking for someone else. Drugs, she suggested as she poured Dixon a cup of coffee. He was probably looking for a stash of drugs.

Dixon didn't buy it any more than Bridger had. As Frannie handed Dixon his coffee, Bridger, always the gentleman, pulled out a kitchen chair for her. She glanced up at him sharply and started to protest. She could stand just fine, thank you, and look down at the photos.

But if he thought she needed to sit, maybe she did. Without actually uttering a word, Frannie lowered herself slowly into the chair.

"Is this the woman you passed in the stairwell?" Dixon placed one photo in front of her, and Frannie glanced down. A quick peek, that's all she needed. But once she looked her eyes felt glued to the photo.

This particular photograph was chosen for its sterility, perhaps. It had been taken in a morgue or a funeral home, she guessed. The body was lying on a metal bed, and there was no blood to be seen, no visible wound. A sheet covered her to the chin. Her hair had been combed, and she looked almost as if she were sleeping.

Almost. There was no life left. The face that had been flushed was now white, the mouth that had been painted red and that had moved to speak was still and pale. The blonde was dead. Someone had purposely taken her life in a most violent way.

"Frannie?" Bridger whispered as he placed a steady hand on her shoulder. Had she really tried to push him away? She raised a hand and placed it over his, finding strength in the simple touch. How odd. She barely knew him, and yet somehow she knew him better than anyone else.

What if he was right after all? What if the man who had done this was the same man who'd broken into her house and pointed a gun at her last night?

"It's her," she said softly. "Does she have a name?"

"Not yet," Dixon said, reaching out to scoop the photo off the table and add it to the stack. Thank goodness, he wasn't going to ask her to look at any more of those pictures. Perhaps they were of the crime scene. She didn't want to know, and most especially she didn't want to see.

Harry Dixon slipped the pictures into an inside pocket of his jacket, leaned back in his chair and sipped at his coffee. "Paula's trying to get me to give up caffeine now," he said as he savored the hot coffee on his tongue.

"You've given up everything else for the woman," Bridger said from his position behind Frannie. "Why not coffee?"

"A man's gotta draw the line somewhere," Harry said gruffly, and then unexpectedly the most satisfied, most sentimental smile bloomed on the man's otherwise rugged face. It was quite a transformation. "I have news, Mal." He glanced at Frannie and paused.

"Should I..." She started to rise, to leave the two of them alone for a few minutes, but Bridger's hand on her shoulder stopped her.

"Don't tell me," he said wryly. "Paula's got you taking yoga classes. You're moving to the country to raise cows and apples." He leaned slightly forward. "You're a vegetarian."

Harry just continued to smile. "Paula's pregnant."

"Oh, that's wonderful," Frannie said. She could tell by the look on Harry's face that he was happy about the baby. Ecstatic even. "Congratulations."

"Thank you."

Bridger was oddly silent. There was no immediate congratulations for his friend; no amiable gibe, either. Frannie glanced over her shoulder. Bridger's face was stoic, unreadable, but the pressure of his hand at her shoulder increased slightly.

The hand left her shoulder suddenly, and Bridger took the chair to her right, sitting down to face his friend across the table. "Are you out of your mind?"

Frannie expected Harry's wide grin to disappear at this rude question, but he kept smiling. "Probably."

"Don't you remember the summer Leigh Ann was sixteen? How about Mark's senior year?" Bridger wagged an accusing finger in the sergeant's direction. "You had brown hair in September, and by May you were as gray as you are now. You said—"

"I said a lot of things," Harry interrupted.

"You said kids make you old before your time," Bridger said through gritted teeth. "You said, more than once, that if you were smart you never would've had kids. Dammit, Harry, Mark and Leigh Ann are grown and out of the house, and here you are nearly fifty years old and you're going to *start all over?*"

Harry ignored Bridger and turned all his attention to Frannie. "I knew he would do this. Ignore him, he'll get over it in a minute. This is good coffee."

Bridger mumbled something, and Frannie ignored him just as Harry did. "Thank you."

"You see," Harry said as he leaned slightly toward her. "Paula's my third wife. I have two kids, Mark and Leigh Ann, by my first wife, and none, thank heaven, by the second." He grinned. "You'd like Paula. We should get together, the four of us, and maybe..." He glanced at Bridger and changed the subject. Frannie didn't want to look to her right and see exactly how Bridger had squelched the invitation. A glare would do it, she supposed.

"Paula doesn't have any kids of her own," he continued. "Everything I said to Mal about having kids was true...at least, I meant it at the time. But there are good things about babies, too. When they're little they're so cute, and helpless, and pure. We don't see a lot of pure in our business."

Bridger stopped mumbling. Frannie risked a glance in his direction to see that he stared at Harry, listening closely. "Well, hell, congratulations, old man." The beginnings of a smile might have touched the corners of his mouth. "If you're happy, I'm happy for you."

"I never doubted it," Harry said as he offered his coffee mug for a refill.

The phone rang while Frannie was pouring Harry his second cup of coffee. Bridger answered it quickly, obviously expecting it to be for him. He said hello twice and then returned the receiver to the hook.

"Wrong number, I guess," he said to Frannie as she placed Harry's coffee on the table.

Mal didn't like leaving the house without Frannie, not even for a few minutes, but she'd insisted, and Harry had insisted. In the end, he'd simply been outnumbered.

He needed a shower, a shave and a change of clothes, but he wondered if Frannie would open her door to him when he returned. Maybe. Maybe not. She didn't see danger the way he did, didn't seem to see any threat at all.

Frannie Vaughn was such a naive, trusting woman. The thought didn't comfort him at all.

She was so certain last night's break-in had been a simple mistake. Maybe she didn't want to face the fact that she might be in serious trouble. Hell, he didn't *like* it, but he didn't dismiss the possibility because it was unpleasant.

Much as he hated to admit it, she was right about one thing. He couldn't simply move in and take over her life. He didn't know what came next any more than she did.

His own apartment was familiar and uncluttered, unlike Frannie's little house. He'd never been one for fussing over the place where he slept, as she obviously did. The furniture in his apartment had been reasonably priced and comfortable, and he'd never had the urge to pretty the place up with pillows and little doodads here and there, the way women did. There was a place to lay his head, a television, a microwave and a functioning refrigerator, and that was all he needed.

Away from the situation, distanced from Frannie for the

space of time it took him to drive to his apartment and take a shower, he realized that this situation was going to be a tricky one. The man who'd broken into her house might try again tonight, next week, next month…or not at all. How could he expect to watch her all that time? Especially since she obviously didn't want his assistance.

Mal towel-dried his hair vigorously as he walked down the carpeted hall to his bedroom. He couldn't move in with Frannie, he couldn't adopt her, he couldn't devote his life to watching over her, but he still felt responsible for her. He grumbled as he tossed the towel onto the floor. Dammit, he didn't want to feel responsible for her.

It was not his job to baby-sit witnesses and crime victims, no matter how physically appealing they might be. His duty was to find the man who had killed the blonde in the stairwell and get him off the street. His only obligation was to the woman who'd been murdered.

As he chose a dark blue suit from the closet, he mumbled to himself. Well, that reasoning *sounded* good, but he didn't feel any less responsible for Frannie Vaughn.

In front of the mirror he straightened his blue and burgundy tie. Why couldn't Paula have introduced him to Frannie over a barbecue and idle conversation? Why couldn't it have been Frannie as a blind date instead of that whiner with the three kids or the skittish woman who had jumped every time he opened his mouth? Frannie wouldn't have asked him to fix her speeding tickets, or wondered aloud at the end of the evening if he wouldn't mind having a talk with a thirteen-year-old who'd decided he shouldn't have to do his homework anymore.

It would've been different with Frannie. Could've been. Would never be…

He strapped on his gun and then his badge. No, he couldn't make a life's work of looking out for Frannie, and if she kept pushing him away every time he got too close they'd never get to finish what they started at the River-watch Hotel. But he could, and he would, make damn sure she could take care of herself.

This afternoon, he was taking Frannie shopping for a gun.

Frannie glanced over her shoulder one more time. Her house was a couple of blocks behind her, and there was no one else on the sidewalk that was shaded by ancient trees and lined, in places, by low-growing flowering plants. So why couldn't she shake the feeling that someone watched her?

Nerves, she decided as she looked ahead once again. Last night's excitement had shaken her, and she wasn't quite over it yet. She wondered, as she remembered the man pointing the gun at her, if she would ever get over it.

She'd have to, wouldn't she? God, she refused to be afraid all the time, to stay locked in her house behind shuttered windows, afraid of every sound and every shadow. Afraid to live.

Frannie tried to dispel the feeling that someone was watching. She needed a new cable for her phone, since the intruder had frayed the connection when he'd ripped the cord out of the wall. Fortunately the wall jack itself seemed to be fine, and they'd surely have phone cable at the hardware store on the corner.

Harry had suggested that she wait for Bridger to get back before running her errands, but she'd stood firm. She would not let the creep who'd invaded her home change her life, would not let him make her afraid to venture out in her own neighborhood.

The small hardware store had just what she needed, and Frannie purchased the cord and stuck it in her purse. She'd sleep better, she knew, if the bedroom phone was in good working order.

That errand done, she walked another block and a half to a neighborhood drugstore. The prices were a little bit higher here than at the discount stores, but it was convenient and she stopped here often. The large, friendly woman with big red hair at the cash register recognized her, then smiled and waved before returning to her magazine. *Cosmo*.

Frannie walked toward the cosmetics section. She needed a few things, and killing time here was definitely better than sitting at home all alone, all day long. She had no idea how long it would be before Bridger returned, but if he got there before she did, well, it wouldn't hurt him to wait in his car for a while and wonder where she was.

She smiled as she looked over a selection of lipsticks. Bridger was obviously not often kept waiting. There wasn't a patient bone in the man's body.

The bell above the door rang softly, and she heard the cashier say hello again. The greeting was more subdued this time, and Frannie lifted her head to see who the new customer was.

She recognized the little man as soon as her eyes lit on him. By the light of day the Riverwatch Hotel's desk clerk looked even more wrinkled and sour and *old* than he had two nights ago.

Frannie lowered her head, hoping he wouldn't see and recognize her. She stared at the lipsticks, and after a few seconds of perusal she moved on to the nail polish.

"Well, hello."

She lifted her head slowly to see that the old man stood right beside her, an unexpected and somehow *wrong* smile on his wrinkled face.

"Hello," she said softly.

"I remember you," he said, shaking a gnarled finger in her direction. "You were with that cop the other night."

She nodded once.

"Did you hear what happened?" He lowered his voice to ask the question. "Did you hear about the murder?" His eyes gleamed, bright in a grayish face.

"Yes." She didn't like the expression on his face, not at all. She reached out and picked up a bottle of red nail polish, just to have something else to study. That smile gave her the creeps. "It's such a shame." She started to walk past him, to steer around the old man and make her way to the cashier with a bottle of nail polish that was much too red for her tastes.

"A shame? What for?" His whispered response stopped her, and she made herself look up at him. "She was a tramp, and she got what she deserved…I imagine."

"You knew her?" Bridger had said they didn't even have a name for the victim, but this man was condemning her. Maybe he knew something, more than he was telling the police.

The old man caught her eye, and his grin turned into a smirk. "Nope. Don't have to know her to know what kind of woman she was. The only kind of women who frequent the Riverwatch are tramps. We get hookers, adulterers, loose women. We don't exactly get good girls renting rooms for an hour or two, or a night or two."

His eyes and his smirk were condemning, and Frannie wanted nothing more than to escape. She turned her back on him and decided to take the long way around to the cashier.

Frannie didn't look back. When she reached the cashier she placed her nail polish on the counter. "You know," she said softly, "I changed my mind. This isn't my color."

The cashier didn't seem to mind. She shrugged and set the bottle of nail polish on a low shelf behind the counter, and Frannie stepped through the door and onto the sidewalk with a sigh of relief. What an offensive old man! She would have argued with almost anyone else, and told them that she *was* a good girl, thank you very much, but she really didn't care what that creep thought, at least not enough to endure a longer conversation.

There was a small antique store a few doors down, and that's where she headed. It was a good place to browse on a lazy afternoon, and she had time to kill. Lots and lots of time.

Terri, the owner, stood behind the desk with a stack of bills and a checkbook. She glanced up and smiled and said hello, and then she went back to her work. She knew how Frannie liked to come here and rummage through the merchandise, searching for treasures.

There was something so comforting about these old things that she quickly put the creep from the Riverwatch from her mind. These objects had a history—every book, every chair, every odd and every end. Frannie and her mother had moved so often, there had never been any time to make a history of their own. No family heirlooms passed from hand to hand, no single pieces that were constant from year to year. Everything changed, frequently and usually without warning.

She picked up and studied a pair of ceramic mushroom salt and pepper shakers. They were ugly as sin, so ugly Frannie was tempted to buy the pair just to save them from the inevitable junk pile. But she eventually returned the mushrooms to the table and continued her journey through the store.

After a while she felt almost calm. Things here were familiar and safe. Some of these pieces had been here for months, and the smell of old books and dust tickled her nose in a comforting way. Not everything changed in a heartbeat. Some things were constant and solid and real.

As she neared the end of a table of knickknacks she saw the angel.

The ceramic figurine was no more than six inches high,

a fat-faced cherub with wings and a halo and a flowing blue robe. There were a number of small chips around the hem of the gown, and some of the gold halo paint was scratched.

She smiled as she approached the counter with her prize. "Fifty cents?" she said to Terri as she fished through her purse for change. "That's a bargain I can't pass up."

The phone near the cash register rang as Frannie dug up a second quarter, and Terri snagged it as she opened the cash drawer.

"Terri's Trash and Treasure," she drawled, and then she handed the receiver to Frannie. "It's for you."

She knew who it was, and her peace of mind fled as her anger grew. Bridger! He'd had her followed, and he was checking up on her as if she were a child. How many times did she have to tell him that she did *not* need him to take over her life?

"Hello," she snapped.

Frannie heard a long sigh on the other end of the phone, Bridger searching for patience she supposed. She was about to hand the receiver back to Terri when he spoke.

"Where is it, Frannie?"

Not Bridger, that was the first thought that went through her mind. Not Bridger, but she recognized his voice. She remembered too vividly the deep whisper that had come to her in the dark last night.

"What do you want?" she asked softly.

"You know what I want. She gave you something."

"No," Frannie insisted, shaking her head as she answered. "You're wrong."

That sigh again. "I'm running out of patience, Frannie." And then he hung up.

She held on to the phone even after the dial tone replaced the harsh whisper. Terri tilted her face to look into Frannie's eyes.

"Are you okay?"

Frannie returned the phone. "No," she whispered.

Bridger was right. The man who'd broken into her house, the man who'd called her—she shivered as she realized that she had not *imagined* she was being followed as she'd walked down her street—was the same man who'd killed that poor woman in the stairwell. And for some reason she could not fathom, he thought she had something. Something worth killing for.

Frannie glanced through the big window at the front of the store. She saw no one unusual on the sun-washed street, but that didn't comfort her at all. That old man who thought she was a tramp could be out there. The intruder who'd placed the phone call might be out there. Either or both of them might be patiently waiting for her to leave this place. Alone.

Bridger had been right, dammit. She wasn't safe.

Frannie pointed to the telephone moments after Terri had set the receiver in place. Her hand shook slightly, the finger that pointed, trembling. "Can I use your phone?"

Chapter 7

Mal wanted to ask Frannie why she hadn't called him from the antique shop, but he didn't. He decided to be satisfied that she'd had the sense to call the police station, and that the officers she told her story to had paged him so he could pick her up and drive her home.

He was angry, much angrier than he was willing to let Frannie know. While the words "I told you so" hadn't once left his lips, he kept wanting to remind her how he'd insisted that she play it safe. Walking off to run a few errands had been carelessly foolish, and he knew Frannie Vaughn was not normally a careless lady.

That carelessness wasn't all that had him steamed. Right now, Harry and at least one other detective were paying a visit to Clarence Doyle, the unsavory Riverwatch Hotel manager who had confronted Frannie in the drugstore. That encounter seemed to bother her almost as much as the phone call she'd received.

She hadn't recovered from the shock yet. Pale and

shaken, she sat on the fat white sofa in her living room, feet tucked beneath her, eyes locked somewhere around her knees, arms crossed as if the room were chilly. It wasn't.

Frannie lifted her head. "You were right," she said softly, and then she smiled. It was a slow, reluctant smile that tugged at something deep inside him. "I can be so blind sometimes. If I don't want it to be so, then it must not be. I really, really didn't want that man who was in my house last night to be the same one who killed that woman."

Mal's simmering anger was replaced by something near fury—at the man who'd turned Frannie's safe and comfortable life upside down, at her for sitting there with an accepting and peaceful smile on her face, at himself for being in the middle of it all. "We're going to take care of this," he said. "Tomorrow morning we'll file for you to get a gun permit. I'll take you to the shooting range, and until your permit is approved—"

"No," she said firmly, her smile gone. "No gun."

He took a deep breath to calm himself. "Frannie, you have to be able to defend yourself."

"No."

"You're being unreasonable."

Her eyes were an unwavering and steady blue fire. He expected an argument, an angry response he could answer in kind. Unfortunately, what he got was an unruffled, very calm reply. "I know myself better than you do, Bridger. If I had a gun, I wouldn't use it."

"You don't know what you'd do if you needed protection."

"But I do know," she whispered. "I'd take that gun and I'd point it at the man who threatened me, and then I'd begin to wonder. I'd wonder if he had a family, if he was high on drugs and had no idea what he was doing, if he was really, really the danger he seemed to be. And in that instant he'd have the opportunity to take the gun from me or fire his own. I lose, any way you look at it.''

So she was one of *those:* a peacemaker, a dove, a woman who shuddered at the sight of a gun. But then again, she hadn't shuddered at the sight of the Smith & Wesson revolver on his belt, the backup weapon he wore in place of the Colt that had been confiscated right after the shooting on Tuesday. She hadn't so much as cringed as he'd told the story about Thrasher's death.

''Don't get me wrong,'' Frannie continued as if she could read his mind. ''What you do is important, and honest, and brave. Without you, who would look out for that woman and other victims like her who can't look out for themselves? But not everyone is cut out to be a cop, and not everyone is cut out to carry a weapon.''

''Frannie…''

''I won't have one,'' she finished in a voice that was soft and yet so strong he knew he didn't have a prayer of changing her mind.

Mal came up out of his chair. ''You won't have one,'' he mumbled. He paced the small room, glancing down at the collection of angels on her end table. She'd added the new one immediately on arriving home, making space for it between a tall, skinny, winged figurine and a brass angel with a bent halo.

He finally stilled himself, sitting on the sofa next to Frannie. As he had been since he'd seen her at the antique store this afternoon, he was consumed with the urge to touch her. So far he'd controlled the urge. After all, it wouldn't do to scare her off, not now when he needed her to allow him to stay close.

With one very easy hand, he touched her shoulder. The solid contact gave him an unexpected comfort, but it wasn't nearly enough. ''I understand your reservations, I really do,

Frannie. But you have to understand that this guy means business. He's killed once. He'll do it again.''

He wanted to scare her, and from the look in her eyes he'd succeeded.

''Do you know what I was thinking last night when that man was pointing his gun at me?'' Her whispered question was breathy, somehow insubstantial. ''I was remembering my stepfather, the second one, who liked to wave his gun around as if it would make him big and strong and special. He was none of those. He was just…mean.''

His hand traveled up to her cheek. ''He hurt you.'' The very thought filled Mal with an unexpected rage.

''A little,'' she whispered. ''But you see, I can't…I don't want to…''

The kiss that silenced her was instinctive. Mal covered Frannie's mouth with his and tasted her sweetness and fear and confusion. He wanted to erase every bad memory she held. He wanted to replace each and every one with something good. A slow dance, a kiss in the rain, a lurching elevator…and much, much more.

She melted against him, her mouth surrendering first, her body following inch by inch as she fell against him until it seemed she touched him everywhere. Just as surely she drifted back until Mal was leaning over her, his body taut, his mouth slanted over hers to deepen the kiss. Together they generated a mindless, all-consuming heat that drove away everything else until all that mattered was this touch.

They could finish their one-night stand here and now, on a plush sofa with angels looking over his shoulder and a hint of the little remaining daylight slicing through the venetian blinds. That would suit him just fine, and apparently it suited Frannie, as well. She had to be able to feel the ridge pressing against her thigh, had to know that all he had to do was touch her and he was ready, and yet she didn't back away.

Her tongue slipped inside his mouth, and her hand moved slowly up his back, the caress feathery light as her mouth and his found a rhythm that promised so much more. Yes, here and now, just this once.

It wasn't until he lowered his head to kiss her throat that he realized she was hanging on to his necktie as if she were holding on for dear life. Her eyes drifted closed, her head dropped back as he touched his lips to her long, white throat.

She smelled and tasted wonderfully female, deliciously sexy, and Mal was overcome with a primitive urgency to touch and taste more, to savor every newly heightened sensation.

Frannie was as wonderfully lost as he was. He knew this as a fact, could feel as well as see it. With a series of subtle shifts of her body she came closer to him, as if to leave a breath of space between them would be a sin.

He slipped a hand beneath her pale pink sweater to touch her breasts, his thumb finding and flicking over one hard nipple beneath a thin, silky bra. The front closure snapped open easily in his fingers, and he touched the bare skin of her breasts, running his fingers over the soft globes as he took her mouth again.

''Bridger.'' His name was whispered between a series of soft, swift, endless kisses. He didn't want to take his mouth from hers. Heaven help him, what if she was trying to tell him to stop?

''What?'' he whispered, his mouth a hairsbreadth from hers.

''We're too different, you and I,'' she said as she kissed him quickly again.

''I know.'' Dammit, she was going to call an end to this, and he wasn't ready or willing to walk away. But if Frannie said to walk away...

"No future," she whispered. "But we have to finish this, don't we? I need to finish this with you."

All he could do was mutter something between a moan and a contented hum.

"But not here," she said, and this time she did draw away slightly. "We're only going to do this once, Bridger, and I'd rather it be in a big soft bed than on a couch that's much too small for you."

It should have surprised him that she thought so much like he did, but it didn't. Different as they were, he sometimes knew what she was thinking and there had been moments when she seemed to read his mind, as well. Finally they were going to finish their one-night stand, and they were going to do it right.

She was so caught up in the kiss that nothing else mattered. Sandwiched between Bridger's hard body and the soft couch, she was caught in a gentle trap she had no desire to escape. His tongue swept inside her mouth and a hand settled in her hair.

From the moment he'd placed that gentle hand on her shoulder, she'd known this would happen. The very air in her lungs changed when he touched her, and she came truly alive. And with every caress that followed, with every kiss, she fell deeper and deeper until there was no way out.

They sat up, still kissing, and when their mouths broke apart Bridger stood. Both hands clasping hers, he pulled her to her feet. She didn't feel steady, not steady at all. Her insides churned, her knees quivered. As if he knew how she felt, Bridger put his arm around her shoulder and steadied her as they walked away. Across the living room and down the hall, he supported her. And touched her. Fingers in her hair, across the back of her neck, up and down her arm.

Frannie shuddered, and she didn't know if it was anxiety or anticipation. Maybe it was both.

Standing beside her bed, Bridger undressed her slowly. He took the hem of her sweater in his hands and very easily pulled it over her head, and then he slipped the unfastened bra from her shoulders. Some of the fire of their fumbling on the couch was changed, but it wasn't gone. It simmered now, slow and steady and certain.

She wanted this. More than that, she had to have it—just one night. His fingers brushed over her skin lightly, barely there, and yet she could feel the warm touch more intensely than she'd ever felt anything before.

He finished undressing her with a slow deliberation, never hurried, until she stood before him wearing nothing at all. Strangely enough she felt no shyness or trepidation, just a mounting desire and a certainty that this was right.

Frannie wondered, as she reached out and grabbed Bridger's tie and kissed him hard and quick, if this connection, this conviction she felt, was love. She had a curiously sinking suspicion it was.

She helped him undress as he had helped her, her fingers slowly unfastening the buttons of his white shirt and loosening his tie. He'd already taken off his weapon and his badge, leaving them discarded on a table by the bedroom door, so she had only to unbuckle his belt and slide the zipper down.

Bridger had a hard, beautiful body—not too wide, not too thin, all muscle with a sprinkling of soft dark hair. The very structure of his body was such a contrast to her own that it was fascinating to watch the way his chest pressed against her breasts, the way his long leg looked next to hers, the way his hip curved and his shoulders overpowered her.

He was big and hard and on the brink of losing control—she could see that truth in his eyes and in the tension in every muscle in his body, in the heat and silent demand of the arousal that pressed insistently against her. And still she felt undeniably safe here.

They didn't fall to the bed, but practically floated there. Bridger supported her, and the slow, leisurely process seemed to take forever. Her legs were parted and he rested between them, fitting to her body as if they'd been made for each other, as if they'd been made for this.

Where the tip of his arousal barely touched her, she throbbed, as if every beat of her heart pulsated there. Her body was ready for him now, waited impatiently to be filled and stroked and fulfilled.

But he didn't thrust to fill her. Instead he kissed her again, a long, slow, deep kiss that made her feel as if she were dissolving into the bed, as if she were fusing with Bridger. He became, in that instant, a real and true part of her. Even though they were not yet together, even though he waited, he was a part of her, a part she'd never let go.

His mouth left hers and slowly traveled lower, kissing her throat and the side of her neck, mumbling soft words she couldn't understand, finally settling over one breast and suckling until she thought she would scream from the sheer pleasure.

When he placed his hand between her legs and touched the nub that was hidden in her pale curls, she practically came up off the bed, the sensation was so unbearably intense. He continued to stroke her, his fingers dancing over and just barely inside her, until every semblance of peace was gone and she was aching for him.

From out of nowhere he pulled a foil-packaged condom, and while she watched he ripped it open and started to put it on. She helped, to hurry the process along, and to touch him, each need coming to her in equally powerful waves. He was hard and hot in her hands, and when his shaft was sheathed in the protection, she took her hands away and he surged to fill her.

Yes. Frannie closed her eyes and reveled in the fullness and pressure of their long-awaited joining. *Yes.* Bridger rocked his hips, withdrawing and filling her again, impossibly deeper. *More.* She moved with him, as they instantly found the primal rhythm that had drawn them to each other from the beginning. It was the most amazing feeling, to so truly and fully be a part of another human being, heart and soul, spirit and mind—one body.

Waves of pure pleasure grew and changed and washed over and through her body, until there was nothing *but* pleasure so intense she cried out and arched off the bed and into Bridger. The sensations overcame her, shooting through her body as she grasped him to her. He drove impossibly deep, deeper than ever before, and she felt his own shudders as he held her tight.

Together they practically melted into the bed. Frannie felt as if she could hardly breathe, and Bridger's breath was coming as labored as her own.

At that moment she was sure she could stay in this bed forever and be wonderfully, blissfully happy in Bridger's arms. There was beauty here, and passion, and love. Everything she'd ever wanted was in her arms. A small frown wiped away the smile that was trying to form. No, she couldn't stay here forever. Not with Bridger.

"I'm glad you had a...that you thought of..." All of a sudden she was tongue-tied.

He cured her with a kiss.

Rather than leaving the bed, Bridger pulled the covers over them and held her close. He seemed content—as content as a man like Bridger could ever be. Her head rested against his shoulder, and his hand played mindlessly with her hair.

"I just have one question," he muttered.

"What's that?"

"When you said 'just once' did you mean one time, or one night?"

She considered the question, but not for more than a split second.

"One night."

She glanced up to see him smile softly. A moment later he leaned over the side of the bed to retrieve his trousers. From the fat wallet in the back pocket he removed three foil-wrapped condoms, and with a casual flick of his wrist he deposited them on the bedside table.

"Confident, weren't we?" Frannie asked, teasing.

Bridger leaned over her, blocking out the last of the day's light that broke through the white lace curtains. Still there was enough light for her to see him smile. "Optimistic," he whispered.

Mal didn't know what woke him from a sound sleep, but he immediately tried to recapture the dream that had faded as he opened his eyes. He was on his stomach, a soft, white pillow was pressed against his face, and there was just a hint of sunlight outside Frannie's bedroom window. Very early morning sunlight.

His stomach growled, and he remembered that he and Frannie had skipped dinner last night. As his eyes drifted closed he was assaulted with vivid images of the night that had passed. The thought of food had never entered his mind.

When he realized Frannie was not in the bed he came fully awake, pushing his head off the pillow and glancing around the feminine bedroom. The white lace curtains, the pale and flowery bedspread that covered half his body, the pink and green pillows that were usually stacked neatly on the bed but had been pushed to the floor during the night, the silk flowers and colorful pictures and the pink ceramic jewelry box on the dresser, they were all hints of who Frannie was.

He'd made his own mark here. There were four discarded condom wrappers on the floor by the bed, and a variety of masculine and feminine clothes strewn about.

He could hear her in the bathroom down the hall, as she sighed and water slapped the side of her tub. Slowly he left the bed. This was a sight he had to see.

The bathroom door stood open, and he stopped to lean against the doorjamb and look his fill. Frannie's back was to him, and pale blond hair curled softly against her neck. Everything about her was feminine and sexy and alluring, and she didn't even seem to try. She just *was*. The curve of her pale shoulder, the legs she'd wrapped around him last night, that was all he could see, but it was more than enough.

Dammit, a night like the one that had passed should have cured him for good, he should be sick to death of lollipops.

"Maybe I'm developing a sweet tooth," he mumbled, and Frannie glanced over her shoulder.

Her smile was quick and real. "What?"

"Nothing."

"I hope I didn't wake you. But I swear, every muscle in my body aches. I woke up and just had to have a hot bath." She drew her legs up and her smile widened. "Join me?"

The tub was long enough, and deep enough, and Mal didn't hesitate to accept her invitation. He stepped into the claw-foot tub and lowered himself slowly, facing her. The hot water surrounded him, and the heat seeped wonderfully into his own sore muscles.

Once he was seated the water lapped dangerously near the rim of the tub. He took Frannie's feet and drew them around him, so her legs rested atop his. His arms hanging over the sides of the tub, he leaned his head back and closed his eyes.

He should be ready to make his getaway, call a patrol car to keep an eye on Frannie, and leave her and her broken angels and those big blue eyes behind. But he wasn't even close to ready to let Frannie go.

One eye drifted open, and he saw that Frannie had adopted a pose much like his own. Head back, eyes closed, arms spread, it was a vulnerable position. She trusted him that much…as she'd trusted him throughout the night.

Mal leaned forward slowly and brushed aside a wayward blond curl that touched Frannie's cheek. It was damp from the steam that had risen off the water. She didn't flinch at his touch, didn't even so much as open her eyes. Instead, she smiled.

The smile was more than he could take. He cupped her head in his hands and pulled her to him for a kiss he shouldn't crave so damn much but did. She kissed him back, giving as good as she got in every measure. The kiss was lazy, at first, decadently slow, but it gradually changed, becoming harder, deeper.

He'd never known a woman to respond so completely to his touch, had never gotten so much joy from watching a woman fall apart in his arms. Frannie made love as if she'd never known the sensations that came with every stroke, as if she were loving for the first time.

She came toward him until she was practically sitting in his lap, her legs wrapped around him, her wet arms around his neck. Steam from the hot bath had dampened her hair, making it curl around her face and dance as she moved her head to kiss his neck and shoulder, gently sucking at his damp skin.

Mal dipped one hand beneath the water, finding the place where their bodies almost touched, his fingers caressing the nub that was hidden in thick blond curls. Frannie's response was powerful and immediate, as she drew in her breath and rocked slightly against his hand.

She brought her mouth to his, and he kissed her deep, beneath the water stroking her with fingers that teased her entrance. Slowly but surely she surged against him, oblivious to the water that crested and lapped over the edge of the tub, splashing onto the bathroom floor. Her mouth left his and she let her head fall back.

Watching Frannie's face, as he'd watched so often during the night, was an unexpected and intense pleasure all its own. Her eyes were closed, her well-kissed lips slightly parted, and he knew without a doubt that she was the most beautiful, most extraordinary woman he had ever known. She felt everything deeply. Pain, fear, pleasure, love.

She came apart in his arms, climaxing with a ragged whisper and an undulation that sent another wave onto the floor. Her mouth found his again, and she kissed him hard and deep and almost frantically. *Frenzied.* He knew how she felt. The night was over.

A hint of alarm welled up deep inside him. He wasn't ready for this night to be over.

"It's just after six," he whispered as Frannie took her mouth from his.

"I know." Slowly she distanced herself from him.

"What time is the night over?" he asked. "Maybe…nine o'clock?"

Frannie gave him a crooked smile. "Maybe noon."

He wanted her right now, and that was impossible. He should have nothing left to give, no energy, no desire…no damn strength at all. Just looking at Frannie made him strong, in more ways than one.

"I used all the condoms I brought. Hell, Frannie, I thought sticking four of those things in my wallet was being *really* optimistic." He ran one hand down her wet leg. "You don't by any chance have any lying around?"

"No." She shook her head slowly and then took a deep breath. "And if I did they'd probably have dry rot."

He lifted his eyebrows.

"It's been a long time, a very long time since I had any use for one." Her smile faded.

For some reason he couldn't explain he was very, very glad to hear that. He didn't like the idea of any man touching Frannie the way he had. It was a curiously possessive feeling.

"There's an all-night drugstore around the corner. Shouldn't take me more than ten minutes to get there and back."

She smiled again, and it was a real, true, unfettered grin that tried to grab at his heart.

"I'll make breakfast while you're gone. I don't know about you, Bridger, but I'm starving."

Chapter 8

Frannie put coffee on, then scrambled eggs and made toast. Bacon or biscuits would take much too long.

She went about making breakfast with a smile on her face. She'd never in her life experienced anything like last night, hadn't even known it was possible. She ached everywhere, in spite of her hot soak, but she wouldn't change anything that had happened, or anything that had yet to happen.

She set two plates of eggs and toast on the table as Bridger let himself in with the key he'd taken with him. He strolled into the kitchen, in his rumpled trousers and white shirt, and slapped an entire box of condoms on the center of the table.

Frannie stared at the box as she placed two white coffee mugs beside the plates. "Now, *that's* optimistic."

"Well, I figured if we could extend the one night to noon, we might as well make this a day instead of a night, and a day is twenty-four hours."

He eyed her over scrambled eggs and coffee, pretty much ignoring the box that sat between them. His eyes were harsh and his face was hard, but there was tenderness in him, too, in his touch and in his heart. Oh, if she thought they could make this work…

She nearly jumped out of her skin when the phone rang. Bridger stood to answer, checking the caller ID box he'd attached to her kitchen phone yesterday afternoon.

"They don't have it working yet," he said as he placed his hand on the receiver. "Do you usually get phone calls at six-thirty in the morning?"

Frannie shook her head slowly as he lifted the receiver.

"Yeah," he barked into the phone. "Who is this?" Very quickly his entire body relaxed, the tension leaving his shoulders and his arms. He turned to face Frannie. "It's for you," he whispered. "Your mother." He mouthed the silent words.

Frannie rolled her eyes as she left her chair. In a way, she'd rather carry on a one-sided conversation with a cold-blooded killer than have this talk with her mother. At least, as long as Bridger was around. He could protect her from the bad guys, but no one could help where her mother was concerned.

Bridger didn't return to his breakfast, but stood very near and listened. She didn't mind. In fact, she rather liked it.

"Hi, Mom," she said as she placed the receiver to her ear. "What's up?"

"Who was that who answered the phone?"

Frannie closed her eyes at the sharpness of her mother's tone. This was not going to be pretty. "Just a friend. You don't know him."

"I knew it wasn't Reese. He was always so *polite* when I spoke to him on the phone. Have you managed to patch things up with him yet?"

Not again! "No, I thought I made it clear—"

"You did, you did," her mother said, and then she affected the long-suffering sigh that came over the phone lines so well. "So, this rude man who answered the phone, he's the new boyfriend? It's about time, Frances Marie, that you got serious and—"

"Detective Bridger is just a friend, Mom."

There was a long, telling silence. "You're dating a cop?"

Frannie could almost smile. She did lock her eyes to Bridger's, and as she'd known it would, that simple connection made this conversation easier. "No, I am not *dating* a cop. Bridger and I have never been on a date and we never will." *More's the pity.* "He's just a friend."

There was no real change of expression on Bridger's face, but he did lift his eyebrows slightly.

"You're in some kind of trouble," her mother accused softly, her voice lowering to a harsh whisper. "What's going on?"

"Nothing." Frannie felt not a twinge of guilt as she lied. She'd been doing it for so long it was second nature to tell her mother what she wanted to hear.

"You're sure?" Frannie could almost imagine a hint of maternal affection in the question.

She took a deep breath. Telling all would only worry her mother, and heaven forbid, she might decide to come to Decatur to *help*. "I'm sure."

"Good. The reason I called…"

Of course there had to be a reason she was calling at this hour. Lois Annette Wylie Vaughn Henderson Stone McAnally Barry had never been a morning person.

"I'm getting married!"

Frannie felt as if someone had knocked the wind out of her. Her knees went weak, and she very gingerly fell against the wall. Why was she surprised? It had been what, six months since her mother had managed to get rid of the last loser in her life? "Again?" she whispered. "To who?"

"Oh, you don't know him. His name is Charlie Bedfield, and I met him a couple of weeks ago at a—"

"You met him a couple of weeks ago and you're already talking about getting married?" Frannie snapped.

"He asked me last night," was the dreamy answer. "We're flying to Las Vegas this morning, that's why I had to call so early."

All her life, Frannie had felt she was the adult and her mother was the naive child. Lois was not a bad person, she was just a terrible judge of character and a dreamer who believed that every flutter of her heart was true love. In her kinder moments, Frannie tried to convince herself that her mother had known love once, with Joey Vaughn, and had been trying to recapture that feeling since the day he'd died too young and without warning. But she couldn't escape the fact that when it came to boyfriends and husbands, Lois had the worst of luck.

"You should think this through," she said calmly. "Get to know this guy a little better before you do anything rash. A couple of weeks, Mom? Really, how…" Frannie's eyes found Bridger's and stayed there. Realization hit her like a ton of bricks. Dear God, what had she done? After all these years of being so careful, *now* she finds out she's just like her mother. How long had she known Bridger? Two days. *Two days!* And here she stood thinking these impossible romantic thoughts, just like her mother, convincing herself that the flutter of her own heart when Bridger looked at her was love. "How foolish," she finished in a whisper.

Her mother either ignored her or didn't hear. "I've got to go, baby. Charlie says we have to get to the airport an hour early. Love you."

"Love you, too." She heard the dial tone in her ear before she said, even more softly, "Good luck."

Frannie gently returned the receiver to the hook, and for a long moment she stared at the phone. "She's getting married again," she said to Bridger without turning to face him. "This will be hubby number six. My mother is a hopeless romantic. She keeps finding these guys she thinks she can change. Drunks, one druggie, bad boys with mean tempers, she convinces herself that all they need is the love of a good woman." She could hear the bitterness in her voice. "The problem is, love is never enough."

"Frannie." She stiffened as Bridger's hand touched her shoulder. As if he felt and understood her response, he removed that hand quickly. "You're not responsible for your mother's decisions."

No, but she was responsible for her own, wasn't she? "I never thought I could be as reckless and foolish and downright stupid as my mother. After all, I had the perfect bad example in front of me every day for eighteen years. But last night…"

"Don't you dare say last night was a mistake."

She turned to face him, then. "No," she admitted softly. "I won't say it was a mistake." Thinking she was falling in love with Bridger, that was the mistake. Confusing gratitude and lust with love, that was a mistake. All her life she'd been searching for a love that was safe and sure, something that wouldn't fade in the sunlight or disappear in the night.

Bridger made no secret of the fact that he wanted her body, but that was all. They'd had one night, and that was all she could afford. Anything more would surely destroy her, because in the end, loving and losing Bridger would be more than she could stand.

He cupped her chin and forced her to look into his eyes. "But it is over, isn't it?"

"Yes," she said, relieved that he saw it as well as she did. "It's over."

He scooped the box of condoms off the table—maybe he didn't want to look at it any more than she did—and headed for the bathroom. She heard the cabinet door beneath the sink open noisily and bang shut, and she placed her forehead against the doorjamb and closed her eyes tight.

The Riverwatch Hotel looked even worse by daylight than it did at night. Every chipped brick, every suspicious stain and winding crack in the sidewalk, screamed rat trap. Frannie had wanted to stay home while he visited the site of the murder, but there was no way Mal was leaving her alone again—not after yesterday's disasters. He knew at least part of the reason she wanted to stay home was her reluctance to face that jerk Clarence Doyle. That was one reason for the timing of this visit. Harry had assured him that Mrs. Doyle was on desk duty during the afternoons.

Mal took Frannie's arm as they stepped into the lobby and faced a different desk clerk than they had the last time they'd come to the Riverwatch.

The woman was as wrinkled and openly suspicious as the old man who'd been working here that rainy Tuesday night, watching the two of them through narrowed, colorless eyes. Her loose paisley dress from another era was faded and shapeless, but her steel gray bun was neat as a pin. Harry's description of Violet Doyle had been right on target—if perhaps a little kind.

Mal released Frannie's arm and flashed his badge. She stayed silently behind him as he faced the desk clerk. "Mrs. Doyle, I'd like to ask you a few questions."

The old woman sighed and leaned against the counter. "All I've done the past three days is answer questions."

Mal smiled. "I'm sure you won't mind answering a few more."

Violet sighed again. With her gray bun and polyester paisley dress, she looked like someone's grandmother, a sweet old lady who should be baking cookies and reading bedtime stories. But there was something bitter in her eyes, and her wrinkled face sported more frown lines than laugh lines. Her bedtime stories were likely to give any kid nightmares.

"The girl who was murdered paid cash," she said as he drew near, "received no visitors that I know of in the three days she was here, and she signed her name in the guest book as Jane Doe. No," she said tiredly, "I did not ask for identification. No, I did not see her driving a car and I did not see her with anyone else at any time. Once I got a look at her, I knew who she was and the cops searched her room good. There wasn't nothing there but a few clothes and a ton of makeup."

"Thank you," Mal said, leaning against the counter casually. "I just have a couple more questions."

"And by the way," Violet added angrily, "the city of Decatur will be getting a bill for what I paid to have that room put back in order. There was no call to rip it apart the way they did."

"That shouldn't be a problem," Mal said calmly. "Now, just a few more questions."

Violet glowered in his direction. "Well, let's get it over with."

"Were there any other unusual guests here the same time as Jane Doe?"

The old woman positively cackled. "You and your girlfriend, Detective Bridger." She shot a glance at Frannie. "Yeah, my husband Clarence described you both real well. He thought it was a hoot that there was a homicide detective sleeping upstairs while the first murder ever in the Riverwatch Hotel takes place."

Mal did not think it was funny, not at all, but he wasn't about to let the old woman make him lose his cool. A small smile silenced her laughter. "Yeah, that's very amusing," he said flatly. He reached out and snagged the leather guest book, and before Mrs. Doyle could so much as complain, he flipped through a few pages. "Oh, look. Jane's brother John was staying here," he said, pointing at a sloppily scrawled John Doe. "And damn near the entire Smith family, it seems. Bob, Joe, little Billy." He slapped the book shut. "Do you have any customers who sign their own names?"

She wasn't intimidated. "Just you, Detective Bridger."

He leaned slightly forward and lowered his voice. "You know, if I can't get the answers I want out of you, I might just have to knock on every door in this hotel. Your clientele seems to come and go with great frequency, so I might have to come back every night for, oh, a couple of weeks."

Finally the crone was worried. "I won't have no business left."

"Probably not." It was a promise, to her and to himself.

She straightened her spine, but there was a hint of reluctant surrender in her eyes. "She's been here before."

"Jane Doe."

"Yes, Jane Doe," the old lady snapped. "Only the other time she was here she wasn't Jane Doe, she was Jane Smith. It was a few weeks back, I can't rightly remember exactly when. She had a male visitor. I saw them come in one night, late, when Clarence was sick and I had to cover his shift."

"I don't suppose you got a name for this male visitor." It was too much to hope for, but he had to ask.

"No, but I'd recognize him if I ever saw his face again." She smiled. "He was purty one. Looked kinda like Tyrone Power, when he turned his head just so. He had dark hair, cut nice and neat, and he was dressed right sharp."

It wasn't much, but it meant Jane Doe had a boyfriend in Decatur. It was better than nothing. Mal flipped a business card onto the counter. "You think of anything else, you call me. Leave a message at the number on the front."

"Sure." She studied the card, holding it at a distance to read the words. "You wouldn't think a nice-looking clean-cut fella that looks like Tyrone Power would have a tattoo," she muttered.

Mal had turned to leave, but her words stopped him in his tracks. "A tattoo?" It was better than a name, which probably would have been John Smith anyway.

"Yep," she said conversationally. "That pretty Jane, she got one on her ankle, and her fella musta got his on his forearm. He was kneading on it like this." She demonstrated, rubbing her own forearm, "and they were laughing and talking about how much it hurt." She leaned forward with a gleam in her eye. This wasn't cooperating with the police, this was gossip, and she loved it. "I think they'd been drinkin' heavily."

"You think so." He nodded knowingly.

"I do. Pretty young girl like that, all that drinkin' will make her old before her time."

Mal didn't remind the old woman that Jane Doe wasn't going to ever have a chance to grow old badly.

Frannie stepped out of the kitchen, leaving Bridger alone to make his phone calls. For the life of her she couldn't figure out why he was so excited about a tattoo. It was a clue, but not much of one in her opinion. Still, he said it was a step in the right direction. One step at a time, he said. One step at a time.

At least the investigation took his mind off last night and this disastrous morning. They both ignored the recent past quite well.

He wanted to fill Harry in on the news and then call the phone company and insist that her caller ID be operational within the next hour. Frannie didn't want to hover over him, so she puttered around the house, listening to the distant vibrations of his deep voice. She picked up and dusted a little, straightened the pillows on the sofa, and finally she had to make her way to the bedroom.

The pillows were scattered all over the room, and her own discarded clothes were where she'd left them last night. She made the bed, snapping the sheets and trying to erase the too-clear memories that lingered here.

She quickly decided not to bother. She'd never forget, and why should she? In her heart she knew she'd never feel that way again, so maybe she should savor the memories instead of trying to chase them away.

She wouldn't make the same mistakes her mother had made again and again. Men didn't change. Bridger didn't want the same things she did. He didn't like kids, he didn't want to settle down, he thought the solution to her problems was to buy a gun, for God's sake.

But, oh, last night had been so perfect, so beautiful and exciting and…unexpected. Frannie had never been one to trust her passion, but Bridger made her trust. He made her feel and want and love too much.

The room looked almost normal again. All that was left was to remove the four foil condom wrappers from the floor. She scooped them up and balled her fist, and as she left the room a smile crossed her face. There had been a few hours when she thought she'd never be comfortable in her bedroom again. After all, an intruder had walked into this room uninvited and pointed a gun at her and threatened her life. She'd been terrified, sitting on the floor in a defenseless position.

But last night had exorcised any demons that remained in the room. Love was stronger than fear, she supposed.

She dropped the foil wrappers into the bathroom wastebasket. One night, and it was over and done.

The ring of the doorbell made her literally jump. Dammit, she had to get over this! No man was going to make her afraid in her own home.

Since she hesitated in the bathroom, Bridger was at the front door before she was. He looked through the peephole, one hand resting comfortably on the revolver at his waist.

"Looks harmless enough," he said softly as he opened the door, but his hand remained over the gun.

Frannie saw the familiar fair head long before Reese spoke. She closed her eyes and took a deep breath and silently swore, using every curse word she'd ever heard.

Bridger filled the doorway, silently looming over Reese. Reese, at the disadvantage of his height and a single step from the doorway to the porch, craned his head to look into Bridger's face. "What are you doing here?" he demanded. His voice got a little whiny when he got excited, and it was *very* whiny now.

Bridger leaned against the doorjamb, effectively blocking Reese's entrance and Frannie's exit. "No," he said calmly. "What are *you* doing here?"

"Has something happened to Frannie?" There was real concern in that whiny voice, and Frannie realized that from where Reese was standing he couldn't see anything but Bridger, his badge and weapon on full display.

"No, nothing's happened," she said brightly, moving Bridger aside with a hand on his arm so she could see Reese's face and he could see her. She thought about smiling to reassure him, but then she remembered that he had just recently fired her without good cause. "What do you want, Reese?"

Bridger looked down at her. "*This* is Reese?"

Frannie ignored the insulting question and focused on her ex-fiancé, ex-boss, ex-friend. Reese had his pale, thin hair pulled back in a ponytail, and his gold-rimmed glasses gave him a scholarly look. He looked more like a college student or a young professor than an entrepreneur. In his well-worn khakis and blue-and-white-checked cotton shirt, he was the picture of casual youth and vigor, of beauty and intelligence, appearing to be easily a full five years younger than his thirty-three.

Next to Bridger he was pale and small and, well, insignificant. She couldn't believe that she'd ever shed a tear or lost a minute's sleep over this man. "What do you want?" she asked again.

Reese glanced up at Bridger. "Can I come in?"

In defeat, Frannie turned away from the door. "Sure. I'll make us a fresh pot of coffee." Just what she needed—Bridger and Reese sitting, together, at her kitchen table. The only two men she'd ever slept with, staring at each other over coffee while she tried to make inane small talk.

Reese glanced suspiciously at Bridger, who was right behind him, as he entered the kitchen. "Can I speak to you privately?" he asked softly.

Frannie barely looked at Bridger as she answered. "No. Anything you have to say to me you can say in front of Detective Bridger."

"Detective Bridger," he repeated suspiciously. "Are you in trouble?"

"No." She made the introductions briefly and almost painlessly, while Reese and Bridger sized each other up in a way that was, well, primal. They were two males challenging one another over the only female in the area, and she could practically smell the testosterone flying about the room. It was no contest: in the wild or in civilization, poor Reese didn't have a prayer.

While they glared, she realized that she had *never* loved Reese. Somehow he'd convinced her that their dreams were the same—family, home, commitment. She'd tried to make herself love him, perhaps, since he not only professed to want the same things from life she did, but because he so perfectly fit her notion of the ideal man. Handsome, gentle, intelligent...this was not a man who would ever raise a hand to another living being, or express his anger by shouting or slamming doors. He'd be a good father, as gentle with his children as he was with the rest of the world.

But he was also somewhat passionless, and next to Bridger he positively paled. Her few awkward couplings with Reese bore little resemblance to last night's remarkable events. She'd never loved him; no wonder their relationship had unraveled.

Reese looked away first, breaking the staring contest. "Frannie, I need you to come back to work. I really need that on-line catalog completed by the end of next month, and if I don't do something fast I'm going to lose my biggest client." He appeared to be disturbed. "You know how Teddy Rigsby can be. He loses his temper over the smallest things. He got too many pralines and not enough divinity in the last shipment for his specialty shops, and he called, raising hell as usual. Sharon burst into tears and told him we didn't need his business if he was going to talk to her that way." He glanced up sheepishly. "When he asked for you and she told him you'd been fired, he hit the roof." What came next obviously pained him. "The office is falling apart without you."

It was evil, perhaps, but she smiled. "What's the matter, the new girl can't handle it?"

He took the mug of coffee she offered. "Sharon can hardly type," he muttered.

"And you thought she could do my job?"

Reese took his coffee to the kitchen table and sat down as if he were very, very tired. "She took a few computer classes, and she said she could handle it, and...I hate to admit it, but she insisted that I fire you. She was jealous."

Frannie laughed out loud. "Of what?"

Reese lifted sad, green puppy-dog eyes to her. Oh, he always did this when he wanted something! "She sensed that there was something between us, still, and she just wouldn't let it go.''

Frannie took a chair, not too close to Reese. He'd known first that marriage for the two of them would never work, and after a difficult discussion she'd had to agree he was right. Sharon thought there was something between them? She and Reese both knew there had never been anything real between them.

''So because your girlfriend is delusional, you want me to come back to work for you, work long, extra hours for little or no extra pay, and pull your fanny out of the fire with Rigsby.''

''Basically, yes.''

Yesterday she would have jumped at the chance to have her job back without so much as a second thought. It would mean security, stability, it would mean no job hunting and she wouldn't even have to consider selling her house. ''No,'' she said softly and surely. ''More coffee?''

Reese knew her too well. Obviously he'd expected her to jump at this chance. ''No?'' There was a moment of puzzlement on his face, and then a smug satisfaction crept in and took its place. She positively hated this expression This was the *Reese wins* look. ''I get it. You want a raise. Okay, I can give you five percent now and another five percent in six months.''

''You promised me that raise last year.'' Frannie sipped her coffee, and as she returned the cup to the table she glanced at Bridger, who continued to stand behind her like a sentinel. She knew him well enough to know that the very small twitch at the corner of his lips was the beginnings of a smile.

''Ten percent now, then,'' Reese said.

Frannie smiled. ''No.''

The smug expression disappeared. ''You want me to eat crow, is that it? Okay, I was wrong, I'm sorry. If you'll come back you'll get the raise and I swear I won't dock you even if you come in an hour late.''

Frannie took a deep breath. ''No,'' she said as she exhaled. ''I've decided to look elsewhere for employment. There are lots of companies in the area who would appreciate a good computer programmer. If I have to drive to Huntsville every day, so be it. If I have to look for a while to find the right place, I can do that, too.''

Once the decision was made she was happy with it. It was long past time to move on.

''You've made up your mind, haven't you?'' Reese pushed his half-empty mug to the center of the table.

''Yes.''

''Well, then,'' Reese said as he stood. ''I'm wasting my time here.'' For a long moment he looked down at Frannie, and she could see that he was irritated and out of sorts, and yet he remained amiable. Nothing ruffled Reese's feathers for long. His glance shot quickly to Bridger and then back to her again. ''Who *is* he?''

She didn't hesitate. ''A friend.''

Reese leaned slightly forward and whispered, ''I think he's a bad influence on you, Frannie. I've never known you to be so reckless.''

He sauntered toward the door. ''I'm going to make a pit stop.'' Just outside the doorway he halted. ''I *can* use your bathroom, can't I?''

''Sure.''

Bridger waited until the bathroom door closed. ''A friend,'' he muttered. ''First your mother and now this jerk. A *friend*.''

''What did you want me to tell him—the truth?'' Frannie said. ''I don't think so.''

They waited in the living room, side by side but not too close, until Reese came out of the bathroom. If anything, he looked more agitated than he had when he'd gone in.

"Frannie," he said tensely. "Can I speak to you privately? Please."

Frannie nodded to Bridger, and he rambled into the kitchen, perhaps to make a phone call, perhaps to pour himself the cup of coffee he'd refused earlier. When he was gone, Reese lifted and opened a fist. A ball of foil lay on his palm.

"What is this?" he asked softly.

Frannie swept the condom wrappers off his palm. "None of your business, that's what they are."

Reese took a deep breath. It was, she knew, his way of calming himself. "When did you meet this Detective Bridger, Frannie?"

"A few hours after you fired me," she snapped.

She shocked him. His face turned red, and he damn near sputtered. "You barely know the man and you're... you're..."

Frannie walked past Reese, opened the door and showed him the way out. "Good luck finding a new programmer," she said with a smile.

He came to her but didn't leave. Instead, he took her hand and held it tenderly. "I'm worried about you, Frannie," he whispered. "You're not yourself. I only want to help, and that's the truth."

"Trust me," she said as she removed her hand from his. "I have all the help I need."

Bridger chose that moment to saunter back into the living room. *And more help than I want.*

Reese didn't need another invitation to leave. One quick look at Bridger and he was gone.

Bridger was quiet as they listened to the car on the street being started and driven quickly away. But when all was silent he stared her down.

"You were engaged to that?"

Frannie clutched the foil wrappers in her hand. "For a few months, yes."

"Why?"

She turned away and headed for the bathroom and the trash can there. Why? It was a question she wasn't ready to answer, any more than she could answer the question that had been popping into her head all day. *Why did she have to fancy herself falling in love with Bridger?*

Chapter 9

About two in the morning, Mal accepted the fact that he wasn't going to get any sleep. Frannie's couch was too soft and too short and too damn lumpy.

And try as he might he couldn't forget that Frannie was sleeping somewhere on the other side of this wall, curled up in the big bed all alone. With no effort at all he could practically see her. She was probably wearing her football jersey instead of sleeping naked, as she had last night. Her knees would be drawn up, the cover pushed down to just past her waist, her head would be turned so that one side of her long throat was exposed. Oh, this was not good.

He should be happy. The investigation into the convenience store shooting had cleared him of any wrongdoing, as he had known it would. Next week he would be back on full duty. Harry was still after him to talk to the psychiatrist, but today's demands to schedule an appointment had been less frequent and much less ardent. Poor Harry had his own problems to occupy his time and mind, impending fatherhood among them.

Every good homicide cop knew the majority of evidence was collected in the first twenty-four hours after a murder, and as far as Mal was concerned they didn't have nearly enough. Stanley Loudermilk officially remained a suspect, and after the way Clarence Doyle had accosted Frannie in the drugstore, they had to consider him a suspect, too. But until they identified the body or found the murder weapon, they were stalled.

Mal had great hopes of identifying the body soon. There weren't that many places in the area to get a quality tattoo like the one on Jane Doe's ankle, and every possibility was being checked out.

Frannie had tried to send him home, but she'd stopped short of tossing him out. Knowing that the man who'd broken into her house was the killer scared her, as it should. She'd be a fool to run her only protection off, and Frannie Vaughn was not a fool.

Last night's delayed but spectacular one-night stand should have him smiling, still. It had been everything he'd dreamed of, and more, and when he closed his eyes he could see and smell and taste and feel the woman on the other side of this wall, his senses coming alive with a memory so sharp it amazed him.

He couldn't remember ever losing control the way he had with Frannie, couldn't remember ever feeling so contented and unsatisfied at the same time. The more he had her, the more he wanted her, and no good could ever come of that. No good at all.

He'd seen her face light up when Harry had shared his disastrous news. Babies! They were nothing but trouble. They ruled your life and changed everything by their very presence. He'd seen it happen, with his sisters' kids and with strangers' children. Sure they were adorable when they were little, but like everything else in this world they grew up and changed—not always for the better.

But Frannie wanted babies. He had seen it in her eyes as she'd listened to Harry talk about how pure and sweet they were. Those eyes had positively sparkled, and if he hadn't already known, if she hadn't already told him that they had no future, he would have known it then.

He should be happy, but he wasn't. Sure he'd been cleared in the convenience store shooting, but that didn't change the fact that he'd killed a man. The Jane Doe murder and Frannie had distracted him from that fact but couldn't change it.

Yes, they had leads in the murder, but they weren't enough. Would Frannie ever be safe if they didn't catch the butcher who'd slashed that blonde's throat?

Frannie was at the center of it all, when you came right down to it. The upheaval, the dread, the certainty that they were *still* unfinished. The woman had worked her way into his mind, had wormed her way in so completely she was constantly there. Mal suffered—and, man, did he suffer— the strongest urge to leave this couch, collect the box of condoms from under her bathroom sink, and spend the entire weekend in Frannie's bed.

But she'd made it clear they were done, and he wouldn't do anything to risk the uneasy balance they'd found. If she kicked him out, who would watch over her?

He raised a hand to brush his fingertips across the wall that separated the couch from Frannie's bedroom. She was there, sleeping, resting, dreaming the sweet dreams of the innocent.

She was exhausted, so why couldn't she sleep? Frannie rolled over again and again, trying to get comfortable. The last decent night's sleep she'd enjoyed had been in the Riverwatch Hotel, so her body should insist on a deep and complete rest in spite of the fact that her mind was spinning.

Thoughts of Bridger, more than the memory of the intruder, kept her awake. The sound of his voice, the touch of his lips, the way his body molded perfectly to hers. She could smell him on the pillow, musky and soapy and male. Heaven help her, she could almost *feel* his body against hers when she started to drift off, had actually reached out once in a half-asleep moment to touch him. He wasn't there, of course, and the realization brought her to full awareness again.

They'd had their night, and whatever had drawn them together was over. Finished, done, complete. Bridger was satisfied. He must be, since he hadn't once in this entire, long day tried to so much as kiss her.

Frannie pulled the covers over her head. She wished with all her heart that she could forget her mother's numerous mistakes and just take what life handed her without question. So what if Bridger was all wrong for her? There were moments, wonderful, crystalline moments, when he was all *right*.

Frannie was making coffee when the phone rang. Even though it was after nine she was groggy and still half-asleep. Of course, the sun had been coming up when she'd finally succumbed to exhaustion.

The caller ID was working, and she smiled when she saw Dixon on the display.

"Hello."

"Well, good morning," Harry said in a very cheery voice. He sounded as if he'd gotten a great night's sleep. "Is Mal up and about?"

She sighed into the phone. Naturally Harry knew that Bridger had spent the night here. "No, he's still asleep. On the couch," she added.

"Wake him up," Harry said with a hint of poorly disguised glee. "This is important."

Frannie left the receiver hanging from the curling cord. She'd peeked in at Bridger on her way to the kitchen, and he'd been out cold. Sprawled across her too-small couch, he looked uncomfortable and rumpled and big. He was sleeping in his clothes, though he'd discarded the tie and his shoes. Pajamas would be better, but she had a feeling Bridger didn't own a pair of pajamas. He didn't wear his gun, of course, but it was on the coffee table, close at hand.

"Phone," she said from a safe distance.

He didn't stir.

"Bridger." She raised her voice slightly. "Harry's on the phone."

Nothing.

She crossed the living room to shake him gently, laying her hand on the arm that crossed his chest. As soon as she touched his arm he came awake, his eyes opening slowly and one hand drifting sensually over hers. His fingers closed one at a time, as he took that hand and held it gently.

She could lean over and give him a kiss, as if he were her own sleeping beauty. A kiss on those full lips, or perhaps there at his throat where his heart beat so steady and true, to wake him, that was just what he needed. Maybe it was just what she needed.

Oh, he looked so tempting it was gut-wrenching and heart stopping and completely unfair. Dark stubble covered his chin and his cheeks, and he was warm and wide, and the hand that held hers was firm and gentle. And his eyes, still more asleep than awake, looked at her with such longing and affection that she was sure, for an instant, that it didn't matter that they were totally unsuited for each other.

"Some watchdog you are," she said softly. "An entire army could tramp through here and it wouldn't disturb your sleep."

He came instantly awake and bolted upright, releasing her hand.

"Phone," Frannie said, backing away. "It's Harry."

Apparently in no hurry, Bridger rose from the couch, unfolding himself slowly and raking a hand through his short, dark hair. Standing, he no longer looked charmingly tempting. He was too tall, too big, too male.

"You were sleeping soundly," she said as she turned and headed for the kitchen. "I was afraid the couch would be too small for you."

He mumbled something that sounded vaguely obscene.

"Anyway, I'm glad you got a good night's sleep," she said, forcing a false cheer into her voice. "I slept like a baby, myself." *Up half the night.* "As soon as my head hit the pillow I was out like a light." She didn't want Bridger to think she'd been mooning over him all night while he slept peacefully, without regrets and temptations.

"Great," he mumbled sleepily as he grabbed the receiver.

The conversation was brief and one-sided, and when Bridger hung up Frannie had no idea what the conversation had been about. Then she turned around, his cup of black coffee offered in her hand, and he smiled.

"Jane Doe has a name."

Coffee, a bath and a change of clothes later, Mal led Frannie down the narrow hallway of police headquarters to the detectives' room. She'd insisted that she could stay home on her own, but wisely she hadn't insisted very hard.

Jane Doe's name was Miranda Jane Fossett. As soon as he'd heard Harry utter the name he'd made the connection. Her brother was Jacob Fossett, a once promising young, idealistic boy who had died a terrorist in jail last year.

Fossett had been a member of a group that touted themselves as red-blooded, true-blue freedom fighters. The Decatur Legion for Liberty, which Harry had quickly renamed the Decatur Legion for Wackos, was a paramilitary group that held meetings and training sessions in all parts of Morgan County, their members dressing in camouflage and carrying enough ammo to start a small war.

They were an equal-opportunity army, banding against everyone and everything that didn't conform to their beliefs, but their number-one target had always been government. State, federal and local, they protested any claimed right to govern their lives, while citing their constitutional rights to protest. Morons.

No one had taken them very seriously, at first. People were drawn in by the word *liberty,* a powerful, patriotic word, but they didn't stay long. The Decatur Legion for Liberty began to dwindle in numbers. There were rumblings in the department that they started selling drugs and guns to raise funds for their cause. They were under investigation for those crimes when they planted a bomb in the Morgan County courthouse.

The explosion had been a small one, but the bomb had been built to kill and it had. A lawyer and a woman who was going to court over a speeding ticket were both killed, and three others had been injured.

Everything led to Fossett. He'd been seen, they could trace the bomb materials to him, and he was a vocal member of the Legion for Liberty. Within two days they had him in custody.

Fossett had not acted alone, and he was not the leader of the Decatur Legion for Liberty; he simply wasn't smart enough, and he was a follower, not a leader. He would have talked eventually to save his hide, Mal knew it, but within days Fossett was dead in his jail cell.

They said he hanged himself. There was even a note that rambled on about not giving in to the pressures of the establishment, about how he'd rather die than live in a cage. The legion had become quiet after that. Some said they'd disbanded but Mal didn't believe it. Fanatics didn't scare that easily.

Mal hadn't bought the story surrounding Fossett's death then, and Miranda Fossett's murder just made him more certain that the nuts weren't only still out there, they were still active.

Frannie wasn't leaving his side if that was the case. Until they had all these bastards accounted for, she wasn't safe. If only he knew who they were looking for.

"Wait here," he instructed, pulling out his chair for Frannie. She sat slowly, her eyes taking in everything.

"This is not what I expected, Bridger," she said, swiveling to face him. "Looks too much like my first cubicle." She grinned and picked up his coffee mug. The one Harry had given him that said *If I Knew Any More I'd Be A Threat To National Security*.

She eyed the file folders and the computer as she replaced the mug on his desk, and he could almost see the housekeeping plans in her eyes. Yes, it was a mess, but it was *his* mess and he knew where everything was.

"Don't touch anything," he ordered as he left her there.

He almost ran Jerry Kruse over as he made his way to Harry's desk. Jerry was new to detectives, and had been working in the burglary division. Young and energetic, he had been a good uniformed cop and was working out to be an even better detective.

"You on call this weekend?" Mal asked as he passed.

"Yeah." Kruse smiled. "Thought I'd hang around here and catch up on some paperwork instead of sitting at home and waiting for my pager to go off."

The paperwork never ended. Once you got behind it was a nightmare to catch up. "Good plan." Mal headed on to Harry's desk, but Kruse's lowered voice stopped him.

"Is that your witness?"

Mal turned around as Jerry nodded slightly toward Frannie. "Yeah."

"Not exactly a tough assignment, watching over that one, huh?" Kruse didn't exactly leer, but Mal didn't like the gleam in the detective's eyes. "Pretty lady."

He rejected the number of angry responses that came easily to his lips. "Finish your paperwork, kid."

Kruse ignored him. "Are you two…" He waved his hands, palms up, in the air, leaving the question unfinished.

"We're friends," Mal said, gritting out the word Frannie used to inadequately describe their relationship. "Just friends."

Frannie's fingers positively itched to reorganize Bridger's cubicle. What a mess! But on closer inspection she noticed that there was a kind of order to his disorder, so she left it alone as he'd requested.

"Ma'am, can I get you a cup of coffee while you wait?"

Frannie spun around in the comfortable swivel chair and faced a nice-looking man who wore a friendly grin and a suit as immaculate as the one Bridger had taken from the trunk of his car this morning.

"No thanks," she said, instinctively answering his smile. "I'm fine."

He didn't leave but leaned up against the edge of Bridger's cubicle and made himself comfortable. He wore the standard short haircut, his brown hair neat except for the one strand that fell over his forehead in a casual manner he'd probably sculpted before the mirror. Instead of a conservative tie like something Bridger would choose, this detective wore one that sported a vivid image of Bugs Bunny.

"I understand you've had a rough week," he said in a lowered voice that was kind and soothing, rather like Harry's. She wondered if the pleasant, intimate tone was something these guys practiced as surely as they practiced firing their weapons.

"You could say that," she admitted. Every detective, uniformed policeman, dispatcher and desk clerk probably knew exactly what had happened to her this week, including the fact that Bridger had all but moved in with her.

His smile faded slowly. "Are you handling it all right? It's not easy to have your whole world turned upside down, I know."

Frannie took a deep breath. "I don't have any choice but to handle it, do I?" That was the truth. Hysteria would get her nowhere. Panic wouldn't help at all.

The man offered his hand and tried a gentler smile. "My name's Jerry Kruse," he said as Frannie took the extended hand. He didn't shake her hand, simply held it easily for a moment. "And I have to say, Miss Vaughn, I think you're handling this very well. I'm sure it helps your peace of mind that Detective Bridger is helping you out. He's the best."

Yes, he is.

Kruse took his hand from hers and crossed his arms over his chest. "If anyone can solve this case, he can."

"I'm sure you're right."

"Like I said," Kruse said with real admiration, "Mal's the best."

"Have you worked with him long?"

They fell into an easy, comfortable conversation. Jerry told her about his promotion to detective, and Frannie told him about getting fired. Only now she could smile as she told him that Reese had offered her the job back and she'd turned it down.

"So what are you going to do now?"

She'd given it a lot of thought last night as she tossed and turned. "I think I'll get a part-time job, just to supplement my savings, and then see if I can line up some free-lance work.''

He seemed to like the plan, and even encouraged her when the old doubts about taking a risk came to her. And then the conversation came to a natural end.

Kruse shifted, moving his weight from one foot to the other. ''Maybe, when this mess is all over, I can give you a call? There's this great Chinese restaurant in Huntsville. Do you like Chinese?''

''Yes.'' He was flirting with her! Frannie would have laughed if she hadn't been afraid of offending him. He was a nice guy, and more than a little good-looking, but right now she most definitely was not interested. Still, it was interesting to note that she'd been looking in the wrong places for her Prince Charming. All she had to do was get arrested. ''But I don't think—''

''Don't turn me down now,'' he interrupted. ''It's just a thought, that's all.''

Bridger saved her, appearing behind Kruse with a scowl on his face. ''What's a thought?''

''I just asked Frannie if she'd like to have dinner with me sometime.''

Bridger forcibly moved Kruse back and away from his cubicle. He lowered his voice, but Frannie could hear every word. ''It's very bad form to hit on the witnesses, Kruse. Lay off.''

Bridger came around the corner and offered his hand to help Frannie from the chair. ''Let's go.''

Frannie laid her hand in his and let him pull her to her feet. She stifled a small smile. Was he jealous? Maybe just a little bit?

Of course not. What wishful thinking that was! He let go of her hand once she was standing, and turned to walk toward the exit. She followed, watching his back.

Bridger was always wound pretty tight, as if he were

constantly waiting for some disaster to occur, and right now he looked even more unyielding than usual. His shoulders were squared, and the muscles in his neck were strained. She knew how to make him feel better, how to make him forget that all was not as it should be, but she didn't dare.

Harry waited near the door that led to the hallway. "Hey, I have a great idea. How about tomorrow you two come to the house. Paula is dying to meet Frannie. We'll grill steaks and play cards and discuss baby names."

"No," Bridger said sharply.

Frannie was disappointed. It would be nice to spend an afternoon with Harry and his wife and Bridger, almost like a real date.

"Come on," Harry said, his voice cajoling. "Prove to me that you haven't forgotten how to have fun."

Bridger opened the door. "We have plans."

"We do?" Frannie glanced up, and the look Bridger gave her was one that hinted at apology.

"I almost forgot. I have this family thing tomorrow, and like it or not it'll last all afternoon." His dark eyes were pinned on her, and at the moment they were completely unreadable. "Food, kids, relatives coming out of the wood-work."

It sounded so wonderful, but where would she be while Bridger got together with his family? "I'll call Darlene and see if she's busy. Maybe I can spend the day with her. Or maybe…"

"Oh no, you're not getting off that easy. You're coming with me," Bridger commanded, leaving no room for argument.

They decided on take-out from Mal's favorite Mexican place for dinner, and the meal was spread out over her kitchen table, along with two tall glasses of sweet iced tea.

After eating a pitifully small meal, Frannie declared that

she was stuffed, then she pushed her plate away and leaned back.

"So," she said, her eyes unerringly on his face, "tell me about your family."

He narrowed his eyes. "Can't this wait until tomorrow?"

She grinned at his discomfort. "No."

He pushed his plate away. "I hate to do this to you, I really do. My family is definitely best met one at a time. The whole clan at once is enough to scare off even the toughest person."

She heard the touch of humor in his voice and laughed out loud. "That bad, huh?"

He didn't answer, but simply stared at her over leftover tacos and burritos and a half-eaten Mexican pizza. He didn't want to talk about his family, not now.

Another celibate night in this house was going to kill him, although he didn't dare take the chance of telling Frannie that and scaring her off. If she kicked him out, there wouldn't be anyone to keep an eye on her, and it was much too soon to have even a glimmer of hope that she'd be safe alone.

Maybe she felt the same frustration he did. He could almost see it in her, as she starting clearing the table. Every now and then he'd catch her fingers trembling slightly, or he'd watch closely and see that she held her breath. At this particular moment she couldn't quite look him in the eye. She looked at the dishes in her hand or the leftover food, and once he caught her staring at the salt and pepper shakers as if they were fascinating.

If only he could be sure that what he saw was a frustration similar to his own, and not fear.

"What do you usually do on Saturday night?" he asked.

She didn't turn to answer him as she wiped off a dish and spoke into the sink. "Oh, nothing. Watch TV, maybe rent a movie. What about you?"

"Same thing," he grumbled. "Usually." It was going to be a damned long night.

If it wasn't for this case he would take a chance and kiss her again, just to see if she melted the way he was almost certain she would, just to see if the feeling would be as powerful as he remembered. If she reacted the way he thought she would, he'd have her right here on the kitchen table. He stared at the pale oak as the too-clear fantasy filled his mind.

It was a chance he couldn't take. Frannie was skittish, and who could blame her, after what she'd been through this week. He didn't want to scare her away.

Maybe the silence got to be too much for her, because she reached across the counter to turn on the radio. They caught the end of an old song, a fast and silly tune that had played at Rick's on Tuesday night, and then a booming voice said, "An all-eighties weekend!" Frannie laughed as she reached out to change the station.

He loved her laugh. It was so real, never forced, never phony. He loved so many things about her, and that real laugh was just one.

In her search for an alternative to the retro weekend music, she found a station that played a soft and easy song, an instrumental with strings and a softly played piano. Evidently that satisfied her, because she went back to washing dishes.

Watching her was not a chore, not at all. He loved her long legs, and her delicate fingers, and her blue eyes, and her funny haircut. Taken one at a time, maybe there was nothing extraordinary there, but together, oh, together they made a fine picture, the kind of picture a man could get lost in.

Outside, the light faded to gray, and the light over the sink illuminated this particular picture for him right now. Frannie was all soft edges and golden halos, gentle and unconsciously seductive motion. As she washed the dishes she never once looked over her shoulder. She either didn't know he was sitting at her kitchen table studying her, or else she didn't care.

All of a sudden her head snapped to one side, and she stared wide-eyed at the back door. "Bridger," she whispered without so much as glancing in his direction. "Somebody's out there."

He stood slowly, his eyes on the back door. There was nothing to be seen through the parted yellow curtain and the glass beyond it. "You sure?"

"Absolutely," she whispered. "I saw a face in the window, just a glimpse, but I'm sure."

He moved quickly toward the kitchen door and threw it open. The bushes to his left rustled, and a man in a baseball cap burst from his hiding place and took off running.

Rage and adrenaline rushed through Mal's veins. He cleared the low back porch with one leap, reaching for his weapon as he landed.

The man skittered around the corner, plowing into a flowering bush and then trampling a small tomato plant in his clumsy attempt at escape.

Mal pursued the man, easily hurdling the remaining tomato plants and a few freshly planted beans, gaining on the clumsy trespasser with every step. His anger grew with each pounding step he took, with every inch he gained on the Peeping Tom.

"Police!" he shouted. "Stop!"

Surprisingly the trespasser in the baseball cap did as Mal commanded, coming to an abrupt halt in Frannie's front yard.

Mal raised his revolver and pointed it at the man's back. If this was the same man who'd broken into Frannie's house on Wednesday night, he might very well be armed.

"Hands in the air where I can see them," he ordered as

he took a step closer, and once again the man obeyed readily.

"Turn around."

The man was circling slowly when Frannie opened the front door. Frannie and Mal both recognized the Peeping Tom at the same time.

"Reese!" she said, about the time the man faced Mal.

"Frannie," Reese said testily. "This man has a *gun* pointed at me."

Mal lowered his weapon. "What the hell were you doing prowling around this house? And why did you run?"

"I was not prowling," Reese defended himself. "I saw the car out front, and I just peeked in the kitchen window to see if Frannie was here and if she was alone. And I ran because—" the man blushed easily "—well, it's an embarrassing situation to be caught in."

Mal grinned, though in truth he didn't feel at all like smiling. "You can put your hands down now."

"You scared the life out of me," Frannie said from her position in the open doorway. "What were you thinking?"

"I wanted to talk to you again, to see if I couldn't change your mind about coming back to work." Reese, who looked maybe eighteen years old with his hair tucked under the baseball cap, cast a suspicious glance in Mal's direction. "But I didn't know *he'd* be here again."

As Mal passed Reese he couldn't resist whispering, "Still, not again."

Chapter 10

Bridger kept his eyes on the road, so Frannie felt free to study his profile and give the view the full attention it deserved.

He looked as if his second night on the couch had been as restless as her nearly sleepless night in her own bed. His eyes were slightly squinted, as if the day were bright and sunny instead of gray and overcast, and his mouth was set in what might have passed for a small frown. It was a face set in granite, harsh and uncompromising.

"What are you staring at?" he growled without taking his eyes from the road.

Frannie was embarrassed to be caught watching so blatantly. There had to be an excuse. She reached out and plucked at the sleeve of his green knit shirt. "I didn't mean to stare. It's just that until this morning I thought maybe you'd been born in a suit and tie." The jeans and knit shirt looked good on him. If only he'd lose the gun.

"I don't remember," he said dryly. "You'll have to ask my mother."

Frannie leaned her head back. "A clan of Bridgers," she said dreamily. "I can see it now. Target practice in the backyard for the men. Glum-faced women in the kitchen. Lots of coffee and Jack Daniel's and—" She smiled, remembering his mild protest that he didn't dance, ever, even though he'd danced with her beautifully. "No dancing."

She peeked out of the corner of her eye to see that he smiled. Better, much better. "So," she said softly, "how right am I?"

"You couldn't be more wrong. First of all, it isn't a clan of Bridgers. I'm the only one. My father died when I was twelve, and while I was in college my mother remarried. Tim had this peach farm then, and three kids of his own. My four sisters, all younger, have married and are reproducing as if the fate of the world rests on their fertile shoulders."

"You have four sisters?" There had been so many days she'd prayed for *one*. Unfortunately, complications of her own birth left her mother unable to have more children. In truth it was just as well. Lois couldn't have handled more than a single child; there had been times when that one was too much for her.

"Yep, and three stepbrothers I don't know very well. I just see them a couple times a year, at Christmas and this annual spring get-together." He was silent for a few moments. "You were right about the dancing, though, unless you catch my sisters dancing in the kitchen while they wash dishes."

Frannie glanced out her window. The skies were filled with fat, gray clouds, and had been all morning. "I hope it doesn't rain."

"It won't," Bridger sighed. He'd assured her of that earlier, as she'd taken her raincoat from the hall closet.

"How can you be so sure?" She glanced at the dark gray all-weather coat that was lying on the backseat. Of course she hadn't listened to his assurances. No matter what he said, it looked an awful lot like rain.

He glanced briefly at her and almost smiled. "Mom would never allow it. In all the years we've been doing this, it's not rained us out once. Thank God. I can't imagine squeezing everyone into the house, even as big as it is."

Bridger returned his eyes to the winding two-lane road. Frannie sighed. Did he know how lucky he was? This was her dream—a big, happy, close family, with family reunions and Christmas parties in a big house in the country. While she'd never actually thought of it before, sisters dancing in the kitchen sounded wonderful.

"You're not going to wear *that* all day, are you?" She nodded to the gun on his belt.

He didn't even look toward her, or ask what she was talking about, even though he couldn't possibly see the nod of her head. "Yep."

"Why? Do you expect trouble? It's because of me and this investigation, isn't it?" Oh, she didn't want to bring trouble to this day. What would the family think when Bridger showed up wearing a gun?

"It has nothing to do with you. I wear my weapon pretty much all the time," he said softly.

"Why?"

He didn't answer for a few moments, as he steered the car around a sharp turn. Maybe it was none of her business, but she did wonder.

"To be honest, I feel naked without it."

She could make a joke, tell him she'd seen him naked and it wasn't a bad thing. But she didn't. She had a feeling that Bridger didn't share much of himself with anyone, and if he would talk, really talk to her, she wasn't about to spoil it.

"But surely with your family…" She hesitated when he shot her a sharp glance that told her clearly that this was none of her business. "You could leave it in the glove compartment and lock up the car. It would be close if you needed it, but not so…there."

Bridger didn't say anything for a while, and Frannie decided that he'd dismissed the subject. She should have kept her mouth shut or made her little joke. She didn't want to ruin this day, didn't want to put a damper on it, for her or for Bridger. One perfect day surely wasn't too much to ask.

"It bothers you, doesn't it?" he finally asked.

"What? The gun?"

He didn't look at her or answer. But then, it wasn't necessary. They both knew what this discussion was about.

"Not really." She placed her head against the headrest and closed her eyes. It was easier this way, not having to look at him. "It's a part of who you are, I guess, and it doesn't *bother* me."

She was answered with complete silence.

"But it seems to me there's a time and a place to let your guard down, to relax and have fun and forget about the bad guys for a while." In her bed he'd forgotten, she knew it. The unexpected thought made her insides tighten and her skin tingle as if it came to life at the vivid memory.

"Maybe I've forgotten how."

"I don't think so," she whispered.

Mal had the sudden impulse to pull the car onto the next dirt road and into the wooded countryside. He was hard and aching and he wanted this woman now. Damnation, he hadn't had the urge to have sex with a woman in the back seat of a car since his seventeenth birthday had passed, but he needed Frannie *now,* and it didn't matter where. How could a mere whisper do this to him?

He drove past the next dirt road without so much as slowing down.

The following twenty minutes passed in complete silence. Frannie closed her eyes and pretended to be asleep, and so on occasion he took his eyes from the road to watch her.

She'd emerged from the bathroom this morning in a flowing, flowery pink dress that was much too nice for this occasion. Sleeveless and soft, it fit her form from the waist up, and the full skirt ended at mid-calf. The material was so lightweight that it moved when she did, swinging with every step, every turn. Flat-heeled, cream-colored shoes covered her feet. The entire outfit was flagrantly feminine.

The rest of the clan would be in shorts and T-shirts and jeans—well, except for the teenage nephew who had spent the past two years shrouded in black from head to toe, no matter what the weather.

Frannie would stand out in any crowd like a bit of summer in the wintertime, like a flower in the mud or a ray of sunshine on a gray day like this one. But then, he had a sinking feeling he'd react the same way if she was wearing a burlap sack.

She wanted him to leave his weapon in the car. After Daphne's whining demands and hysterical pleas, he'd sworn to never again let a woman tell him to leave his gun at the door. Frannie didn't whine or plead. She reasoned, she whispered. She worked her way into his head.

But the result was the same, wasn't it? She wanted him to sacrifice a part of himself, deny who and what he was. Frannie's whispers did something to him Daphne's demands never had. They made him question his certainty that the gun and the badge were all-important, that they defined him completely.

A grove of peach trees replaced the evergreens that had tunneled most of their trip. It was a sign that they were almost at their destination. As if on cue, the clouds broke and a ray of sunshine brightened the day and sliced across Frannie's face. She opened her eyes and smiled.

"Looks like you were right and I won't need my raincoat after all."

He pulled into a long, winding driveway, and Frannie was immediately alert, leaning slightly forward and watching with big blue eyes. The house at the end of the driveway was a sprawling white farmhouse, and there were already a number of cars, everything from Lisa's Mercedes to Tim's rusted pickup truck, parked in and along the long driveway. Somebody had a new minivan, he noted as he pulled into the grass.

He shut off the engine and, for a long moment, stared through the windshield, his fingers tapping gently on the steering wheel. A couple of kids, nephews whose names he couldn't remember right now, ran around the corner of the house, laughing and tossing a Nerf football from one hand to the other.

He reached for his belt, wondering exactly why he felt compelled to do this, wondering if he was trying to grasp at something he would never have, something he had never even wanted. For a moment he hesitated, as he wondered what the hell he was doing.

The holster and weapon came off as one unit. He reached across Frannie and opened the glove compartment. The revolver fit snugly there, atop a map and a rarely used ice scraper. He slammed the glove compartment shut and locked it before he looked at Frannie.

He half expected her to make a playful comment about him being naked, but she wasn't even smiling. Her face was close to his, and she didn't draw back, didn't make a crack about him going to the family reunion naked, didn't throw open her door to escape. Instead she leaned forward just enough to touch her lips to his.

The kiss was soft and easy and comforting, a light touch of her lips to his that was all too brief.

"I'm sorry," she said as she backed away, obviously embarrassed. "I shouldn't have."

He cupped the back of her neck with his hand, threading his fingers through short blond curls, and brought her mouth to his. This time the kiss was neither easy nor brief. Mal closed his eyes and lost himself in the sensations of his mouth against hers, of his tongue inside her mouth and the way she swayed against him. Frannie tasted of sunshine and—impossibly—lollipops. If beauty had a flavor, this was it.

He should have taken that dirt road after all, he decided too late. One night, hell. It wasn't enough, it wasn't nearly enough. They weren't done; he had a feeling that they hadn't even started.

If Frannie pushed him away he'd know he was wrong. If she didn't *feel* this…ah, but she did. She answered this kiss in kind, her tongue teasing his lower lip before flicking into his mouth.

A thud and a slight jarring of the vehicle brought Mal to his senses. He opened his eyes just in time to see an orange and yellow football bounce off his windshield. A couple of laughing kids were right behind it.

One of the boys waved and the other collected the ball and then they were off.

"Maybe we should go in now," Frannie said, only slightly breathless.

"In a minute." Mal leaned his head back and closed his eyes. He told himself, in the passage of a split second, that he didn't want any of the things Frannie wanted from life—family, stability, white picket fences and babies. The certainty didn't make him want her any less.

"Let's talk about —" he glanced to the side while Frannie waited anxiously, her eyes wide and her mouth just slightly swollen from the kiss "—baseball. Batting averages and bull pens and ERAs. The Dodgers, the Mets, the

Mariners. Dammit, Frannie.'' He smiled. He almost laughed. ''I can't go in there like this.''

She didn't make him explain, didn't even glance at his lap to check for herself. ''How about those Atlanta Braves?'' she asked in a voice that was innocently seductive.

It was obvious to Frannie that Bridger had never brought a woman to one of these get-togethers before. She was the center of attention for a while as each and every one of his sisters and their husbands gathered around for introductions and a nice, long, good look.

Bridger's mother, Katherine Gilbert, was sweet and lovely, the very picture of Southern grace and charm. She welcomed Frannie with open arms—literally—and a bright smile. A pretty woman who had to be nearing sixty, she wore her thick gray hair in a short, neat style that complimented her oval face.

Frannie realized right away that she was overdressed for the occasion, and she wished that Bridger had warned her. Even Mrs. Gilbert was dressed casually, in faded blue jeans, an oversize button-up shirt and a pair of comfortable walking shoes.

Bridger's four sisters were especially curious about her. They gathered around at one point, all but looking her up and down for flaws and checking her teeth for cavities. Denise and Robin had dark hair and brown eyes like their big brother, though their features were soft and pretty where his were harsh. Mindy's hair was dark blond, and Lisa's was chestnut, and they both had strikingly square features and hazel eyes. Frannie felt all those eyes on her, at one point.

When they smiled, all at once, Frannie decided she'd passed the inspection.

Eventually, thankfully, the novelty of her presence wore

off. While everyone continued to be friendly, they were too busy eating and playing games and tossing footballs and horseshoes to bother much with her.

In a rare, peaceful moment, Frannie sat on the edge of the porch and watched. Goodness, she'd been to county fairs that had fewer attendees than this reunion! There was Tim and Katherine Gilbert, his three sons and their families, and Bridger's four sisters with their husbands and children. He was right about the girls producing children at an alarming rate. The youngest, Denise, had three boys, and according to the other sisters she had some catching up to do. Lisa and Mindy had four children each, and Robin had five!

It was a madhouse, a loud, chaotic melee…and Frannie loved every minute of it.

Her feet dangled over the edge of the porch, and she sipped on the tall glass of iced tea Mrs. Gilbert had pressed into her hand. A cool breeze ruffled the skirt that brushed her calves. No wonder Bridger had been so confident that it wouldn't rain today. Nothing but perfection would suit a day like this one.

"Hi."

The greeting startled her, and she glanced around to see a baby-faced little boy in a bright red T-shirt and a pair of faded jeans. He held two cookies, one in each hand. If she remembered correctly this was Denise's oldest, Parker, who was six years old. His short dark hair had been mussed by all the running and jumping he'd done this afternoon, and his deep brown eyes—Bridger eyes she surmised—were looking just slightly weary.

"Hello." She smiled at him, and he took that greeting as an invitation and sat close beside her.

"Wanna cookie?" He offered one to her, a chocolate chip cookie that was clenched in filthy fingers.

"Thanks, but I'm still pretty stuffed from lunch." While

she had no desire to take a cookie from that dirty hand, her protest was the truth. She'd never eaten so much at once in her entire life!

Parker munched on one of the cookies, and then took a small bite out of the other. His sneakered feet swung lazily from the porch.

Frannie looked for Bridger. He was easy to spot even in a crowd. He was taller, darker, broader than the others, and her eyes always seemed to be drawn to him. As she watched, he tossed a football to another nephew, the one who apparently had a penchant for all things black.

Parker took a bite out of one cookie, and then he nibbled at the other. "Why didn't Uncle Malcolm wear his gun today?"

"I don't know," she said, looking down at a tousled head. "Maybe he didn't think he'd need it."

"Uncle Malcolm *always* wears his gun." Parker glanced up, wide-eyed. There was a smudge of chocolate by his mouth. "He never lets me touch it, though."

Frannie was horrified at the very thought. "Of course not," she said calmly.

"He says I can hold it when I'm thirty, maybe."

She could see it so clearly, Bridger stern and protective, Parker wide-eyed and innocent. "Sounds like a plan to me."

Parker finished off his cookies and leaned back on his hands, a little man with his adopted pose and curious eyes. "When I grow up, I'm going to be a policeman just like Uncle Malcolm."

"You are?"

He looked directly at her then. "Well, either that or a ninja. I haven't decided."

"A policeman or a ninja. That's a tough choice." Frannie kept her voice low and serious as she fought back a joyful laugh. Parker was certainly not joking.

"Maybe I could be both," he said thoughtfully.

Frannie reached down and brushed away the chocolate smudge with her thumb. She half expected Parker to turn his face, but he obediently held still as she wiped off the chocolate. "What does Uncle Malcolm think about your plans?" *Uncle Malcolm.* She couldn't help but give in to a smile as she said the words.

"He says I should be a ninja."

With his cookies gone and his questioning done, Frannie expected Parker to jump off the porch and join the fun in the big yard. But he remained where he was, at her side and watching his large family play. Frannie sipped at her sweet tea.

"My daddy says Uncle Malcolm needs a woman."

If she'd been swallowing tea she would have choked on it. "What?" Surely she'd misunderstood.

But Parker looked up at her unflinchingly, eye to eye, and repeated the statement. "My daddy says Uncle Malcolm needs a woman."

It was surely a whispered statement the child should not have overheard or remembered. "Well..." she began, searching for a way to handle this explosive comment.

Parker didn't wait for her explanation. "I need a dog."

She laughed. Maybe it was the wrong reaction to the perfectly serious statement, but she couldn't help it. It was a laughter that came from someplace deep inside, from the heart and the soul and the magic of a day like this one. Parker smiled, apparently pleased with himself that he'd made her laugh.

"Do you have a dog?"

Her laughter faded. "No, I don't."

She looked up to see that Bridger walked toward her, his football game forgotten.

"I don't like the looks of this," he said, unsmiling but

with a touch of humor in his voice. "What have you two been talking about?"

"You don't want to know," Frannie said softly.

Parker piped up. "*She's* a woman," he said as if he were imparting great wisdom.

"Why, yes she is," Bridger conceded.

"But she doesn't have a dog."

Bridger stood a few feet away, arms crossed over his chest, face flushed with color from the exertion on this warm afternoon. He was achingly handsome today, for some reason she couldn't define. Maybe it was the way his knit shirt and jeans fit him, or the way the sun shone on his face. Whatever the reason, she found it difficult not to gawk.

"No," he said, staring at her. "No dog."

She could not for the life of her understand why Bridger was so dead set against having this for himself. Today had been one of the most perfect days of her life, and she was an outsider, a stranger intruding on this family reunion. But this was all his. How could he not appreciate it?

Parker leaped to his feet. "Catch me, Uncle Malcolm," he said, and then he jumped with all the strength his short legs could muster, flying off the porch and into Bridger's arms, never once doubting that his uncle would catch him and lower him safely to the ground.

She wondered if Bridger had ever trusted anyone that completely. Sadly, she thought not.

Chapter 11

He never should have brought her here.

Mal sat on the porch, near to the place Frannie had been sitting earlier, and watched her through the kitchen window. She smiled, and danced with Robin and Lisa to an old Mellencamp cassette Robin had fetched from her car.

He couldn't remember ever seeing a woman as openly happy as Frannie was right now. Her cheeks were flushed, her eyes were bright, and she was so obviously delighted by this simple, silly moment. She laughed as she twirled around Lisa, drying a plate as she went, dancing past Robin, who was standing at the sink doing her own stationary shuffle.

Mal knew without a doubt that Frannie belonged here more than he did.

When his father had died he'd instantly become, at the age of twelve, man of the house. The heart attack had been unexpected, taking the life of a seemingly healthy man in an instant. His mother had fallen apart, his sisters had been

too young and confused to be of any help, and Mal had—
in every way he knew how—taken care of them all.

The girls had cried on his shoulder, one at a time and
together. His mother had sleepwalked through the next year
or so, and it had been Mal who made sure his sisters were
eating, that they did their homework and got to bed on time.
By the time his mother recovered it was too late. His childhood was gone, and his sense of responsibility was so
deeply ingrained he was unable to let it go.

Even now, he felt more father than brother to the girls.
His heart had broken for Mindy when she'd had her mis-
carriage four years ago. She didn't talk about it anymore,
but he knew she still felt the pain. Hell, he felt it for her.
When Robin had considered marrying that lowlife longhair
right out of college, it had been Mal who'd gently but
firmly dissuaded her. Of course, even with his rap sheet in
hand and every logical reason in the world to dump the
guy, she'd ignored his advice. She'd had to find out for
herself that he was an unworthy bum, and that had hurt,
too.

Illnesses, injuries, children who wouldn't behave, Mal
had seen it all. Frannie saw only the good side of this family life, the fun and the laughter. She didn't know that there
was sometimes heartache behind a laugh.

Then again, maybe she did. From what she'd said after
talking to her mother on the phone, it was clear that her
own life growing up hadn't been any bed of roses. Her
mother had dragged her from place to place, from one hell
to another, and still she had this unrealistic craving for love
and family, for the ideal that didn't exist. She was so naive.

"I like her."

He'd been staring at Frannie, and hadn't even heard his
mother approaching. She plopped down beside him, her
descent just a little bit slowed by age.

"Frannie?" *Who else?*

"Yes, Frannie."

Mal could still hear the music and the occasional laughter, but he couldn't very well stare at Frannie while his mother watched. "Yeah, she's a nice girl." What every mother wanted for her son—a nice girl.

"How long have you known her?"

Ah, the questioning had begun. "Since Tuesday."

His mother's smile faded and she stared at him hard, bringing her eyebrows together in a knot. "Tuesday? Goodness, Malcolm, you barely know her."

He knew her better than anyone else. The way her mind worked, the way she laughed, the way she gave everything she had when he touched her. "I know her well enough."

She glanced beyond him to the kitchen window, and without looking, Mal knew what she saw. An honest, smiling face, bright eyes full of hope and wonder, beauty and light. "Well, she does *seem* like a nice girl."

"Trust me, she is."

"So," she said, turning her eyes back to him. "Where did you meet her?"

Mal hesitated. *I picked her up in a bar* wasn't going to do. "I met her in a little restaurant on Bank Street." It was true enough. Frannie had said herself that Benny made a mean salad.

"Someone introduced you? A mutual friend?"

He couldn't very well tell her to butt out. After all, he'd never brought a woman to one of these functions with him. Not even Daphne. She was entitled to be a little curious. "Yeah. Benny."

"Do I know him? I don't remember ever hearing you mention his name before." She squinted slightly in his direction, interrogating him as surely as he interrogated his own suspects. "Is he a detective?"

"No, Mom, you don't know him."

She nodded her head and let the inadequate explanation

go. For now. "I'm glad you have someone with you this week. I know it's been…hard."

She'd called him at work on Tuesday afternoon, after seeing the story about the shooting on the noon news, and he'd assured her that he was fine. As a matter of fact, during that conversation he'd had to assure her at least five times that he was *fine*.

He was saved from continuing the discussion when Mindy came running up, the newest addition to her family comfortably perched on her hip. "Here," she said, thrusting the baby into his arms. "Mom, I need you for just one minute."

They scrambled off the porch, leaving Mal alone and helpless, with a baby that was not yet six months old in his hands. As soon as the women were gone, the baby started to squall.

"Stop that," Mal ordered softly, to no avail. The kid screwed up his face and screamed louder.

He didn't like babies, and Mindy knew it. Once a kid got to be two or three they could be fun, as long as they were someone else's.

He heard Frannie step onto the porch through the kitchen door, knew it was her by the soft fall of her step and the hint of pink he saw out of the corner of his eye. The wind caught the skirt and lifted it gently, so that the material danced seductively around her long legs.

"Now, this is a sight I never expected to see," she said softly. "Uncle Malcolm doing baby-sitting duty."

He glared at her. "Do *not* call me Uncle Malcolm," he whispered.

Frannie only smiled wider as she sat beside him. "Here, let me try." She took the baby from him and cradled it gently in her own arms, and almost immediately the crying stopped. It was her smile, he imagined. What kid could look at that bright smile and cry?

He realized with a sinking heart that this picture was perfect. Frannie wanted and needed children. Dammit, that baby looked so natural, so comfortable in her arms, and Frannie's face was impossibly brighter and more attractive as she cuddled it to her chest.

"Isn't she beautiful?" she whispered.

"He," Mal corrected, leaning forward to take a peek at the peaceful face pressed against the pink pillow of Frannie's breast.

"And such a happy baby," she said in a high, soft voice. Baby talk.

"I'd be happy, too," Mal said softly, "if my nose was buried where his is."

She glanced sideways at him, and readjusted the baby so his head was a little higher. "That's your Uncle Malcolm," she said sweetly to the child. "He's a bad, bad boy, and you don't want to grow up to be an old curmudgeon like him, no you don't."

Mal leaned forward to look down on his newest nephew. "Don't listen to her..."

The baby answered by reaching up and grabbing his nose. Hard. Frannie laughed, and out of the corner of his eye Mal saw an approaching brother-in-law with a damned camera that was quickly raised. He heard the snap and whir of the camera before he could disengage his nose.

The brother-in-law in question grinned from ear to ear. "Don't worry," he said as he wandered off. "I'll have a few extra copies of this shot made."

It was an almost perfect ending to a perfect day. Parker had decided she was his new friend, and tagged along after her now and again. She liked all of Bridger's sisters, but Lisa and Robin were especially nice. She got to hold Mindy's baby all she wanted. It was heaven.

If only Bridger wasn't in such a foul mood, all of a

sudden. Ever since his picture had been taken, he'd been grumpy. It was as if he didn't like being caught on camera being human.

She was holding the baby again, walking around the big house and talking the baby talk that seemed to appease him. He felt so heavy and warm and right in her arms. She wouldn't say the words aloud to anyone, not to anyone, but she wanted one. She wanted a baby of her own one day.

There had been a time, years ago, when she'd sworn she wouldn't have children. She'd been afraid, uncertain, sure that she'd do no better with a child than her mother had. A few years back she'd changed her mind. Babies were hope for the future, unconditional love and the greatest responsibility in life. Harry had it right—they were pure in a world that too often wasn't.

"With my luck," she said softly to the baby in her arms, "I'll be one of the women who makes the news for being so old when I finally give birth. Very, very old," she said in a voice that nearly squeaked. "Horribly, incredibly old."

"Who's incredibly old?"

Her head snapped up and Bridger was there, standing right before her, looking at her with intense, tired brown eyes. How much had he heard? Not much, hopefully. "You," she answered. "Incredibly old and cranky Uncle Malcolm."

He scowled at her, and she answered with a smile.

"Time for us to go," he said softly. No smile, no wry remark.

Frannie wasn't ready to go, but she had a feeling that she could stay here all night and not be ready to go. "Sure."

Her purse and raincoat were still in his car, so she didn't have to collect anything. She did have to thank Bridger's mother and say goodbye to everyone. Robin and Lisa hugged her, and she hugged them back. Parker gave her a big hug, too, throwing his arms around her neck when she bent down to tell him goodbye.

Katherine had to pack up lots of leftovers in plastic containers for Bridger, choosing his favorites from the huge amount of food that remained. Chicken casserole and peach cobbler and corn pudding.

Taking their leave took a good half hour, but finally they headed for the car. Bridger's mother walked with them down the driveway, and it seemed to Frannie that she was reluctant to see her son go. He was thirty-seven years old— a cop, a tough, no-nonsense man who led a life filled with violence and death and danger—and his mother worried about him, still. The realization made Bridger much more vulnerable in Frannie's eyes.

Katherine kissed Bridger on the cheek, handed him the brown paper bag filled with containers of leftovers and ordered him to call more often, and then she turned to Frannie.

"You'll come to see us again?"

She didn't know what to say. Oh, she wanted more than anything to come here again, to see everyone and hold babies and laugh and dance in the kitchen. "I'd like that."

Katherine started to give her a hug. Her delicate arms were barely around Frannie's neck when Bridger spoke. "She's a witness, Mom."

Katherine Gilbert drew slightly away and looked at her son. "What?"

"Frannie's a witness," he said, throwing open the back seat door on the driver's side and setting the brown paper bag on the floor. "I've been keeping an eye on her, and today..."

"He just brought me with him so I wouldn't get in any trouble while he was away from Decatur," Frannie finished for him, and she smiled brightly. Oh, she smiled brightly.

Katherine was clearly confused. Damn Bridger's hide, why couldn't he keep his mouth shut!

"Well, it was nice to meet you," Katherine finally said, offering her hand this time. "I hope everything works out all right for you." She shot Bridger a questioning glance.

"I'm sure it will," Frannie said as she opened her own door and slipped into the car. The smile made her face hurt, and she was suddenly chilled, cold to the bone. It would soon be dark, and she supposed the sudden chill came about because the sun was gone. Once she was in her seat and had her seat belt buckled, she hugged herself, searching for warmth.

Bridger didn't say a word as he started the car and they drove down the gravel driveway to the winding two-lane road that would take them home. It was just as well. She had nothing, nothing at all, to say to him. She stared out the window, away from him, and watched the trees fly by in a blur.

They were well down the road before he spoke. "I had to say something," he said softly. "She was getting this look in her eyes."

"What look?" Frannie asked without turning her head to look at him.

"A serious, *when is the wedding* kinda look."

"Oh," she said softly. She kept watching the trees fly by as the light of day faded. "Well, we can't have that, can we?"

"No."

She was a complete and utter fool. She'd allowed herself to fall in love with a man who not only didn't want her love, he probably didn't even believe it existed. He was surrounded by love, with a family like his, and he could still deny it. Bridger didn't appreciate what he had! He was the fool.

His headlights lit the road before them, a road they had all to themselves.

Would he expect to sleep with her tonight? After the kiss in the car and the following necessary conversation about baseball, she had a feeling he would. All he had to do was ask, or look at her, or lay his hands on her, and she would give him anything he wanted, everything she had. Eventually she wouldn't have anything left.

The more she loved Bridger, the harder it was going to be to let him go when this was over. And she would have to let him go when this was over.

"I don't want you in my house tonight," she said softly.

Eyes on the road ahead, he sighed. "I didn't mean to make you mad."

"You didn't make me mad." She faced him at last, studying his granite features by gray light. "It's just better if we don't spend so much time together. Arrange for another bodyguard, if you still think it's necessary, or put me in a hotel somewhere until this blows over. I don't care."

"A few more days…"

"No."

He took a deep breath. "Frannie, just because I told my mother that you were a witness, that doesn't mean we have to change anything."

"This doesn't have anything to do with you telling your mother why we were together today." Not directly, anyway. "It's for the best if we just call a stop to this now."

He shot her an angry glance. "I don't think so."

Bridger was incredibly stubborn, and so used to having his way that he couldn't imagine anyone arguing with him, telling him that he might actually be *wrong*.

Ah, but she knew him too well. She knew how to scare him off, didn't she? She knew exactly how to send Malcolm Bridger screaming into the night. All she had to do was tell him the truth.

"I'm falling in love with you."

The car swerved slightly, but he managed to keep the car on the road. "Frannie." His voice was tight, low and full of regret.

"I'm not asking you to love me back," she said. Bridger kept his eyes on the curves ahead. His jaw clenched, his neck was taut with tension. "But if you continue to stay with me, we'll end up in bed again. You know it and I know it. I'll fall a little deeper every time you touch me, and you won't ever love me back."

He took a deep breath but said nothing.

"You're a one-night stand kinda guy, Bridger, and I'm a forever woman. Nothing good can come of this."

After a long and mostly quiet ride, they came upon the bright lights and traffic of Decatur.

Frannie continued to stare out the window, silently brooding. She'd said the words on purpose, to confound him, to get back at him for telling his mother the truth before she started planning a wedding. She told him she was falling for him just to shake him up, to make sure he ran like hell when they got back to Decatur.

It had almost worked.

"Tomorrow I'll set something up," he said in a voice that left no room for argument. "For tonight—"

"No."

He only glanced at the back of Frannie's head. "Will it make you feel better if I promise not to touch you? I'll spend one more night on that damn couch."

"No." Her voice was soft, lifeless, and still she didn't turn to face him.

He clutched the steering wheel tight. "Dammit, Frannie, don't get unreasonable on me all of a sudden."

Her head rotated slowly until she was staring directly at him. "Unreasonable? *Unreasonable?*"

He kept one eye on the road and one on Frannie. Color flooded a pale face, and her eyes flashed. Anger. Good, he could handle anger.

"I tell you I'm starting to love you and you call me *unreasonable?*" With one hand she swept back a strand of curling blond hair that touched her cheek.

His mother's words came back to him. "You barely know me. How can you possibly think you…" The words caught in his throat, and the argument remained unfinished.

"Love you," she said softly. "You can't even say it, can you?"

He kept both eyes straight ahead. They were almost to the turnoff for Oak Street. Hell, maybe he should arrange for a policewoman to spend the night with Frannie. Let someone else watch over her, someone who wasn't treading in dangerous territory. Someone else, starting tonight.

He pulled up to the curb. Frannie unbuckled her belt and reached beneath her seat for her small purse. She took out her keys without so much as glancing in his direction, and threw her door open.

"Good night, Bridger," she said as she stepped out of the car.

He threw his door open and stepped onto the street, ready to follow her no matter how much she protested. She wasn't safe, not yet. "Frannie, dammit—"

"Put a patrol car in the driveway, if you want, but I don't want anyone in my house tonight." She slipped her key into the lock. "Especially not *you.*" She turned the key and pushed the door open. He watched as she tossed her purse onto the sofa.

Dammit, she was not going to run him off, not like this and not because she imagined herself in love with him.

His weapon. A hand fell instinctively to his belt. "Hell." He wasn't going to watch over Frannie unarmed. Impatiently he turned back to the car to fetch the gun from the glove compartment.

"And another thing," her angry voice called. He turned to see Frannie step through the open door, watched as she stormed down the steps toward him, her stride powerful and quick. There was anger in every step. "Why did you have to tell your mother as we were leaving that I was a witness? I swear, Bridger, you must have a black hole where your heart is supposed to be."

Mal leaned against the passenger door and stared at her as she came toward him. "It was the—"

He never got to say the word *truth*. The blast was deafening, the light that exploded directly behind Frannie so bright it hurt his eyes. Momentarily Frannie was backlit by a flash of white light, before she fell to the ground and orange and yellow flames erupted behind her.

He ran toward her. "Frannie!" She lay still on the ground, facedown in the grass. She'd covered her head with her arms, and she didn't move.

Mal dropped down beside her, his heart in his throat as he laid his hand on her back. She'd been far enough from the blast that it shouldn't have injured her, but she was so still, hiding with her face against the grass and her ears covered with trembling arms. A small spot of blood bloomed on the back of one arm, and then another, and another.

"Frannie?"

An inferno claimed her house. Fire licked from every window, and already danced from the roof, alive and deadly. That quickly, the entire house was engulfed in flames. Waves of heat washed over him, an unnatural assault of warmth. Neighbors left their homes and congregated on the street, their eyes on the fire. One elderly man carried a cordless phone with him, and Mal could see that he practically shouted into it.

He put his hand in Frannie's hair, against her neck. "Come on, honey, say something to me."

She lifted her head at last, and Mal closed his eyes. She was all right.

The heat from the fire grew hotter, and flames lit Frannie's face as, with his help, she sat up. He'd never seen such heartbreak on a woman's face before. There was a pain so deep in her eyes that he ached for her, and he would have done anything, anything, to take the pain away.

"My house," she whispered once, and he took her into his arms and held her face against his chest. She didn't need to see any more, didn't need to feel the heat of those flames against her face. She could hide here, in his arms. She *should* hide here.

In the distance, he heard the wail of sirens.

"Come on." As gently as possible, he half carried, half dragged Frannie away from the heat. The fire was smaller now, but just as fierce. Black smoke rolled upward, thick and ominous.

When they were beside his car he stopped, sat down and gathered Frannie into his lap. She shuddered once, as she laid her head against his shoulder, and the rage he felt as he absorbed that deep tremor welled up in him and wouldn't subside.

Neighbors rushed forward, asking if they were all right, and Mal waved them back, barely lifting his head as he dismissed them. He should be doing something, he knew, taking charge, making phone calls, getting things in order. But he stayed right where he was, holding Frannie close.

She buried her face against his chest, hiding perhaps, and then she turned her head and forced herself to look at the fire. "Everything's gone," she whispered. "Just like that. I tried so hard to make it mine, to make it home. It's the only true home I ever had." She took a deep, ragged breath. "What happened?"

Mal forced Frannie's face against his chest again. She didn't need to watch this.

"It's okay," he said softly, knowing as he said the words that nothing was okay. "We'll find another house, I promise. A bigger, better one." *We,* he said without thinking. He couldn't take it back. And at the moment, he didn't want to take it back.

She lifted her head and looked at him. She didn't turn her head again toward her burning house. Maybe she didn't want to see. He smoothed her hair away from her face and looked into those big blue eyes that were colorless in the fire-filled night. She was stunned, scared, confused. He wanted to make it all go away.

"Something old and battered we can paint and fix up," he whispered. "We can buy more angels, and you can make more afghans, and I'll plant a garden in the back-yard." He could imagine it too well, and dammit the very thought comforted him. That wasn't his intent, as he said the words. The picture he painted was meant to soothe Frannie, and yet he found an unexpected hint of peace for himself, as well. "You can make a home anywhere."

She started shaking, and so did he. Sitting on the ground while the fire blazed hot and all-consuming, he shook. "All that matters is that you're okay." It was the truth. She could have been in there, she could have been trapped in the fire, heat and flames all around. He could see it too clearly. If she hadn't come back outside to tell him he had a black hole where his heart was supposed to be, she'd be in the burning house right now.

And he'd be with her. There was no way he could stand by and watch Frannie die. Watch her *burn.*

The fire engines arrived, and the firefighters set about trying to save the two houses adjacent to Frannie's. Hers was beyond saving. Paramedics were right behind the firemen, and they tried to take Frannie from him. Mal wouldn't budge and neither would she.

She leaned against him and held on tight.

The medics checked Frannie's heart rate and pupils, right there where she sat, and they bandaged the small cuts on the back of her arm. Flying glass. Mal's stomach twisted at the very thought of what might have happened had she been closer to the house at the time of the explosion.

Frannie was silent as the commotion that surrounded what had been her home continued. Fat hoses were dragged across the yard, and firefighters sprayed an endless stream of water into her burning house and the homes on either side.

When the medics suggested taking Frannie to the hospital where she could stay overnight, she held on to Mal even tighter and shook her head.

Frannie didn't need to be in the hospital, she just needed to be held and comforted and reassured. That's all. He could do that.

He was, he knew, the only one who could.

Chapter 12

Frannie sat in the tub with her knees drawn up and her head resting on those knees, while warm water rained on her from the showerhead set into the tile wall high above. She felt every drop of water that hit her skin, heard very clearly the sound of drizzle against flesh, and the roar of the shower above, and the gurgle of water going down the drain.

The droplets were soft, her hair was soaked through, and rivulets of water ran down her skin to pool beneath her and run lazily toward the drain. The cuts on the back of her arm stung a little, and she tried to ignore the pain. The sting was a too-clear reminder of exactly what she was trying to forget.

She watched the water run, concentrating on the little streams so maybe, for a moment, she wouldn't have to think about what had happened tonight.

Her house was gone. Her house and everything in it. Every time she felt she was beginning to think straight, she remembered something else that was gone. The new angel, her favorite dress, the afghan she'd crocheted last year.

Frannie lifted her head and allowed the water to wash over her face, closing her eyes as the droplets rained, soft and warm. Surrounded by warmth and pelted by the caressing sprinkle, she could almost forget that she'd watched her home go up in flames tonight.

It came to her, as she sat there, that she'd always planned to put a showerhead in her bathroom, over the big clawfoot tub. She'd never gotten around to it. Now it didn't matter.

This was Bridger's bathroom, in his apartment, and he paced in the hall outside the door. She shouldn't be here, it was a bad idea, but when he'd put her so gently in his car and brought her home with him she hadn't protested. Not once.

We'll find another house, a bigger one. Did Bridger even know what he'd said as he'd held her after the explosion? Probably not. He was surely in shock, as she was. Then again, maybe he was just fine and her memory was failing. Maybe she'd only heard what she wanted to hear.

The water turned cold, and still she sat there. She couldn't move, didn't want to move. With her eyes closed she allowed the cold water to rain down on her face. She wasn't comfortable anymore, and she couldn't forget anything so she stopped trying. Her favorite mug, the brass angel, her jewelry box All gone. Her haven, her home…destroyed.

"Frannie?"

She opened her eyes to see Bridger standing over her, a fat white towel in his hand, an expression of confusion and concern on his face. Looking at him, really *looking* at him, she knew that everything she'd said to him on the way back from the peach farm was true. She'd love him, and he would never love her back.

He turned off the shower and very gently helped her to her feet, even as she argued halfheartedly that she didn't need any help. Her knees trembled when she stood, so maybe it was a good idea that he held on to her arm so securely as she stepped from the tub.

"You're cold," he said as he began to dry her body with the fat towel. He didn't look her in the eye, but very carefully patted the towel against her skin, taking great care with her arms. He might have been drying an egg, his touch was so easy. Did he think she would break?

His body leaned close to hers, so close that he almost enveloped her. He towered over her, his long arms and legs sheltered her. Was he trying to protect her, still, or was she just imagining things again?

"Oh, Bridger, I used all your hot water. I'm sorry." Her voice shook slightly, and now he did glance up to look her in the eye.

She wondered if she'd fallen in love with him the first time he'd looked at her this way, wary and weary. His brown eyes were ancient, somehow. Deep, determined, somber. Yearning. There was love hidden in there, she knew it. If he was capable of love, why couldn't he love her?

"It doesn't matter," he said softly as he continued to dry her body. "The hot water tank will refill quickly, and I can take a shower later."

He moved the towel to her hair and rubbed it gently over her scalp. "I can dry myself, Bridger," she said shakily, but she didn't make any move to take the towel from him.

He shook his head. "I should have let them take you to the hospital."

"I hate hospitals."

"Me, too." He brushed the towel over her already dry shoulder, leaned close and rubbed her back, the towel raking down her spine.

"I went to the hospital once, when my father died," she whispered. "I was five years old, and I still remember the smell and the bright lights and the icky green walls." And most of all she remembered her father—a man she'd been sure, as she looked at the battered patient on the bed, was not her daddy—bruised and bleeding and dying, the victim of a drunk driver who would walk away without a scratch or a single day of jail time.

"Okay," he said as he stepped back and dropped the towel to the floor. "No hospital."

He took a white dress shirt from a hook on the back of the bathroom door. It hadn't been there before, so she assumed he had brought it in with him. With as much care as he'd used when drying her body, he slipped her arms into the shirt and buttoned it from the second button down to the hem. The shirt hung almost to her knees, but for the vented sides that revealed her thighs. She watched Bridger's hands as he rolled up sleeves that hung well past her hands. They were strong, capable, steady hands.

When he finished she was well covered, almost as well covered as she'd been in her football jersey. She flinched as she realized that even that was gone.

"We're alive," she whispered, and the truth of that statement hit her like a thunderbolt. Everything else could be replaced. They were things, possessions, inanimate objects that didn't feel pain or love. "If we hadn't been arguing, if we'd just walked into the house, we'd both be dead now."

"I know."

She reached out and stroked Bridger's cheek. His face was rough with stubble and warm beneath her fingertips, and there was comfort in the easy caress, a giving and a taking comfort. She needed to touch him, and whether or not he knew it he needed that touch, as well.

He needed her to love him. Maybe it wouldn't last,

maybe there was no future for a one-night stand kinda man and a forever woman, but Bridger needed to be loved as much as she needed to love him. It was as simple and as complicated as that.

Her fingers traced a lazy trail down Bridger's face to his throat, a trail as winding and certain as the water that had run off her body and down the drain. He answered with an easy exploration of his own, a finger that brushed across her temple and down her cheek. A soft kiss followed as he laid his mouth on her forehead and her cheek and, finally, her mouth.

Her knees went weak again, her body turned to liquid fire as Bridger kissed her. The kiss was gentle for a moment, soft, easy lips moving against hers, as if Bridger were still afraid she would break, and then it changed. His tongue plunged into her mouth, and the kiss became demanding, probing, fierce.

He touched her, a palm against her breast, against the nipple that hardened to his touch. His hand brushed lightly over the fabric that came between her hardened nipple and his touch, and a burst of lightning cracked through her body. She trembled, down deep, and her inner core quaked. A wordless plea escaped from her throat.

The moment Bridger lost control she knew it. He trembled, too, as deeply as she did, and a plea of his own rumbled in his throat. He pulled her close, held her impossibly tightly, and she felt the hard ridge of his arousal pressing against her.

He lifted her easily, and she wrapped her legs around him. As he carried her into the hallway they kissed, dancing tongues and hungry mouths mating and searching. She cupped the back of his head, threading her fingers through short hair and pressing his mouth tighter, ever tighter, against hers.

Bridger carried her into his bedroom, the neat, semidark

room that was illuminated only by the light from the hall-way. A double bed covered with a forest green comforter sat in the middle of the room. At the moment, it was the only piece of furniture Frannie noticed.

He crossed the room and lowered her slowly to the bed. Her legs were still wrapped around him, still held him close. She heard the rasp of a zipper, a low moan, and then he thrust to fill her.

It was impossible to separate the sensations—his mouth, the stroke of his body inside hers, the love that filled her. They were wonderful, magical sensations that rocked her body and made Bridger, for this moment, hers. Completely, totally, hers.

He moved rhythmically, filling her with hard, quick thrusts until she was certain their hearts beat together, their lungs breathed together. She felt his pleasure and pain and he felt hers. One. One being, one soul.

She shattered, the climax bursting through her body like yet another, more powerful, bolt of lightning. She arched her back, coming off the bed and crying out, a cry Bridger caught in his own searching mouth as he drove deep one last time and shuddered above and inside her.

Yes, they were definitely alive.

And being alive meant *living,* loving, taking chances.

"I love you, Bridger," she said breathlessly.

He lifted his head slowly and looked down at her. Oh, those eyes got her every time. "Don't," he whispered.

She didn't get angry. She smiled at him and cradled the back of his head with her hand. "You can ask me not to say the words out loud, but you can't ask me not to love you. I do love you," she confessed. "You're going to break my heart, because there's no way you can give me what I need, but I can't help it."

The pain in his eyes was clear.

"But I promise not to tell you again." She pulled his

mouth to hers for a brief kiss. "Because we've still got some of the night left just for us, and I don't want to spoil it."

Was she a complete fool to offer herself up this way? She knew Bridger could never give her what she needed from the man she loved. He would never love her back. She wished she could convince herself it didn't matter.

But it did.

He might never sleep again.

Mal lay on his back in his own bed, Frannie's head against his shoulder as she slept peacefully. The hall light was on, illuminating the room faintly, and the comforter was covering the two of them from the waist down.

Someone had tried to kill her. The investigation into the fire wasn't over, probably hadn't even begun, but he knew in his heart they wouldn't find any gas leak or electrical problem in what had once been Frannie's home. The explosion he'd seen behind her wasn't a natural disaster, and it sure as hell wasn't any accident.

Someone had tried to kill her, and the very idea kept him enraged enough to stare at the ceiling half the night.

That, and those words that wouldn't leave his head. *I love you, Bridger.* She was in shock, she was scared, she'd had her world turned upside down in less than a week. She thought she loved him because he watched over her, protected her, and because they had great sex.

Really, really great sex.

He'd never lost control with a woman before, never. He'd never been so blinded by what his body demanded that he forgot everything else.

Forgot that she said she would love him more every time he touched her, forgot that he didn't want or need a forever woman. Forgot that his box of condoms was under Frannie's sink, burned to a crisp along with everything else.

He'd never been inside a woman without one. Never. Malcolm Bridger was a lot of things, but he was not stupid, and he was never careless.

The hand that rested against his stomach moved, ever so slightly. "You're awake," she whispered.

"Yeah." He placed a hand in her hair. "Go back to sleep, Frannie. You need your rest."

She hummed, apparently in agreement, but her hand didn't still. Warm fingers raked across his chest, across flat nipples that hardened at her touch. "If you can't sleep, I can't sleep." Her hand moved lower, slipped inside the waistband of his silk boxers and cupped his erection. "Oh, my. No wonder you can't sleep."

He flicked open the buttons of his shirt, the white dress shirt that looked so right and sexy on Frannie, revealing bare skin that shone in the pale light. He touched the swell of her breasts, flicked a thumb over a nipple that puckered at his caress. She closed her eyes and breathed deep, delighting in, he knew, the feel of his hands on her flesh.

He tasted her there, lashing his tongue across her pebbling nipple, suckling gently until she arched into him. He drew her soft, warm flesh into his mouth as one hand dipped to delve between her legs to touch her where she was already wet for him.

He wanted her, again. He wanted nothing between them, again. This time he would relish every stoke, every shiver, every breath she took. This time he would watch her fall apart before allowing himself release.

It was reckless, he knew, foolish and weak and unlike him. But the full knowledge of his failings didn't make him want her any less.

Frannie slithered carefully from the bed in the early morning hours, finding Bridger's shirt on the floor and slipping it on as she made her way to the doorway. Before she entered the hall she glanced back once and smiled at the sight of Bridger's peaceful face.

He did care for her. Maybe he didn't know it yet, maybe he was trying to convince himself that he didn't feel so much, but he did. He couldn't have loved her so completely last night if he didn't.

Her smile faded as she made her way down the hallway to the kitchen. Was she thinking like her mother? The idea scared her, as much as losing the home she'd fought so hard to make for herself scared her. Had Lois convinced herself that she loved each and every one of those men she lived with or married, and that they would come to love her, too? Had she convinced herself that she could love enough for both of them?

It was a thought that made Frannie shiver as she searched the cabinets for coffee. There was a coffeemaker on the counter, so there had to be coffee.

"Cabinet beside the sink."

She snapped her head around and, in spite of her sobering thoughts, managed to grin at the sight before her. Bridger was leaning against the doorjamb, wearing green silk boxers and a day's growth of beard and looking absolutely, positively adorable. Adorably masculine, hard and relentless and rugged.

"Has anyone ever told you that you look adorable in the morning?"

"Not since I was five," he muttered.

"I tried to be quiet," she said as she opened the cabinet and reached up for the can of coffee. "I didn't want to wake you."

When she glanced over her shoulder she saw that he hadn't moved. Tense and silent, he leaned against the door frame. He stared at her hard, without a hint of a smile on his lips or in his eyes.

"So," she said casually, giving her attention to the task of making coffee. "What do we do today?"

"I go to work."

"I'll call Darlene and see if I can hang out at her place today." She tried to make her voice cheerful. "Maybe Newton will have my car ready, and I can go to the bank and take some money out of savings." Her hand trembled as she measured out the ground coffee beans. "I'll need new clothes, a purse, makeup…" Her hand shook harder. *Everything.* She needed everything.

His steady hand snaked past her shoulder and covered hers. Dammit, she hadn't even heard him coming, sneaking up behind her like a cat. But, oh, she was glad to have him close.

"I'm sorry," she whispered. "I shouldn't…"

"You have every right to shake a little." His voice was soothing, deep and smooth and Southern. He took the coffee and finished the chore she'd started, and as the coffeemaker gurgled he pinned her against the counter and placed his hand beneath her chin, lifting it to force her to look into his eyes.

"You're not going anywhere today." It was a soft, sure command. "I've got a steel door and the best deadlock money can buy, and I haven't told anyone you're here. You're going to stay right here until I get home, and then I'll take you anywhere you need to go."

"I can't just…"

"Yes, you can."

She wished he would kiss her, but he didn't look as if that were his intention. He was solid as a rock, motionless, emotionless.

"Frannie," he whispered. "The explosion wasn't an accident. You know that, don't you?"

She trembled again. "It might have been a gas leak."

"There was no gas leak." The words were cruel, and

she didn't want to hear them, but the voice was soothing. Loving. It made the truth easier to take.

"Someone tried to kill me."

He nodded once.

"Someone tried to kill *us*." He was in danger because he was protecting her. Why had she never seen that before? "Oh, Bridger. You could've been killed, and it would've been all my fault. Your mother would never forgive me."

She was perfectly serious, but he smiled as if he found her worries amusing.

"I don't know why you're smiling *now*," she said, frustrated. "I swear, you are the most perverse man I've ever met."

"Am I?" He actually began to move forward, slightly, his mouth headed toward hers, but at the last minute he broke away and turned his back on her.

"Yes!" she said to his back, which she noticed was quite finely shaped and muscled. She'd touched it, but she hadn't really studied it until this moment. Was there anything about the man that was less than perfect? "You are incredibly perverse."

He was entering the hallway when he answered. "Frannie?"

"Yes?"

"You look damn good in that shirt." He sounded as if the admission pained him, and Frannie's smile crept back.

The explosion had been just the beginning. By the time Mal arrived at the police station, the place was in a state of controlled chaos. Harry pulled him aside as he came through the door and gave him the news.

Violet Doyle, the old lady who was half of the management team of the Riverwatch Hotel, the one who had said Miranda Fossett had been seen weeks earlier with a man who looked like Tyrone Power from a certain angle, was dead. She'd been hit by a car in the early morning hours. Hit-and-run.

Overnight there'd been a grisly murder at a tattoo parlor in Huntsville. They didn't have the proof yet, but Harry and Mal were both sure the victim was the man who'd given Miranda and her gentleman friend tattoos.

Everyone who'd seen the suspect was dead. All their possible witnesses were dead. All but Frannie.

He'd left her this morning with strict instructions to bolt the door and not open it or answer to anyone but him. She'd been ordered to look at the caller ID if the phone rang, and to answer only if the number that came up was his cell phone number or this office.

She would do as he asked. He'd made her promise, and Frannie wasn't the kind of woman to break a promise. Since no one knew where she was, no one but him…and anyone who had watched them drive away from her burning house last night…

Mal picked up the phone and dialed home. "Come on," he whispered when Frannie didn't pick up on the first ring. He didn't breathe again until she picked up, after the third ring.

"Hello?"

He breathed deep, once.

"What is this?" she asked, and he could hear the teasing note in her voice. "A heavy breather at the Decatur Police Department?"

He couldn't tell her what had happened, not over the phone. She didn't need to be frightened any more than she already was. "Just checking in," he said, keeping his voice calm. "You checked the caller ID before you picked up?"

"Yes, sir."

"And remember, you promised you wouldn't open the door to anyone but me."

"Scout's honor."

He wondered if she was still wearing his shirt. With no effort at all he could close his eyes and see her, long legs peeking out from beneath that white shirt, thighs exposed by the vents on the sides, throat framed by a sharp and precise vee. When she'd reached for the coffee this morning it had ridden high, teasing him with the promise of what he might see if she reached a little higher.

"Bridger? You still there?"

"Yeah." He pulled himself to the present. "Listen, I'm going to try to take off early, so be looking for me this afternoon."

"Sure."

"And Frannie? Don't answer the door to anybody, you got me?"

"Yes, sir," she said again, with mock severity.

He didn't realize Harry was standing behind him until he hung up the phone and swiveled around. Harry looked every one of his forty-nine years today.

"Is she all right?"

Mal nodded. "I don't want anyone to know where she is. For now, we keep this between the two of us." He didn't really believe she was safe in his apartment, not safe enough. But until he was able to make other arrangements it just might do.

"Sure." Harry shoved his hands into his pockets. "Have you two figured out what this guy's looking for?"

Mal leaned back in his chair and shook his head. "If Miranda Fossett gave Frannie anything before she died, it's a mystery. And ash, now," he added, remembering the flames that had licked at Frannie's small house. "I think maybe Miranda told the killer she'd passed something to Frannie, hoping to buy time. The lie could end up..." *Costing Frannie her life.* He couldn't say it aloud.

"Yeah," Harry said, understanding. "What now?"

"You talk to Loudermilk and Clarence Doyle. Find out

what they were up to yesterday and where they were this morning when Mrs. Doyle was hit.'' He wanted to talk to them himself, but not yet. He was still too angry. "I'm going to check out the fire scene. I imagine the investigators are there already?''

Harry nodded and turned around, and almost ran Jerry Kruse over.

"Hey,'' Jerry said, glancing past Harry to Mal. "I heard about your friend's house. Is she okay?''

Mal tried not to glare at the man who'd had the gall to ask Frannie out on a *date*. Just because he'd told the kid there was nothing between them, just because he'd said they were just friends, that didn't give the kid the right to hit on her. "She's fine,'' he said without emotion.

"Well, I'm here if she needs anything…'' Kruse began.

This time Mal didn't bother to squelch the glare, and Kruse said nothing more.

Chapter 13

Mal stepped under the crime scene tape that encircled Frannie's property. What was left of her house sat in the center of it all. The smoldering, blackened sight sickened him, and he swore then and there that Frannie would not see this. She'd been through enough.

The arson investigator, veteran Mike Marchand, was furiously taking notes, but he lifted his head as Mal approached.

"You don't see something like this every day," Mike said with a wide smile that revealed how much he loved his job.

Mal couldn't make himself smile back. He'd seen this house intact, had slept in it, had slept with Frannie in it, and he could see nothing to smile about. "Something like what?"

Mike fairly shook with excitement as he pointed at what remained of the house. "Man, I can't believe anybody walked away from this. The way it was set up, the attention to detail, it's quite extraordinary."

Mal did his best to contain his anger. "Well, when we catch the guy you can write him a fan letter."

Mike shot a sharp glance at Mal, and his smile died. "Straight to business then. There was a tilt detonator on the doorknob, with a delay of several seconds. That way the person walking into the house doesn't get thrown clear. He's inside with the door closed when the bomb goes off." He pointed to the place where the front door had been. "It was set so that the force of the blow was concentrated inward, and there were secondary charges at the kitchen door and every window. It was definitely a high-order explosion."

"No one was supposed to get out," Mal said softly.

"No way. This place was a death trap."

Mal stared at the charred remains of Frannie's home for a long, silent moment. They could have been in there, and from what Mike told him there wouldn't have been a hell of a lot he could have done. If he and Frannie hadn't argued, if he hadn't gone back for the weapon he'd left in the glove compartment, if she hadn't come storming back out into the night to tell him that he had a black hole where his heart was supposed to be, they'd be as charred and lifeless as this house.

He wasn't afraid of death. It was inevitable, it came to everyone, and in his business he saw the harsh realities of life and death every day.

But Frannie didn't deserve this. She was worried about him, about *him,* apologizing for putting his life in danger and afraid that his mother would never forgive her.

The truth of the matter was, if he hadn't taken her to the Riverwatch Hotel the night they met she wouldn't be in this mess. She'd be safe and sound in this very house. She probably would have taken her job back, when Reese offered it. She'd be content and safe. He knew her well enough to know that those securities were important to her.

"Any way to tell who did this?"

Mike shook his head. "I've never seen anything quite like it. It reminds me a little of the bombing at the courthouse last year, but until we do more tests..."

"The Decatur Legion for Liberty bombing?"

Mike nodded once, and looked at the burned building with an expression that spoke clearly of awe and respect and revulsion. "Maybe."

Frannie was straightening up Bridger's living room, dusting halfheartedly and straightening the pillows on his couch, when the pounding knock sounded on the door. It didn't stop, but went on and on. She glanced at the clock on the end table. It wasn't yet twelve o'clock, and Bridger had said he wouldn't be back until afternoon.

"Frannie?" he shouted through the door.

She closed her eyes and breathed a sigh of relief at the sound of his familiar voice. She practically ran to the door to release the dead bolt.

He closed the door behind him and locked it. "You okay?" he asked. His voice was calm but there was something in his eyes she didn't like. Not fear, but uncertainty. Oh, this was not good. Bridger was always very certain of himself.

"I'm fine," she assured him.

"Any phone calls?"

She smiled softly. "Just one obscene phone call from the police department. A heavy breather."

He glanced at her but didn't smile at her joke.

"What's wrong?" she whispered, walking toward him. She never knew what to expect from Bridger. He might walk away before she reached him. Then again he might meet her halfway and greet her with a kiss that sent her insides whirling.

He did neither. He stood stock-still as she approached.

When she stood in front of him, close but not too close, he reached out and gently touched the collar of her pink dress, slipping his finger beneath the pale fabric. That finger barely brushed her skin.

"It was a bomb, Frannie," he said, watching the lazy progress of his finger instead of looking her in the eye.

"You suspected as much."

He took a deep breath and exhaled slowly, calming himself, perhaps. "This may be much more than a mugging that got ugly or one of Miranda Fossett's ex-boyfriends who got angry and lost control. Whatever the killer thinks she passed to you, he wants it bad or he wants it gone. That's why he destroyed your house and everything in it."

She reached out and grabbed the striped tie that hung before her face.

"The old woman at the Riverwatch hotel," he said, as the back of his hand brushed high on her chest. "She's dead. It was a hit-and-run."

Frannie's heart leaped into her throat. "It might have been an accident." She didn't believe it, even as the words left her mouth.

Bridger didn't believe it, either. He was shaking his head. "That's not all. A tattoo artist in Huntsville was murdered last night."

"Could be coincidence," she said softly, not believing it any more than Bridger did.

He shook his head again. "If we'd been in the house last night when it blew up, there wouldn't be anyone connected with this case left."

Frannie hung on to Bridger's tie still, but she laid her head against his chest and he wrapped his arms around her. "What do we do now?"

"I don't know," he whispered.

Now she understood the odd expression on his face as

he'd come in the door. "You're worried, aren't you? You're worried about me."

"Yes."

"And you don't like it one bit." She tilted her head back so she could see his face as she asked this question, though she expected Bridger would be painfully honest with her. He had been from the day they met, she'd give him that. Even when a lie would have been easier, he stuck with the truth.

"No, I don't."

She released his tie and tried to move away, but he continued to hold her tight.

The last thing he needed or wanted was a woman to worry about. No wonder he preferred one-night stands. Love 'em and leave 'em. One woman was just like another in the dark, to a man who not only didn't believe in love, but didn't *want* to believe in love. Bridger didn't want to worry. He didn't want to care.

"Maybe I should go away," she suggested.

"Maybe."

Her heart constricted, and a chill shot through her veins. "I could take my money out of the bank, get my car from Newton and hit the road." She smiled, but it was an effort. "My house is gone, my job is gone, I have nothing to keep me here." *Do I?*

He rumbled something that might have been a reluctant agreement.

"Surely whoever's doing this won't try to follow me, and if he does, well, maybe he won't find me." She tried to sound confident, but she wasn't. If she ran she would be just like her mother, fleeing from every mistake, from every problem as if there were an answer somewhere down the road.

"Maybe," Bridger muttered. And then his eyes locked

to hers. She saw so much there—a longing, an anger, a flash of pain. "Maybe not. It's a chance I can't take."

Poor Bridger, he'd never wanted to be involved, to be worried, to be her knight in shining armor. If she left Decatur and disappeared, it might be best for both of them. "It's not your chance to take," she whispered. "It's mine."

He hadn't seen this side of Frannie before, and it irritated the hell out of him.

Mal stuck close to her side as they maneuvered through the aisles of Wal-Mart. The buggy was half full, with casual clothes, cosmetics, toiletries, cheap tennis shoes and a few pairs of socks. And a suitcase. Not a big suitcase, but a soft tote bag sizable enough to carry her purchases.

Stubborn. He'd had no idea she could be so damned *stubborn.* Dismissing the obvious threat to her life, she'd threatened to call a cab if he wouldn't take her to her bank and then shopping.

And she kept talking about leaving as if it were actually a viable option. As if he would let her leave.

The other shoppers didn't appear to be threatening, but Mal kept his eyes peeled for trouble. Most of the members of the Decatur Legion for Liberty had never been identified. After Jacob Fossett's death they'd faded into the woodwork, becoming quiet once again, but they were still out there. Anyone they passed, any normal-looking person…

"Shampoo!" Frannie said, making an abrupt U-turn in the aisle.

"I have shampoo," he said through gritted teeth.

She glanced over her shoulder and smiled. "I can't very well take your shampoo with me, now can I?"

"You're not going anywhere," he said for what might have been the hundredth time in the past two hours.

She ignored him. He supposed she was tired of trying to argue the point.

Whenever he thought of Frannie packing that little bag and climbing in her car to just take off, it terrified him. *Nothing* terrified him. Nothing but the idea of Frannie on the road all alone, without him to protect her.

Stupid, stupid notion. He couldn't have saved her from the blast that destroyed her home. He couldn't anticipate what was around the next corner, what the man who wanted her dead would try next.

But, by God, he would die trying.

As she paid for her purchases with the cash she'd withdrawn from the bank, his pager beeped shrilly. He glanced at the number that came up. It was Harry's desk.

More bad news, no doubt, he thought as he hurried Frannie to the car. Another dead body, another dead end. He tossed the bags into his trunk, saw Frannie into her seat and then he snagged his cell phone from the glove compartment and dialed the number.

"Mal," Harry said as he picked up the phone.

"Yep." Mal leaned back in his seat and watched the shoppers, people walking by with their buggies filled, many with children in the seats before them.

"There's a woman here to see you," Harry snapped. "She was there last week when the shooting you were involved in occurred."

He wondered if the woman was sitting right there at Harry's desk. Probably so. Otherwise Harry would have said something crude.

"What does she want?"

"She's got her little boy here with her, and she wants to speak to you. Now, if you can manage it."

He remembered that little boy too well. The kid had stared up at Mal with terror in his eyes, and it had been those eyes that had haunted him...until Frannie had made him forget even that. He didn't want to look at those eyes again, didn't want to be reminded that he'd terrified the kid.

"I'll be right there."

There was something so insanely normal about the police station that was situated on the ground floor of Decatur's City Hall. Efficient and well ordered, it might have been any small company, except for the weapons everyone wore and the occasional uniformed officer passing in the hallway.

Frannie followed Bridger down the hall. If anything, he was more tense than he'd been before the conversation with Harry. Since he'd been a bear all day, that was saying something.

She still didn't know why they were here.

Bridger opened the door to the detectives' room, and, ever the gentleman, he allowed her to enter before closing the door behind him.

"You can wait at my desk," he said softly, his eyes on Harry and the woman and child with him.

She should take his advice, she supposed, but perhaps his perverse nature was rubbing off on her. Instead of taking the sharp right that would take her to his desk, she followed as he walked slowly toward the threesome that was silently waiting.

The woman stood and offered her hand. "Detective Bridger." She tried a smile but it was weak, almost watery.

Harry jumped in as Bridger took the woman's hand and shook it. "Mal, this is Maggie Talbot."

"Yes," Bridger said softly. "I remember."

"I never got the chance to thank you—" Maggie began.

"Don't," Bridger interrupted. "There's no need."

Frannie wondered if she was the only one here who knew that Bridger silenced the woman because he didn't want to be thanked for taking a life. Perhaps they thought he was modest, or that he was one of those just-in-a-day's-work kinda guys. But she remembered the look in his eyes as he'd told her he'd killed a man. He'd taken this job to save lives, not to take them.

Maggie Talbot looked as if what came next pained her; and maybe it did. "The reason I'm here..." Her eyes dropped to the child at her side, a fair-haired little boy who was probably about Parker's age. The child held on to his mother's skirt and stared up at Bridger with pure, undisguised terror in his blue eyes. "Joshua has had trouble sleeping, since the, um, incident, and I thought it might help if he spoke to you."

It was unfair to spring this on Bridger with no warning, Frannie thought during the short silence that followed. He was prepared to interrogate, to shoot off sarcastic comments when the moment was right, to be brutally honest, but to soothe a kid? That wasn't something that would come naturally to him.

"Hi, Joshua," Bridger said gently, offering his hand for a manly shake. The kid pulled his mother's skirt in front of his face and hid there, and Bridger let his hand drop.

"Remember what I said?" Maggie Talbot said, her voice as gentle as Bridger's had been. "Detective Bridger is a policeman, and this is where he works."

From the edge of that beige skirt, one blue eye appeared and it was fastened, Frannie saw, to the gun at Bridger's belt.

She'd been terrified to watch Phil Stone wave his gun around, when she'd been a child. How terrifying would it have been to actually see a man shot? No matter that it was necessary, no matter that the shots Bridger had fired had saved this kid's life, and others, it was still a sight no one would ever forget.

Frannie skirted around Bridger. He jumped a bit as she brushed her hand against his back, started so faintly that no one would see it—but she felt it clearly enough. He'd been so intent on the task at hand that he'd probably thought she was obediently sitting at his desk.

She dropped to her haunches, so that she was face-to-face with the blue eye. "Hello, Joshua," she said, and she smiled. The kid was uncomfortable and more than a little scared. He stared at her, with that one wide eye, and held tightly on to his mother's skirt. Frannie lowered her voice. "Can I talk to you for a minute?"

Joshua nodded his head, once.

"This guy right here?" She pointed up to Bridger, without looking his way. "You can call him Uncle Malcolm. He has lots of nieces and nephews, some of them about your age, so there are lots and lots of little boys and girls out there who call him Uncle Malcolm." Who could be afraid of anyone called Uncle Malcolm?

The kid glanced up and stared at Bridger with a new gleam in his eyes. He looked to be more skeptical than terrified at the moment.

She lowered her voice even more, wondering but not really caring if any of the adults surrounding her and Joshua could hear. "He looks pretty tough, but he's really a nice guy, a real sweetheart. I think I know why he's so sweet," she added softly. "Why, just this morning I found an empty Twinkies box in the back of his pantry. And do you know he has three flavors of ice cream in his freezer?"

There were two eyes to stare at now. "What kinds?"

"Chocolate, chocolate chip and cherry vanilla."

"I like chocolate," Joshua revealed in a soft voice of his own.

"Me, too."

A nose peeked out from behind the beige skirt, and the corner of a perfect little mouth that was almost tilted up in a smile was revealed.

"His mom makes really good chocolate-chip cookies. You know, I think Uncle Malcolm has a sweet tooth."

Joshua glanced up again, and this time Frannie was certain she knew what the kid was thinking. Uncle Malcolm had a *mother?*

Frannie reached out and brushed a strand of pale hair away from Joshua's face. "You saw Uncle Malcolm do something pretty scary, didn't you?"

His eyes widened and he nodded.

Frannie cupped the child's cheek. Oh, his skin was so smooth, so pure and untouched. In a perfect world, children would never even know violence existed. But this wasn't a perfect world, not by a long shot.

She could see his entire face now, chubby cheeks and long lashes and just a few freckles sprinkled across a pert nose. "Uncle Malcolm was there that day to watch over you, did you know that?"

Joshua shook his head.

"Well, he was. He was there to look out for you, and your mom, and all those other people. It's his job. It's what he does. Uncle Malcolm is kinda like…" She searched for a description the child would understand and embrace. "A ninja," she finished. "He's one of the good guys."

This time when Joshua looked up there was something new in his expression. Awe, maybe.

Frannie offered her hands to the kid, and amazingly Joshua loosened his hold on his mother's skirt and allowed Frannie to slip her hands beneath his arms and lift him as she stood.

Joshua was heavy, well past the carrying stage, but it felt right, for the moment. He wrapped his legs around Frannie's waist and his arms around her neck, and she looped one arm around his waist. Together they faced Bridger.

Bridger was baffled, relieved, amused. She saw all that and more in his deep brown eyes.

"Joshua, say hello to Uncle Malcolm," she said with a smile.

"Hello, Uncle Malcolm," he said, still shy and a little wary.

"If you ever want his attention," Frannie said, "just try this." She reached out and grabbed his tie and jerked on it gently, once.

Joshua giggled. Out of the corner of her eye, Frannie saw Maggie Talbot smile widely. Maybe this was the first time since the shooting that Joshua had laughed. Children should laugh every day.

"Come on," Frannie urged. "Try it."

Joshua reached out and took the edge of Bridger's tie between two short, chubby fingers, and he tugged once.

Frannie whispered into his ear. "Harder than *that*."

With a wider smile on his angelic face, Joshua grabbed the tie and gave it a good yank. And then he giggled again.

"Now," she said as he fell easily back into her arms, "I want you to give Uncle Malcolm a big ol' hug."

"Frannie," Bridger began, but his protest came too late.

Joshua said, "Okay," and leaned forward, shifting his weight precariously so that Bridger had to either catch the kid or let him fall.

Long arms closed around the kid, as Joshua wrapped his arms around Uncle Malcolm's neck and hugged tight. It was as heartwarming as watching Bridger catch Parker as he jumped from the porch.

A revelation came to her, as she watched Bridger hold the little boy. He didn't know it yet, but he should have children of his own, lots and lots of babies to hold and love and watch over.

They hadn't used protection last night, and she wondered—for the first time—if she might be carrying Bridger's child. She had no job and no home, and Bridger had made it clear there was nothing permanent to their relationship.

And still she smiled, hoping it was true. It wouldn't be

easy; in fact, it would be damned hard. But if there was a baby she would love it with all her heart, and she would never, ever, place her child in danger. She and her daughter or son wouldn't run away in the night. There would be stability and love and security for her child.

That meant she couldn't run. Oh, there probably wasn't a child, not after one night, but in her heart the resolutions were the same. Her home was here, and if she had to fight for it, she would.

Bridger and Joshua held a brief, meaningful discussion about a shared love—ice cream. Maggie Talbot grabbed Frannie's arm and very softly thanked her, while Joshua told Uncle Malcolm that he didn't like nuts in his ice cream. Before Bridger placed Joshua on his feet, the child tugged at his tie one more time. And giggled.

Joshua and his mother left the office, both of them noticeably happier than they'd been when Frannie had first seen them. When the door closed, Bridger and Harry both stared at her, silently questioning.

"All I did was convince the kid that you're a good guy." They stared at her so hard she was a little embarrassed. "And that you're human," she added. "A fact I know you hate to share."

"You've been snooping in my freezer," Bridger said softly. "And my pantry."

Frannie answered with a wide smile. "I was hungry." She turned her back to them and pointed toward the far corner. "Coffee's over there, isn't it?" Without waiting for a reply, she went in search of caffeine.

As she walked away she heard Bridger mumble, "Ninja?"

A moment later Harry said softly, "Marry her."

Chapter 14

Mal leaned against the counter and watched Frannie as she scooped the chicken casserole and corn pudding from the refrigerator. She was bending forward from the waist, and her pink skirt—which was almost transparent with the light from the refrigerator behind her—draped softly around her bare legs.

"I'm glad you thought to bring these in last night," she said as she closed the refrigerator door and placed the plastic containers on the counter. "Otherwise we'd have to make a trip to the grocery store, and after our trip to Wal-Mart I decided that you are a terrible shopper."

"I brought them in after you went to sleep," he said. "Your raincoat, too. It's in the hall closet."

She hadn't mentioned leaving town since they'd left Wal-Mart. He wanted to ask her if she'd changed her mind but was afraid she'd say no. If she left he couldn't protect her, couldn't try to figure out what she knew that made her a target, couldn't touch her.

She popped the lid off one container. "Should I heat it all up or just put a little bit on plates and warm them up in the microwave?"

Earlier today she'd told Joshua that he had a sweet tooth, as she'd done him the great favor of erasing the fear from the boy's eyes. A sweet tooth? She had no idea.

He didn't mean to startle her, but when he placed his arms around her waist she jumped. She even squealed a little and dropped the plastic lid so that it rolled across the counter.

"I swear, I'm going to put a bell around your neck if you don't stop sneaking up on me," she teased as she relaxed, falling back into his arms. Her head rested against his chest as he raised one hand to brush his palm against a full breast. He could feel the nipple harden in response, could even feel the faint tremor that shot through the body that was pressed against his. The way she responded to him, so quickly and absolutely, was as amazing to Mal as the realization that he couldn't get enough of her.

"I thought you were hungry," she murmured.

He bent his head to kiss her neck, to suckle gently at the enticing curve of flesh where neck became shoulder. It was the only answer he was capable of giving her at the moment.

He had never wanted a woman this way—endlessly, uncontrollably, completely. Frannie was inside him, somehow; she had changed him forever. There were moments when that knowledge scared the hell out of him, and other moments, like this one, where he tried not to think about it all, but only to feel.

His ache for her consumed him, until there was nothing but the press of her body against his, the sound of her quickening breath, and the certainty that this was as right and true as anything he'd ever known.

He slipped one hand lower, to flatten against her belly

so that his arousal was pressed snugly against her backside, then lower still, to cup her femininity. Everything about her was warm and welcoming. She was heat and comfort, desire and refuge. Home.

He reached beneath her flowing pink skirt to slip her panties down. The slip of silk fell to the floor and Frannie kicked it away and turned to face him.

When he looked into those big blue eyes he remembered that she thought she loved him. How could he not remember? Frannie's face was an open book. Every joy, every pain, every hunger was there for the world to see. All he had to do was look at her to know what she felt. She was open and honest and trusting. Once those qualities had terrified him, they were so foreign, but right now he was certain they were part of the reason he needed her so much.

Lifting Frannie easily, he spun around and set her on the edge of his kitchen table. He stood between her spread thighs and touched her, his fingers delving into her hot, damp center. She closed her eyes and her head fell back slightly. Savoring. Frannie savored everything—every sight, every sound, every sensation. He loved to watch her relish life; he loved even more to watch her react to his simplest touch.

As he stroked her he kissed her bared throat, tasted her skin as he delved gently within her and she rocked against him, into him, and moaned so deep in her throat he could feel a tremor against his mouth.

Her fingers found his zipper and lowered it, and she slipped her hand over his erection and gently dragged her fingertips up and down its length. That was all it took to send every other thought out of his head.

He freed himself and then he surged inside her, hard and fast. Legs wrapped around him, as Frannie lifted her hips to take all of him, to take everything he had. This wasn't a gentle coming together, but was a primitive, driven mating. She cried out softly, once, and her inner muscles tightened and squeezed around him, and while she was still climaxing he drove deep one last time and found the release he'd been so fiercely seeking.

In that moment when there was nothing in this world but his body and hers and the way they came together, Mal felt a rush of greedy possession for this woman and what they'd found. She was his, and though he had never been a man to give anything of himself easily, he was hers.

Frannie came up slowly, into his arms, draping her limp arms around his neck and resting her head against his shoulder. She turned her head and whispered something softly against his neck, mumbled low words he could not understand into his skin. *I love you?* Or maybe, *What do we do now, Bridger?* He ran his fingers through her short curls, unable and unwilling to ask her to repeat herself.

If she was going to stay and fight for her life and for Bridger, plans had to be made. He'd gone to the office early, making her swear to check the caller ID before picking up the phone, and insisting that she not answer the door to anyone but him, and promising to be home early again.

She'd liked it, kissing him goodbye and straightening his tie as he went out the door.

After she showered and dressed in a pale blue knit sweater she'd found in the bottom of one of Bridger's drawers—a gift, surely, that had probably never been worn—and the jeans she'd purchased from Wal-Mart, Frannie sat on the couch and stared at the telephone on the end table. She could call Reese and have her old job back in a heartbeat. Problem solved. Well, one of them, at least.

She'd stayed with Reese's company for so long because it was safe, the easy thing to do. After the breakup things had been awkward, for a while, but she'd stuck with her job. Frannie Vaughn did not take chances. She was cautious and reserved and she did not throw a perfectly good job away just because life in the office was a little uncomfortable.

Well, she'd been cautious and reserved before meeting Malcolm Bridger. She couldn't help but smile at the thought, and her body warmed at the remembrance of the night that had passed. There was nothing cautious *or* reserved about her relationship with Bridger.

Frannie had never allowed herself many weaknesses. Caffeine, maybe, which she wasn't really convinced *was* a weakness. Her love for old things, which was more a quirk, she decided, than a weakness.

Bridger was definitely a weakness. He made her forget who she was and what she wanted, and when he touched her she threw caution to the wind.

And would again.

Being cautious hadn't been particularly kind to her, over the years. Frannie stared at the phone and decided that in order to have everything she wanted, she was going to have to take a chance.

Mal had always loved coming to work in the morning. He was never late arriving, he never went home early, and the only sick days he'd ever taken had been when he'd been watching over Frannie.

But today he didn't want to be here. When Frannie had kissed him goodbye and reached up to straighten his tie, he'd damn near decided to call in sick again, and spend the day in bed.

But until this case was solved, Frannie was in danger.

He scribbled notes and studied old ones, trying to make things come together in his mind. Too much about this case didn't make sense.

His mind continued to go back to the Riverwatch Hotel. Back to the beginning. Neither Stanley Loudermilk nor

Clarence Doyle had an alibi for the time the man at the tattoo parlor in Huntsville had been murdered, or for the time Violet Doyle had been hit and killed. They both had plenty of unaccounted hours for Sunday, more than enough time to rig Frannie's house to blow to kingdom come. As far as he knew, neither of them had the expertise, but the background checks hadn't been finished. Besides, with the Legion for Wackos behind the killer, there was an unlimited supply of such talent available.

"Hey, Mal."

He glanced up to see a grinning Jerry Kruse bearing down on him. All Mal could manage as a response was a grunt.

Kruse didn't appear to be discouraged. "How's the case coming?"

"It's not," Mal admitted.

"If you need any help, let me know. All I've got right now are a couple of car burglaries and a string of bike thefts. Nothing that won't wait."

Mal could almost remember being this enthusiastic, years ago. "Thanks."

Kruse hung around, and suddenly Mal was certain his offer of help had nothing at all to do with this little visit. "That Frannie Vaughn…" Jerry began.

"What about her?"

"You, uh, said you were just friends, and I was thinking maybe I'd give her a call." The kid shifted his weight nervously from one foot to the other. "You know, she could probably use a night out to forget everything that's happened. Maybe dinner and a movie, you know, or—"

"I lied," Mal interrupted in a deceptively soft voice. "She's not just a friend, and if you ask her on a date I will have to kick your scrawny butt from here to Huntsville."

Jerry didn't seem to be at all offended. In fact, he smiled widely and glanced over his shoulder. "You were right," he yelled, and Mal heard Harry's laughter from around the corner. "Lunch today is on me."

Mal tried to smile, to go along with the joke, but he wasn't in a joking mood. Yes, Frannie meant much more to him than he was willing to admit, and until this case was solved, she was in serious trouble.

It just took a few minutes to drive from City Hall to the Riverwatch Hotel. There was an empty space at the curb, and Mal pulled in sharply and threw his door open. Everything had begun here. Maybe this was where it would end.

There was a new face behind the counter, a young face as surly as Clarence's had ever been.

Mal flashed his badge. "I'm looking for Stanley Loudermilk."

The new desk clerk didn't look impressed or disturbed. "He's not here. He took the day off. I think he said he was going to the river, or something."

Or something. That was a lot of help. "What about Clarence Doyle? Is he around?"

"Give him a break, man," the clerk said with a sneer. "They're burying his wife today."

"I know. I'm investigating her death."

With a shake of his head, the man headed for a door that led to a back room, an apartment where Clarence and his wife had lived for years. A minute later, he motioned for Mal to join him, and held the door open wide.

In a room that was permeated by the faint odor of cabbage and old socks, Clarence Doyle sat on a rust-colored couch that had seen many better days. At one corner a stack of books took the place of a missing leg, and still the sofa canted gently to one side. The old man looked older today. Grayer, smaller. Ancient, in his cheap suit and poorly knotted tie.

"You find the man who killed my Violet?" he asked, glancing sharply up at Mal.

"Not yet. I'm very sorry for your loss, Mr. Doyle." The old man was sour, mean, judgmental, probably crooked, but looking at him, Mal realized he'd loved his wife. In that instant, he relied on Harry's instinct rather than his usual reasoning. He couldn't believe that Doyle had run Violet down.

"Save your sympathy," Clarence snapped. "And find the man who killed her."

Mal sat in a gold wing chair that faced the couch. Here he was face-to-face with Clarence. "That's what I'm trying to do. You can help me," he said in a soothing voice. "The man who killed your wife is the same man who killed Miranda Fossett, right here in this hotel. I'm sure of it. She knew something, she saw a man's face and could identify him for me. Help me catch him, Clarence."

Clarence wouldn't look at him. "I don't know nothin'."

Mal squelched the sudden desire to jump to his feet and demand that the man come clean. "It's connected to the hotel, somehow. I'm not stupid, Clarence. I know there's something going on here. It cost Violet her life. Don't you want to help me catch the guy who did this?"

Clarence lifted angry, rheumy eyes and pinned them to Mal. "Okay, so this isn't the nicest hotel in Decatur. Sometimes I rent a room to a guy who wants to sell a little pot, or to a married guy who wants to get horizontal with a bimbo he met in a bar. Every now and then I'll turn the other cheek when a couple of baby-faced kids carrying six-packs of beer tell me they're twenty-one, or when a fine upstanding middle-aged slut I see in the supermarket now and again checks in with a boy half her age. Sometimes people want to do business for a few days, and they don't want to be disturbed, and I provide them a private place to meet with their associates. That's it."

It wasn't enough. "Have you ever heard of the Decatur Legion for Liberty?"

"Those nuts that tried to blow up the courthouse last year?"

Mal nodded. "Did you ever rent a room to them?"

Clarence frowned. "If I did, I didn't know it. I don't ask my customers what their business is, you see. I just provide a quiet place, that's all."

Another dead end. Mal gave the man his sympathies once again, and then left the Riverwatch Hotel.

Nothing. He had *nothing*. Instead of going directly to his car he walked down the sidewalk, hoping to burn off some of the energy and frustration that made him feel he was about to explode.

Somebody had to know something. This killer wasn't operating in a vacuum. Somebody knew who he was.

He turned onto Bank Street. Small businesses, several antique shops, a café and Rick's stretched before him. Nothing was open yet, but soon things would begin to bustle.

Mal was passing one window when something caught his eye. He stopped, backed up a couple of steps and stared.

The ceramic angel was tall, much taller than any of the ones Frannie had arranged so carefully on her end table. The figure was abnormally slender, and was draped in a mint green robe. The face was angelic, the halo was gold, the wings were wide and white...and one of them was chipped.

He glanced at the sign on the door of the antique shop, and then at his watch. Twenty minutes until opening time. A woman was busy at the cash register, though, so Mal tapped on the door and flashed his badge.

Frannie always felt better when she had a plan. All those rootless years, when she'd often had no idea what came next, had spooked her. Yes, she had to have a plan.

And now she had one. Bridger wouldn't like it, and she

would allow a little time before putting the plan into motion, but she knew where she was going from here.

She recognized Bridger's knock, a snappy, insistent pounding that brought a smile to her face. He was early again, as he'd said he would be. Her lunch of a peanut butter sandwich and coffee was long past, but she hadn't even begun to think of dinner, yet. They'd probably have to go grocery shopping.

"Did you look through the peephole?" he asked as he stepped into the apartment.

"Of course."

He closed the door, and she grabbed his tie and pulled his lips to hers for a quick kiss. The touch of his mouth on hers was a comfort, a relief. She'd been waiting, craving that touch all day. How could she miss him so much?

There was a wadded-up brown paper bag under his arm, and he tossed it carefully to the couch.

"How'd it go?" she asked as he slipped off his jacket and placed it over the back of a chair.

He scowled, but not at her. "It didn't. I talked to a dozen people today, and got nowhere. Even stopped by the funeral home this afternoon, for Mrs. Doyle's visitation, hoping that someone who shouldn't be there would show up." He glanced at her hard, the way he sometimes did. "Any phone calls?"

She shook her head. "Maybe he doesn't know where I am?"

Bridger didn't quite buy that, though he wanted to. "Maybe he knows I've got caller ID."

"Maybe he finally believes that I don't have anything he wants."

He wanted to believe that as much as she did, she thought. She could see his mind working, could see the inner struggle in his eyes. "If that's the truth, he'll disappear and we'll never catch him."

That was a conflict for Bridger. He wanted her to be safe, but he wanted to get the bad guys, too.

She decided to change the subject. "What's in the bag? Dinner? I swear, Bridger, man cannot live by ice cream alone."

He smiled. "It's a little something for you."

"For me?" She was really surprised. Bridger had never struck her as the type of man to court a woman with gifts and flowers. He was a no-nonsense man, who didn't have time for such frivolities.

"What is it?" She sat on the couch and glanced at the brown paper bag. "Twinkies?" she asked devilishly. Since she'd discovered Bridger's weakness, she couldn't let it pass. "More ice cream?" Guessing what was in the bag was bound to be more fun than opening it. "It had better not be a gun, Bridger, I told you..."

He sat down beside her, scooped the bag up off the couch and placed it in her lap. It sat there heavily. "Just open it," he said softly.

She plucked at the wrinkled brown paper, opening it so she could slip her hand inside the bag. Her hand found something hard and cool and smooth, and she wrapped her fingers around the object and drew it from the bag.

The paper bag fluttered to the floor at her feet as she stared at the angel. It was magnificent, almost ethereal, and she'd never seen one quite like it. One wing was slightly chipped, and she placed her finger there to caress the rough edge.

She couldn't see the progress of her finger over the angel's wing, not very well. Tears filled her eyes, blurring her vision. "It's beautiful," she whispered.

"I saw it in a store window, and I thought about you." Bridger's arm was heavy and comforting around her. "That's never happened to me before," he admitted grudgingly. "But when I saw that broken angel I knew you had to have it."

"She's not broken," Frannie whispered. "She's imperfect. There's a difference." Tears slipped down her cheeks, slow, fat tears. Bridger *did* love her. He had to. If he knew how much this meant to her—a new start, a fresh beginning, and still a trace of the past, then he had to love her, a little.

He slipped a hand beneath her chin and forced her to look up, to look at him. "Oh, no," he growled. "Why are you crying? Dammit, Frannie. Stop." When she didn't immediately obey, he growled. "I can't stand it when a woman cries."

"I thought Malcolm Bridger could stand anything." She tried to keep her voice light, but it wasn't easy.

With his fingers he wiped away her tears. "Stop it," he commanded gently. "You didn't cry when that man broke into your house, or when we argued, or even when your house blew up. Why now, Frannie?"

How could she explain? She didn't have to. He kissed her, and her tears began to dry. He touched her, and there was no more reason to cry. He would love her, perhaps right here on this couch, and their coming together would be beautiful and furious, as it always was. They wouldn't use or even mention protection, but neither would they mention babies or love or tomorrow.

Bridger took the angel from her and placed it carefully on the end table. One hand slipped beneath her sweater to touch her skin lightly. "I didn't mean to make you cry," he whispered.

As he brushed his fingers across her skin he lowered his head to kiss her throat. Frannie closed her eyes, relishing the sensation of his mouth on her skin, of his breath brushing against her neck. He wrapped an arm around her and scooted her over so that she was half lying down and he was cradled between her thighs. Nothing felt so good, or so right, as this man touching her.

Before it was too late, she wanted him to know why she cried. She wanted him to know how the simple gift touched her heart. At the same time, she couldn't allow herself to say too much. Opening her heart completely would scare Bridger away right now.

"You just don't know how much an imperfect angel means to someone who doesn't have anything but a misbehaving car and a raincoat with a hole in the pocket," she said softly, trying to make light of the tears she couldn't explain as she lifted a hand to his shoulder.

He growled something against her throat, a wordless response as he feathered small kisses across her skin, and then he stilled suddenly. "What did you say?" He pulled his head back to look her in the eye.

"I said, you don't know what it means—"

"The raincoat," he said impatiently.

"A raincoat with a hole in the pocket?"

He kissed her quickly, and then a grin bloomed on his face and he sprang from the couch, leaving Frannie half sitting, half lying down, and suddenly alone.

"What?" she asked impatiently as she stood and followed him into the hall. He already had her coat out of the closet and was shoving his hands into first one pocket and then another. She saw the satisfaction on his face when he found the small hole in the left pocket.

"Bridger, I know what you're thinking. But what on earth could Miranda Fossett have dropped into my pocket that would slip through that little hole? Besides, I would have felt it if she'd dropped anything in my pocket, and I didn't, so it's not possible that there's any evidence floating around in my raincoat."

He moved his search to the hem of her raincoat, running his fingers from one end to the other until he obviously found what he was looking for. There was an expression of near joy on his hard face. It was quite unexpectedly enchanting.

"Lost a key lately?" he asked with a smile.

"No, I never lose my keys."

He raised the hem of her coat, and with the pressure of his finger on the backside she could see, very clearly, the outline of a small key.

Bridger whispered, "Bingo."

Chapter 15

A locksmith identified the key Mal found in the hem of Frannie's raincoat as belonging to a safe-deposit box in a local bank, and less than an hour later Harry called a judge acquaintance to get a court order giving them the right to open the box and confiscate the contents.

When the bank opened the next morning Mal and Harry were there, waiting as the teller unlocked the door. No one else, but Frannie and the judge, knew what they'd found, and Mal wanted to keep it that way, for now. If word got out, she could be in even worse danger than before.

Anything could be in Miranda Fossett's safe-deposit box. They might find proof positive of the killer's identity, and then again they might find nothing at all. All Mal asked for as they took the metal box into a closetlike room, was a crumb, a decent clue to point him in the right direction.

He turned the key himself, and opened the long metal box. There was cash on top, a good-sized bundle of it. Mal felt a surge of disappointment. Cash would lead them nowhere. He lifted the bundle of bills and revealed an envelope. Even better, in the back right corner of the long, narrow box was an undeveloped roll of film.

Wearing cotton gloves, Mal took the letter between two fingers and opened it carefully. "Prisoner Mail" was stamped on the envelope, and Jacob Fossett's name was written neatly in the space for a return address, along with the PO box number for the county jail.

He scanned the handwritten letter and grinned as he turned to Harry. "I knew it," he said. "Fossett was going to spill the beans, he was going to tell everything." The letter fluttered between his fingers. "This is not the letter of a man about to commit suicide. This is a near-desperate letter to his sister, almost an apology for being involved in the bombing. He was going to name names."

"We have another murder," Harry said. "That does not make me happy. Why are you smiling?"

"At least we have a motive," Mal said as he returned the letter to the envelope and the envelope to the manila envelope he'd brought in with him. The cash followed, and finally the roll of film. "And a reason to reopen the investigation into Jacob Fossett's death. It'll be interesting to see what's on this roll."

Before they left the small room, Harry's pager sounded. A few seconds later, so did Mal's. By that time, Harry had already pulled his cell phone from his suit pocket and was dialing the station.

The conversation was brief, and when Harry hit the end button he practically stormed out the door. "We have another damn body."

Mal and Harry kept their distance while the crime scene tech, Sam Wingate, finished his work. The grotesque body was sitting up in a fat blue chair that was positioned directly before the television. A favorite chair, perhaps.

Martin Blake had been a good friend of Jacob Fossett's, Mal remembered, and that was strike one. They'd suspected him of being a member of the legion, but there had never been any proof. On the end table beside the body was a framed photograph of Miranda Fossett. Strike two. In the photograph she was smiling, standing in the sun near a body of still water. She looked very little like the dead woman he'd seen in the stairwell of the Riverwatch Hotel.

Blake had dark hair, but since half of his face had been blown off it was impossible to tell if he had ever looked anything like Tyrone Power from any angle. The tattoo on the dead man's forearm, a small heart with the name Miranda beneath it, was visible from where Mal stood. Strike three, you're out. What else could they ask for?

"Suicide," Sam said without looking up from the body. "And he didn't plan to fail. Sawed-off shotgun in the mouth."

A messily scrawled note, red pen on a lined sheet of notebook paper, lay on the floor near the dead man's feet. *I'm sorry.*

It was all so neat and tidy, like a present wrapped up in a red ribbon and left at his feet. Mal had a vaguely uneasy feeling about this, but he couldn't ignore the facts before his eyes.

"Why did he kill himself?" he asked, as much to himself as to Harry.

"Guilt?" Harry suggested, nodding to the note on the floor.

It didn't feel right. "*After* he killed four people?" *And tried to kill Frannie.* "Why now? Let's say we were right from the beginning, and this is a simple case of a rejected boyfriend taking his revenge on an unfaithful woman. If he was going to kill himself, why not right after he killed Miranda? Why bother to cover everything up, getting rid of any possible witnesses, and *then* commit suicide?"

"Maybe he knew we were getting close." Harry suggested.

"How?" Mal studied the room they stood in. Blake's apartment was small, but it was neat and clean. There were plants in the windowsill, and Miranda's photograph wasn't the only one in the room. There were pictures of an older couple, of small children and even one of a black lab. It was all very homey, for a man who was capable of multiple murder. "A handful of people knew we'd found the key."

"It only takes one to spring a leak."

Harry was well on his way to being satisfied, but Mal didn't quite buy it. It was too neat.

"You just don't want this to be over," Harry suggested as they worked their way through the house, examining everything with cotton-gloved hands, cataloguing anything that might be of interest to the case. "If this is over, then that means you have to let Frannie go."

"Not necessarily," Mal grumbled. He looked up to see that Harry was grinning widely.

"You're going to take my advice and marry her." Harry nodded his gray head slowly, pleased with himself.

"I didn't say that," Mal said as he opened the refrigerator door. "There's a full gallon of milk in here. Why would he buy a gallon of milk if he was planning to blow his head off?"

"You ask too many questions."

It was late afternoon before they left the apartment, and they had all the evidence they needed. The car in the garage had a crumpled fender and a broken headlight. They were certain the small amount of dried blood would match their elderly hit-and-run victim. There were mechanical parts that might be used in the building of a bomb, and a number of knives. One of them would probably match the wound in Miranda Fossett's throat, and if they were lucky, very lucky, there would be blood remaining in the wooden handle of one of those weapons. And as an extra added bonus, they found a small, royal blue handbag stuffed in the back of the master bedroom closet. Miranda Fossett's driver's license and two hundred dollars cash was inside.

The body was bagged and headed for Birmingham, and Sam said again that he was confident that this was, indeed, a suicide.

Back at the station, Mal headed straight for the evidence room and the officer stationed there. He handed over the letter, cash and roll of film from Miranda Fossett's safe-deposit box.

"See about getting that film developed for me," he said halfheartedly. It was too little too late, but he wanted a look at those photographs that were worth killing for, worth five lives and Frannie's house.

But the photos would keep. Right now he had to go home and tell Frannie that the nightmare was over.

She hadn't started to worry until well into the afternoon, but once she started fretting it was impossible to stop. Dammit, Bridger should have called hours ago and told her what was in the safe-deposit box!

She'd puttered away most of the day, cleaning a little, taking a shower and dressing in one of her new outfits. The lavender skirt and matching blouse were a little big, but the outfit was comfortable and cool.

Frannie sat on the couch with her newest—her only—angel in her lap. It said more about Bridger than he knew, that he'd bought this slightly imperfect angel. Even more, it said something wonderful about him, that he knew how much the figurine meant to her.

The music that played softly helped to calm her. She'd found a few cassettes in the small storage drawer of Bridger's entertainment center, and among them were a couple of old soft rock collections that were familiar and soothing. She let the low music wash over her, and told herself again and again that if anything was wrong Bridger would be here.

The knock on the door was solid but steadier than in the past few days, and Frannie set the slender porcelain angel on the end table as she jumped off the couch and hurried to the door to throw the dead bolt and let Bridger in.

There was something different about him as he stepped into his apartment and closed the door. For one thing, he didn't immediately set the dead bolt back into place.

"Well?" she said as she peeled off his jacket and tossed it over the back of a chair. "What did you find?"

He faced her then. His posture was more relaxed, even his eyes were calmer. "We got him," he said softly.

Frannie practically threw herself at Bridger, tossing her arms around his neck and holding tight. There had been moments when she was sure they'd never know who had threatened her and destroyed her house, terrifying moments when she was certain this would never be over. "Thank you," she whispered.

She felt the gentle sift of Bridger's hand through her hair. The touch was familiar and soothing. "Don't thank me. The guy killed himself and left enough clues in his house to solve the murders of Jacob and Miranda Fossett, Violet Doyle, and the man from the tattoo parlor in Huntsville. A possible murder weapon, Miranda's purse, a damaged fender. There were even electronic components that might have been used to make a bomb, and I'm pretty sure they'll match up with what was used at your place."

He should have been ecstatic, but instead he sounded almost disappointed.

"Sounds perfect," she whispered. "So what's wrong?"

He hesitated for a moment. Fingers were wound in her hair, and one arm was tightly encircling her waist. Her blouse shifted so that one shoulder was bared, and as if it were a kind of invitation, Bridger kissed her there.

"Maybe it's too perfect," he said softly, his breath warm against her skin. "Then again, maybe I'm just looking for trouble where there isn't any."

"Now why would you do that?" she whispered against his chest.

"Harry thinks I just don't want to let you go, yet."

Yet. Frannie closed her eyes tight. "Yeah, well, what does he know?" she asked lightly, glad her face was hidden for the moment. She'd known from the beginning this was a temporary relationship. Bridger had never lied and tried to tell her differently.

"He *thinks* he knows everything."

She brushed one finger against Bridger's white shirt, feeling the warmth of his skin seeping through, warming her fingertip. "I thought that was a trait common to the detectives in the homicide division."

She knew what she had to do, didn't she? Hard as it would be, there was no choice. She didn't doubt for a minute that what she felt for Bridger was love, but this was no way to start a relationship. One really bad day had brought them together the first time, and tragedy had brought Bridger back to her. His sense of duty and intense physical attraction kept them together. But for how long?

"Bridger?" she said softly, not even trying to pretend that this was a lighthearted moment. "I want you to take me home."

"What?" With a finger beneath her chin he forced her to look up, into his face. His features were rugged, the lines sharp and occasionally brutal, but he had always been beautiful to her.

"My house," she whispered. "I need to see it."

He shook his head. "No, you don't. It'll just upset you."

It'll hurt. She knew that. But before she moved forward,

she had to look back. Just once. "If you won't take me I'll go by myself." She would do it, but, God, she didn't want to face the sight alone. She wanted Bridger there, holding her hand.

He didn't make her wait long. "All right."

The sun was low in the sky, but not yet setting, when they arrived at her lot on Oak Street. She could only call it a lot now, since in her view from the passenger window there was nothing resembling a house left.

Where her little house had once stood, there was a charred, black blemish on the earth. All that remained in the burned square were lumps of unidentifiable wood and metal, misshapen, charred lumps of what had been her life. The azaleas were gone, she noted numbly, and then she choked back a hysterical sob that bordered on a laugh. She was worried about the azaleas? *Everything* was gone.

She opened the door, and when Bridger tried to stop her she brushed him off, keeping her eyes on the blight before her. If she looked at him she would cry, and she didn't want to cry right now. He couldn't stand a woman's tears, she remembered.

"I painted last year," she said when Bridger appeared beside her and slipped his arm around her waist. *Good,* she thought as she leaned slightly into his warm arm. *I won't fall now.* Her knees were awfully weak all of a sudden. Bridger kept her standing, with his steady arm and, even more, just by being there as she made herself look at the damage before her.

There was yellow crime scene tape encircling her property, and Bridger held it up so she could go under. The closer she got to the place where her house had been, the more debris she stepped on and around. Then she reached a place where the glass beneath her feet was abundant.

She looked at the numerous small, jagged shards of glass

beneath her feet. Something crunched ominously beneath the soles of her shoes. "If we'd been closer to the house when it blew up, we might have been badly hurt." The healing cuts on the back of her arms throbbed slightly at the reminder.

Bridger didn't say anything. Oh well, it was a statement that didn't require a response.

When Frannie tried to take a step closer to the house, he held her back gently but firmly. "Close enough," he said softly.

Perhaps he was right. This time she didn't try to change his mind or go on alone. She leaned into his arm and stared at the blackened mess before her, trying to remind herself that she and Bridger were lucky to be alive. She knew it was the truth, but looking at what was left of her life still hurt, as she'd known it would.

"I worked so hard at making this home," she admitted. "It was my nest, my haven, my place to hide from everything in the world I didn't want to face. I painted it and decorated it and loved it." *As though if I loved it enough it would love me back.*

"I know you did," he said soothingly. He didn't assure her, as he had the night of the bombing, that they would find another house. A bigger, better house to paint and love. In fact, he hadn't used the word *we* in a while. He'd never used the word *love*.

Frannie rested her head against Bridger's shoulder, and his hand lifted slowly to cup her head. Together they watched what remained of her home as the sun set. They didn't move, they didn't speak.

Everything ended, she knew that. There was a beginning and an end to all things, good and bad. But she'd never expected her time in this house she'd loved to end so suddenly and violently. In the blink of an eye everything she'd worked and saved for and loved was gone.

Even the tender, last light of day wasn't kind to the destruction. What was left of her home remained ugly, until darkness softened the edges and drank in some of the charred blackness.

"I'm ready to go," Frannie said as nighttime finally claimed the sight before her. Bridger turned her about and led her to the car. She didn't look back.

The drive to his place was silent, and seemed to take much longer than the earlier trip from his apartment to what was left of her house. It was fully dark when they arrived, though the complex was well lit with sporadically placed streetlamps and a number of porch lights.

Frannie sat in the car and looked up at the second floor, stared at Bridger's front door as he circled the car. He opened her door and offered a steady hand, a hand she gratefully took.

What would she do when it came time to let go of Bridger? Losing him was going to be much harder than losing a house and everything in it, but she didn't think she could change the end of their tenuous relationship any more than she'd been able to change the violent destruction of her home.

That knowledge didn't make her want him any less.

Inside his apartment he locked the door behind them. Frannie stood over the end table and looked down at the angel she'd placed there earlier. She did her best to think of nothing at all, not the future or the past, not what she'd lost or what she'd found.

She was getting used to Bridger coming up behind her without making a sound. This time she knew he was coming, she felt rather than heard him, and when he put his arms around her she didn't so much as flinch.

"Are you all right?" he whispered in her ear.

"Yes," she said, and amazingly she meant it.

With one slow and easy finger, Bridger slipped her

blouse aside so that her shoulder was bared again. That finger brushed against her skin, warm and light and comforting, as if he were tracing an unseen path. When he kissed her there, she smiled. A kiss really could make everything better.

Turning in his arms, she lifted her face for a kiss, parting her lips as his mouth touched hers. She wanted to memorize this exact feeling—the heat and the flutter, the weakness in her knees and the throb of her heart. When she closed her eyes she wanted to be able to remember exactly how he smelled and tasted. She placed her hand against his chest. She needed to memorize this, too— the steady beat of his heart.

Giving Bridger up was going to hurt worst of all, but it didn't have to hurt tonight.

Chapter 16

"Bridger?"

Mal came awake slowly, gently, the sound of Frannie's voice bringing him to consciousness. He reached out for her, as he had in the night, needing to hold her. When he'd reached out to her in the wee hours of the morning she'd come to him wordlessly, as if it were their first time...or their last.

He didn't want to need anything, not like this, but he couldn't help it. He was past resistance. His hand slid over bare sheet, touched the pillow where Frannie had laid her head last night. He knew she was close, her voice had been practically in his ear.

"Come on, Bridger, wake up."

He opened his eyes to see that she wasn't in the bed at all, but stood over him. She was fully dressed, in her new jeans and the pale blue sweater Robin had given him three Christmases ago.

"What are you doing up?" He glanced at the clock, it

was barely six. She'd already showered—her hair was still slightly damp—and she'd dressed and put on a little pink lipstick. In the faint light from the hallway she looked like his own angel, fresh and good and beautiful. His heart constricted at the unexpected thought.

She smiled at him, but it wasn't the wide, crooked smile that had captivated him from the night he'd met her. This smile was controlled and a little sad. "I tried to leave without saying goodbye, but I couldn't do it."

"Leave?" He sat up quickly, and when he did he saw the tote bag sitting by the bedroom door. The angel he'd bought Frannie was standing beside it.

"It's time," she said softly.

"You can stay here as long as you want." He reached for his boxers and put them on quickly. Frannie took a step back.

"I know." She backed to the door and scooped up her tote bag, tossing the long strap over her shoulder. Then she picked up the porcelain angel, grasping it tightly in one hand. "But it's not a good idea."

He didn't know if he was angry or scared, but something he didn't like welled up in his chest. Why hadn't she mentioned this last night? He could have argued more effectively with her if he was clearheaded. He could have convinced her she was wrong, if she was lying beneath him. "Look, you don't have a place to go, and I'm still not convinced that Blake is the right guy."

"You said yourself that there was more than enough evidence in Blake's apartment to close the case," she said sensibly. "And I do have a place to go." With the weight of the bag on one shoulder, she stood with her arms and legs off center.

"Where?"

She shifted her weight. "I have a part-time job at Terri's Trash and Treasure. It's an antique shop on Bank Street.

Terri has a room upstairs I can live in, free of charge, until I get my life back in order again. It used to be a small apartment, and then it was a storage room for years. There's a bathroom and a small kitchen and lots of closet space. It just needs a little fixing up.''

"Frannie…" Mal took a step forward, and she lifted the figurine in her hand as if he were a vampire and the skinny angel her silver cross. He stopped. "You're going to work part-time in a junk store. That's your plan?"

She smiled, slightly crooked, slightly wide. "Part of it. I'm going to buy a new computer, set it up in my new place, and then I'm going to start looking for work as a contract programmer. I made a few phone calls this week, and there are lots of companies out there looking for programmers to rewrite programs that aren't Y2K compliant. That should keep me busy for a while, at least until the year 2000."

"You're going to do contract work? That's risky." He wasn't purposely trying to scare her, not really, but he knew how careful Frannie was, how neat and secure she liked her life.

He didn't scare her at all. "I know it's risky. Maybe that's a good thing. Maybe it's time I stopped living so cautiously."

Frannie was poised to flee, and he was certain that if he moved forward that's exactly what she'd do. He wasn't ready to watch her run away from him.

"You could do that from here." Was he asking her to move in? Dammit, it sure sounded that way.

She shook her head. "You know how I feel, but let's face it, Bridger. If there hadn't been a dead blonde in the stairwell of the Riverwatch Hotel, I never would've seen you again. You wouldn't have called, you wouldn't have come looking for me. I would've been a fuzzy, funny memory, a story to drag out now and again, maybe. The one-night stand that wasn't. I was dumped in your lap, and eventually you're going to remember that and resent it.''

''We haven't even discussed this.''

''What's to discuss? We've never been on a date, Bridger. You've never called me to see if I'm busy, or just to talk.'' She tried to smile again, but this time he could see it was an effort. ''We need some time apart, I think.''

''You don't even have a car,'' he snapped. ''What are you going to do, walk to Bank Street from here?'' The question sounded bitter, and he didn't want her to know how hostile he felt right now. It revealed too much. ''Never mind, I'll get dressed and drive you.''

''Newton dropped off my car bright and early,'' she said. ''There's no need for you to drive me.'' And then she turned away.

Mal followed her into the hall, watched her walk unerringly for the door. He wanted to ask her again to stay, but he knew what the answer would be. She was determined.

She opened the front door, readjusted her tote bag and glanced over her shoulder. ''Call me sometime,'' she said softly.

Frannie put the last of her things away in the antique dresser Terri was letting her use. There wasn't room for everything downstairs, and the dresser needed a few minor repairs before it could be sold for top dollar. Same with the oddly canted four-poster bed and the ugly orange chair that needed to be reupholstered, and the scratched cigarette table the tall skinny angel sat upon. As of now, that was the extent of the furnishings in her new apartment.

She sat down in the chair, stretching out her legs and leaning back lazily, taking a deep, cleansing breath. Leaving Bridger had easily been the hardest thing she'd ever done. Harder than watching her house burn, harder than listening to her mother tell her she was getting married *again,* harder than facing a man with a gun.

But what choice did she have? She couldn't stay with him, easing into his life so that before he knew what was happening she was there for good. She loved him, but she had to know that he wanted her in his life.

With nervous fingers she plucked at the sweater she wore. Bridger's sweater. Taking it wasn't so bad. He never wore it, and besides, if he wanted it back all he had to do was ask.

Mal grumbled as he sifted through the papers on his desk. Thanks to the excitement of the past week, he had enough paperwork to keep him busy for a month.

His mind wasn't on the paperwork, though. It was on Frannie. He was angry, he was confused. He missed her already, and she hadn't been gone a full day.

She was right, of course. This was for the best. He'd never been looking for more than one night, and if it had turned out to be more spectacular than he'd expected, well, that was just a bonus. He could never give Frannie everything she wanted, he could never be the man she needed.

Perversely, he thought he might like to try. Maybe in a week or so, when things died down and she'd had a chance to settle in her new place, he'd give her a call.

Harry had asked about Frannie right away, as soon as Mal had come through the door that morning, wondering what her plans were and if she would continue staying at his apartment. The sergeant had apparently caught the matchmaking bug from his wife. He was so disappointed to learn that Frannie had moved out, you'd think he was the one who'd be sleeping alone tonight.

He hadn't mentioned Frannie since then, not as they'd shared a quick lunch together, and not as they'd each pored over their stacks of paperwork. Harry had been restlessly in and out of the office all day.

It was late afternoon when Harry burst into the detectives' room, his face red as he threw open the door and headed straight for Mal's desk. "Frannie," he said breathlessly, and Mal's heart stopped. Something was wrong. Something had happened to her or Harry wouldn't be looking at him this way.

Mal slowly came up out of his chair.

"Where is she?" Harry finished. He was winded, as if he'd run all the way here.

Where is she? Didn't he know? Mal's heart rate slowed considerably. "At the antique shop, I guess. What's wrong?"

"I just got off the phone with Birmingham. Martin Blake didn't commit suicide, though somebody went to a helluva lot of trouble to make it look like he did. He had enough codeine in his blood to kill him, and the coroner says there's no way in hell he pulled that trigger himself."

"Somebody did it for him."

"That's not all," Harry snapped. "The tattoo on Blake's arm is only a few days old. The skin was still irritated."

"It was a setup."

He'd known it was too good to be true, too damn neat. Mal thumbed through the phone book quickly, easily finding Terri's Trash and Treasure. He dialed the number but got a busy signal.

He cursed as he slammed down the phone. "I'm headed over there. Send a car that way, but keep trying to call, and if you get Frannie, tell her to stay put until I get there."

"Will do."

The uniformed officer from the evidence room blocked his exit, and he was waving a small flat package. He hadn't overheard, couldn't know that Mal was about to run him down if he didn't get out of the way.

"You want those pictures, Detective Bridger?"

Pictures, what damn pictures? He was in such a panic he almost forgot. "Yeah."

On the chance that there was something valuable here, he took the time to open the envelope, and flipped restlessly through the stack of photographs. These shots were so off kilter and occasionally out of focus that he assumed they'd been taken secretly, at a meeting of the Decatur Legion for Liberty. Fossett was there, as well as a few faces he recognized as known criminals and...as he leafed through...one face he hadn't expected to see.

"Harry, where's Kruse?"

"He took off early. You need his help?"

"No," Mal didn't take time to explain. He tossed the pictures to Harry and took off.

Frannie dusted a display of figurines while Terri chatted on the telephone. She'd been on the phone all afternoon, talking to one friend and then another. It had been slow. A few customers had stopped by earlier, but in the past couple of hours it had been just Terri and Frannie. Terri had already assured her that Saturday was their busy day, and the rest of the week was erratic, at best.

When the bell above the door jingled, both Frannie and Terri lifted their heads to see who the new customer was.

"Jerry," Frannie said with a wide grin. At that, Terri returned to her conversation.

He returned her smile and headed in her direction, hands in his pockets. "Hi."

She continued to dust the figurines. "What are you doing here? You don't strike me as the kind of guy who goes in for antiques." She glanced at the array surrounding her. "Or junk."

"I'm not. I heard Mal telling Harry this morning that you were here, and I thought that maybe, if you guys aren't serious or anything, you might like to reconsider that Chinese. Maybe a movie afterward, or dancing, if you prefer.''

A couple of weeks ago she would have jumped at the chance to date a guy like Jerry Kruse. He was handsome, he had a nice smile, and he seemed to genuinely like her. But Bridger had spoiled her.

''Thanks, but I think I need to step back and spend some time alone, for a while.''

''That's too bad.'' Jerry picked up an old wooden box, turned it over in his hand and studied the wood grain carefully. ''If you change your mind...'' he began in a soft voice.

''Frannie, I'm heading home early,'' Terri said as she hung up the phone. Her smile widened. ''Oh, I'm going to like having you around. I haven't been able to take off early in ages.''

The phone rang before she'd taken two steps. ''Terri's Trash and Treasure.'' She held the receiver aloft. ''Frannie, it's for you. A man,'' she added as Frannie approached. ''Sounds important.'' She winked as she handed over the phone and grabbed her purse from beneath the counter. Frannie waved as Terri sauntered out the door.

No one knew where she was but Bridger. She'd hoped he would call, but never expected that he'd seek her out so soon. ''Hello?''

''Frannie, thank God.''

''Harry?''

She could hear him take a deep breath. ''It was the wrong guy,'' he said softly. ''The killer's still out there. Mal is on his way over right now, and—''

No. ''What do you mean, the wrong guy?''

''Just hang on until Mal gets there. He'll explain everything.''

Frannie tried not to be alarmed. ''I'll be fine until then,'' she said, leaning against the counter. ''Jerry Kruse is here.''

Harry uttered the filthiest curse Frannie had ever heard. "Listen carefully. You've got to—"

"Harry?" Frannie spoke into the dead phone, then moved it away from her ear in time to see Jerry Kruse drop the severed phone line and turn the knife he held in her direction.

"I was hoping this was finished," he said softly. "But I can see by the look on your face that it's not. Too bad. I like you Frannie, I really do. Do they know it's me?"

Frannie took a deep breath. She wanted to scream but couldn't find enough air. She wanted to run, but her legs shook too much. Jerry stood between her and the door. No matter what, she would *not* turn and try to run upstairs to her apartment. She remembered too well what Jerry had done to the last woman he'd caught on a stairwell.

"It was you standing at the elevator, wasn't it?" she asked softly.

He nodded once and took a step closer. "Miranda got greedy. What was I supposed to do? She'd been blackmailing me for months. I tried to romance her into behaving herself, but it didn't work. She just wanted more, and more, and more." He took another step. Frannie answered with a sliding step back.

"And all those other people?" Bridger was on the way. If she could just keep Kruse talking…

"The old lady and the guy from the tattoo parlor had seen me with Miranda. Blake was just easy. He even cooperated when I got him drunk and suggested he get a tattoo in Miranda's honor."

"But what about—"

"We don't have time for this," he said, and with the hand that didn't hold a knife he motioned her forward. "You really did have the film and the letter she was blackmailing me with, didn't you? I'd about decided that Mal had it right, that Miranda lied to me so I wouldn't kill her and all this time you had nothing. But no, I was right from the start. Where was it?''

''I didn't know I had it.'' Somehow she had to get past Kruse and to the door. So far he threatened her only with the knife and not with the revolver he wore on his belt. Blades were silent.

''Where is it now?''

Frannie took a step back. ''Bridger has it.'' She could scream for help, but it would do no good. The coffee shop next door had already closed, and the space on the other side was vacant. No, she was on her own.

Kruse tilted his head to one side. He was calm, still, emotionless. ''That's what I was afraid of. So if he doesn't know yet that I'm the one he's looking for, it's just a matter of time.''

He'd been walking so slowly his sudden lunge caught Frannie by surprise. She dropped to the floor and scrambled away before Kruse reached out. The knife in his hand missed her arm by inches.

She had one advantage. She knew this store, inch by inch. As Kruse came down the aisle after her, she slipped beneath one long table, across another aisle and hid beneath a mahogany occasional table with fat, ornate legs. The space was small, and she was partially hidden by a lace tablecloth that was draped over one edge.

''Come on, Frannie,'' he cajoled in a sweet voice. ''Don't make this difficult.''

She held her breath. His voice was close, and as she held her breath he walked right past her. His shoes passed not ten inches from her knee.

''I have to run now, change my name, hide for a while, but before I go I want to leave Mal a present. You.'' There was a touch of glee in his voice, and it made Frannie shudder. ''If he hadn't taken this case so personally, if he'd just let it go, everything would have worked out for the best.''

His footsteps faded and became louder. Frannie winced at the loud screech of wood against wood as he shifted furniture to look for her. "Miranda would be out of my hair, and in just a few months the legion would be in full swing again. Do you have any idea how much money there is in misdirected patriotism? More than I'll ever make as a cop, that's for sure. Come on, Frannie." He was losing his patience, she could tell. "Mal ruined everything. He had to get involved, he had to take it personally just because he was in the hotel when I killed Miranda." He took a deep breath. "Though I think he took it even more to heart when I broke into your house."

He was coming up the same aisle, again, and Frannie held her breath, again. The clack of his hard-soled shoes were almost as loud to her as the thrum of her own blood rushing through her veins.

"If he has your body to cry over, he won't come after me right away," Kruse said in a frighteningly sensible voice. "And by the time he recovers from the shock, I'll be long gone."

Jerry didn't know Bridger very well if he thought he would cry over her. Maybe he'd toast her with Jack Daniel's, and maybe he would even miss her a little. But Bridger cry? No way.

The shiny shoes stopped right in front of her, and before she could react Kruse dropped down and grabbed her arm. She set her feet so she'd stay beneath the table, but he was too strong. He dragged her from her hiding place and she kicked out hard. The first attempt glanced off his ankle. She tried again, putting all her strength into the simple move. Her foot connected with Kruse's shin but didn't slow him down. He hauled her into the aisle.

Frannie didn't look up at the weapon she knew he held, and she didn't give up. She kept kicking, slamming her feet against his knees. Finally she was able to sweep Jerry's feet out from under him. He fell heavily, and she scrambled to her feet. All she had to do was make it to the front door and onto the street.

Before she'd gone three steps Jerry tackled her from behind, and together with the knickknacks from a small table she bumped against they fell to the floor. All around her was the crash and tinkle of breaking fragile objects, the thud of a heavier item. She was roughly flipped onto her back. Kruse's weight crushed her as he breathed heavily into her face.

She stared up into his handsome, indifferent face and knew he was going to kill her. "Don't," she whispered. She stared him straight in the eye, as one hand searched blindly for something, anything, to defend herself with. Her fingers fell over a solid object, and she lifted it carefully. "You don't gain anything by killing me."

"I have no choice," he said, and he almost seemed to regret the decision.

She brought the object in her hand up with all the strength she could muster, crashing it into Kruse's head. The blow wasn't massive, but she did manage to take him by surprise. A thin trickle of blood ran from his temple down his cheek, and Frannie was able to push Kruse away as he raised a hand to his wounded head. The broken mushroom salt shaker fell to the floor as she scrambled to her feet, shards of glass cutting into the palm of her hand and even through her jeans to cut her knees.

She ran for the door, while Kruse jumped to his feet and circled the table to cut her off. They were headed for the door from different directions, circling almost toward each other. If she ran fast enough, if she didn't look back... When the bell over the front door jingled, they both stopped.

Frannie had a clear view of Bridger's profile as he walked into the store. Unfortunately, Kruse faced him head-on, and he must have seen Bridger coming for the weapon he wore on his holster was drawn and waiting. He fired once.

She couldn't hear her own scream for the blast, but she could feel it in her throat, ripping and silently burning. Bridger grunted and flew back, falling heavily by the front door.

Kruse turned back to her, the gun still in his hand. This time it was pointed at her, and she was frozen. "Sorry, Frannie," he said as his finger tightened, and she closed her eyes.

The blasts were deafening, one and then another, and she waited for the blow to her chest, to be thrown backward and to the ground as Bridger had been. But nothing happened. She opened her eyes as Jerry crumpled to the floor. Blood stained the front of his shirt, and there was a neat hole in the center of his forehead.

Bridger lowered his weapon.

She ran to the door, falling to her knees beside him. Tears filled her eyes, blinding her, as she reached out and touched his face. "Weren't you supposed to wait for backup or something? Didn't you know there was a man with a gun in here? Dammit, Bridger, your mother will never forgive me if you die trying to save me."

"I'm not…going to die," he said, his voice strained. A large, warm hand reached out to dry her tears. Her vision cleared and she gathered the nerve to look down. He wore a thick black vest beneath his jacket, and a bullet was embedded in the material near the center of his chest.

"You're wearing a bullet-proof vest," she said, smiling weakly as she touched the protective gear.

"Yep." He tried to take a deep breath but couldn't quite manage it. "Harry called…cell phone." Each word was obviously an effort. "He said Kruse was…here, so I…I…"

"Don't talk," Frannie demanded. She gripped his arm,

hanging on, wanting more than anything to throw her arms around Bridger and hold him tight, afraid she'd hurt him if she did. A few seconds of silence passed, and it was almost more than she could stand.

"How do you feel?"

He locked deep brown eyes to hers. "Like I've been hit in the chest with a sledgehammer." His words were already coming easier, if not effortlessly.

She glanced to Jerry Kruse's lifeless body, and a terrifying thought nearly stopped her heart. "What if he'd shot you in the head? You idiot!" she said, suddenly angry. "You could've gotten yourself killed!"

He took her hand and held it tight, and worked his way into a straighter sitting position, so that he leaned back against the glass door. "Do you really think that I could sit outside where it's safe and wait for backup while you went and got yourself killed?"

"It would have been the smart thing to do," she said, but she couldn't stay angry. Her heart was still pounding too hard, the blood was rushing at an incredible rate through her veins, and she couldn't make herself look again at what was left of Jerry Kruse.

"It's done," he said softly. "You'll be okay now."

As if she would ever be *okay* without Bridger around! She loved him, she needed him, but it sounded suspiciously as if he were saying goodbye.

His eyes were locked on the body that was sprawled on the floor, the body she didn't want to look at again. The agony on his face came from much more than the ache in his chest, she knew.

"Tell me something, Frannie," he said, lifting the hand that still held a gun to point at the body. "How do you explain this to a kid like Joshua? How do you explain that sometimes the good guys turn out to be the bad guys?"

Sirens were approaching, and suddenly blue and red

lights flashed over everything in the store, over Bridger's face and Kruse's body and tables full of junk and treasure. Bridger held her hand tight, their fingers laced together, and even as the commotion increased behind them he didn't so much as turn his head to look out the window.

"Explain that, Frannie," he said softly.

"I can't," she whispered.

He looked like his heart was broken, and she didn't think there was anything she could say to fix it.

Chapter 17

Mal stared at the picture in front of him. It was propped against his computer monitor, at eye level.

Of all the photographs, this one was clearest. Jerry Kruse was grinning that fool's smile and shaking hands with a scumbag Mal knew was a drug dealer. That's where most of their money had come from. Drugs.

The photographs had helped them to round up what was left of the Decatur Legion for Liberty, all in a matter of thirty-six hours. They called themselves freedom fighters, domestic terrorists, but Mal knew them for what they were—redneck drug dealers with big plans

He could live with that. Bad guys came in all kinds of packages. It was Jerry Kruse's involvement that confused and angered him. What had turned him? Money? Power? There was no answer that made any sense to Mal and, by God, he wanted answers. He wanted there to be answers that were black-and-white, but everywhere he looked.. gray.

He picked up another photograph, one that had come in the mail yesterday. He and Frannie sat close together on the porch at the old farmhouse. She was holding a baby, cradling it as if it were the most precious thing in the world, and that baby was hanging onto his nose with viselike little fingers. And Frannie was laughing. Looking at him, happy and laughing and...hopeful. Always hopeful.

Harry came sauntering around the corner, two cups of coffee in his hands. "How are you feeling?" he asked brightly.

Mal didn't look up, but he placed the photo he'd been studying facedown on the desk. "Like I was kicked by a mule."

Harry set one cup of black coffee on Mal's desk and sipped at the other. "I talked to Frannie yesterday."

Mal looked up at his sergeant and friend. "How is she?"

"Fine. I asked her to have dinner with Paula and me sometime. Paula thought maybe we could introduce her to Peter."

"Peter?" Mal asked calmly.

"Paula's brother," Harry said with a smile. "You know, the one who just got divorced."

Mal picked up his coffee and took a sip. "So, what did she say?"

"She said no."

Why was he so damn relieved to hear that?

"You know," Harry said in that calm, soothing voice of his, the one that sometimes drove Mal mad, "she might wait for you for a while, but she won't wait forever."

"I know that." Mal muttered.

"She's too good for you."

"I know that, too."

"So, get your butt out of that chair and go sweep her off her feet. Frannie's pretty, she's smart, and for some reason she's crazy about you. She deserves to be swept off her feet at least once. Jeez,'' he said as he walked away. "Do I have to tell you how to do everything?''

Mal stared at the photograph of Kruse and the drug dealer, trying to make sense of it all.

It came to him, a good fifteen minutes later, that maybe he didn't have to.

Frannie stood at the counter and looked out over the nearly deserted store. Terri was arranging a new display of collectibles, and a single customer was sorting through some old magazines.

Jerry Kruse's body had been taken away days ago, and a large braided rug covered the bloodstain they hadn't been able to completely remove from the wooden floor.

The old Frannie would have run from this place and the horrifying memories of that afternoon. It had been hard, at first, to look around the room and not remember vividly how terrified she'd been, how her heart had almost stopped when she'd seen Bridger go down, how she'd seen a man die…but she wasn't running. That was her mother's solution, not hers.

Foolishly she kept expecting Bridger to come through the front door, smile at her and take her home. Romantic hogwash. She'd been right in leaving and giving him the choice. Otherwise, she would have always wondered if he cared for her at all.

Apparently, he didn't.

Harry had called a couple of times, to ask how she was getting along. He never mentioned Bridger, though he had suggested that she have dinner with him and Paula one evening. Paula had this really nice brother, who'd just gotten divorced. She wasn't interested.

The phone near her elbow rang, and she picked it up. "Terri's Trash and Treasure.''

There was a short pause, and she waited for the caller to say "wrong number" and hang up.

"Frannie Vaughn, please."

She smiled at the sound of the familiar voice. "Speaking."

There was another small pause, and she could almost see him sitting there at his desk, gathering his nerve for what came next. "This is Detective Malcolm Bridger. I don't know if you remember me or not, but we met a couple of weeks ago at Rick's."

She leaned against the counter. "I think I remember you."

"Yeah, well, I was just calling to see if you'd like to get together for dinner sometime."

Her heart did a funny little flip in her chest. "Detective Bridger, are you asking me out on a *date?*"

"Yeah. What do you say, Frannie?"

Yes! Only she shouldn't be so overly enthusiastic. "Maybe. Say when, and I'll check my calendar."

"Now."

"Now?" She laughed into the phone. To hell with trying to hide her enthusiasm. "Well, give me time to change, and I'll—"

"No need to change." He said confidently. "I think you look great in yellow. Is that new?"

Her head jerked up and immediately she saw him, standing on the other side of the glass door with a cell phone to his ear and a bunch of red roses in one hand. When her eye caught his he opened the door and stepped into the shop, and as she hung up the phone he pressed the end button on his cellular.

He handed her roses across the counter, and when he did, she saw that there was something hidden behind the roses—a large, multicolored lollipop. She took the roses in one hand and the lollipop on the other. "What's this?" She wagged the sucker in his direction and got a wry smile as a response.

"I'll tell you later."

Terri was more than willing to let Frannie go for the day, and together she and Bridger stepped onto the sidewalk. A breeze caught the skirt of her new yellow dress, and she was glad she'd decided to wear it today, rather than her usual blue jeans and casual top. She held the roses and the lollipop, and Bridger took her arm and steered her in the right direction. They passed his car and kept going.

She looked him up and down in his dark blue suit and white shirt and burgundy tie. Something was different.

"Do you feel naked?" she asked softly.

He glanced down to his belt where his weapon usually rested. It wasn't there now. "I didn't think I'd need it tonight."

"Probably not," she whispered with a smile.

They walked to Rick's, and Bridger paused before the door. The sign said Closed and the shade was down.

She was a little disappointed. Rick's wasn't the fanciest restaurant in town, but it was here she'd met Bridger. That made it a special place.

But Bridger didn't turn and walk way. He reached into his pocket and withdrew a single key, a key that fit the front door to Rick's. He unlocked the door, led Frannie inside and then locked it behind them.

She stepped into the main room, where candles burned at every table and a meal was laid out at the bar.

"I rented the place," Bridger said, his words soft behind her. "It's ours for the night."

"You were confident I'd say yes when you asked me out, weren't you?" she asked, her eyes on the romantic setting. There were more flowers here, and candles on the bar, and lollipops. Lots and lots of lollipops.

"Optimistic," Bridger whispered.

Frannie walked through the room, her back to Bridger. He had to care for her to go to so much trouble. *Optimistic.* She was almost certain there hadn't been so much as a smidgen of optimism in Bridger's body before he'd met her.

"It's beautiful."

"It's a date," Bridger said. "You said you wanted a date, and by God you're going to get one."

She turned to face him. In the soft light of the many candles he was beautiful. But then he'd always been beautiful to her because she loved him so much.

"Dinner," he said, gesturing to the bar and the meal that was laid out there. "And dancing." He reached into his pocket, drew out a roll of quarters and slapped them on the nearest table. "If we're going to do this dating thing we might as well do it right."

Frannie walked toward Bridger, needing, more than anything, a kiss. She'd craved a kiss, her mouth on his, his hand strong at her back. When she reached him he took the roses from her, and the lollipop, and set them beside the roll of quarters. Then he took his tie between two fingers and flipped it neatly into her hand.

She tugged gently, and he kissed her, knowing exactly what she needed, knowing without asking, without hesitating.

"I just have one protocol question," he whispered as he took his mouth from hers. "How many dates do we have to have before I can propose?"

"Propose what?"

He narrowed his dark eyes at her. "Marriage."

She placed her head against his chest. "Three, I think."

One hand was flat at her back, warm and comforting. "We danced the night we met, that has to count as a date. And I took you to meet my family, surely that qualifies."

"I guess it does," she whispered against his chest.

"So this is number three."

With a hand beneath her chin he forced her to look up and into his eyes. "I missed you." He whispered the confession. "At first I decided you were right. We could spend some time apart, make sure what we felt was real and not just something fleeting. But every day it hurt worse, like there was a hole in my chest."

She placed her hand over the center of his chest. "You were shot," she whispered.

"Well, that hurts, too, but that's not where it hurts the most," he said. "Where it really hurts is over to the left a little, right smack dab in the middle of my black hole."

She moved her hand, sliding it across his chest until it rested over his heart. "That's it," he whispered.

He reached into his pocket again and came up with a faded velvet box. He flicked it open with his thumb and presented her with a square-cut diamond solitaire set in white gold.

"This was my grandmother's. My mother said years ago that it was mine, when I wanted it." He smiled sheepishly. "I told her to give it to one of the girls because I'd never need it, but when I went out there this weekend to see if she still had it, she did. She wasn't at all surprised that I asked for it."

He took the ring from the box and took her hand, then held the ring over the tip of her finger.

"All you have to do is say yes." He looked her in the eye, dead on. She saw so many things there she loved—determination and longing, persistence and tenderness.

There was something missing, the one thing she didn't know if he could give her. She needed it. "Why?" she whispered.

The ring hovered over the tip of her finger, and Frannie stared at the mesmerizing sight. Her eyes were on the small, candlelit ring in his big hand, as her bare finger waited. All she had to was whisper one word. One simple little word. She waited for an answer to her question. Bridger knew what she needed, didn't he?

"Because I need you," he whispered. "Because without you I'm lost." He took a deep breath and looked her in the eye. "Because I love you."

She smiled. "I love you, too, Bridger. Yes."

He slipped the ring onto her finger, where it fit perfectly. "We can get married this weekend at the farm," he said as he took her left hand in his. "Mom's already called everybody in the family and invited them, and she ordered a cake and contacted her minister. Parker wants to give you away. I hope you don't mind."

Frannie laughed. How could she complain? It sounded perfect. "Of course I don't mind." She leaned close, glancing up at the hard and beautiful face that was all hers. "Such plans you made. You were pretty sure of yourself, Bridger."

He bent to kiss her again. "Optimistic, Frannie. Optimistic."

Epilogue

If anyone had told him, years ago, that he had an appalling weakness for blue-eyed blondes, he never would have believed it. Ah, but he did have a weakness. Especially, he'd discovered, for very short blondes who had big blue eyes and freckles and curling pigtails, who made him necklaces out of macaroni and called him Daddy.

"Daddy, Daddy!" Mal looked up from the barbecue to see his two girls running toward him. Angela, a bubbly five-year-old, was in the lead as always, and Kate, three years old and always behind—because she kept stopping to pick up pretty rocks and discarded bottle caps and pennies—was close. Harry and Paula's redheaded Chelsea, who was six months older than Angela, brought up the rear, a misused doll hanging from her hands.

"Mommy says it's time." Angela said, looking up at him with serious wide eyes.

"Tell Mommy the burgers aren't ready yet." Mal glanced at Harry, who was sprawled in a chaise longue and sipping on a beer. "Being eight and a half months' pregnant makes her a little cranky. And if it's time to eat, it's time to eat *now*."

The doctor had assured them that this would be another girl. The nursery was a freshly painted pink, and Frannie had been going through all the little outfits Kate had outgrown so quickly.

Paula left her chair, a big grin on her face. "Frannie chased me out of the kitchen awhile back. Maybe if everything else is ready she'll let me back in."

The girls were running toward the house, their short legs pumping, Paula following at a distance.

Harry stared at his wife's retreating form. "House looks good since you painted it," he said, taking another sip of beer. "I had begun to think there was no hope for this old place, but you've got it looking good."

It was Frannie's dream house, big and rambling and full of old things and little girls. There was a big garden that had just been planted with vegetables the girls had picked out themselves, including a striped tomato they found fascinating, and the azaleas against the house were in full bloom. Oddly enough, this was Mal's dream house, too. He'd just not known it until he got here.

Angela came bursting through the back screen door a minute later. "Daddy!" she yelled as she bounded from the porch, past the blooming pink azaleas. "Mommy said let Uncle Harry finish the darn burgers. It's time *now*."

Understanding crept into Mal's brain, and he spared a quick glance to Harry. "She's not due for two weeks." He dropped the spatula onto the grill as Harry slowly left his chair, groaning only once with the effort.

"I'll finish the burgers and feed the girls and take them home with us," Harry said in his most soothing voice. "Just give us a call when baby girl Bridger number three arrives."

Mal ran into the house, expecting Frannie to be waiting by the door with her bag in hand. Her first two deliveries had been fast, and she took no chances. That bag had been packed for a month.

But she wasn't waiting.

Angela and Chelsea were standing at the door of the master bedroom, eyes wide and forgotten dolls hanging from their little hands. From beyond that door, he heard Frannie's raised voice.

"Where *is* he?"

Kate came running from the downstairs bathroom, her little legs pumping, her arms filled with sloppily folded towels. "Here are the towels, Aunt Paula," she said, barely able to see over the top of the stack.

Mal took the towels from Kate and sent the girls upstairs to their room to play. He stepped into the spacious master bedroom that he and Frannie had shared for the past four and a half years. His heart stopped when he saw her. She was sitting up in the bed, a sheet draped over her knees and her rounded stomach, her lightly curling ponytail hanging over one shoulder.

Frannie was right in the middle of a contraction. One hand rested over that tremendous stomach, and she was taking short, shallow breaths.

Paula stood beside the bed, talking on the phone. "No, you don't understand," she snapped. "She's having this baby right now."

"Now?" Mal repeated softly, his eyes on Frannie.

The contraction over, she took a deep breath and actually smiled weakly at him. "You do know how to deliver a baby, don't you, Bridger?"

"No." He tossed the towels onto the foot of the bed. "Come on. We can be at the hospital in ten minutes."

"I don't have ten minutes."

As if to prove her point she had another contraction.

Taking short, ragged breaths, she glanced at Paula. "I love you like a sister," she said hoarsely, "but get out."

"But—" Mal began.

"Just you and me, Bridger," Frannie whispered. "Just you and me."

Paula apparently didn't think twice. She thrust the cordless phone at Mal. "They're on their way, but I don't think they're going to make it."

He told the operator on the other end to hang on, and set the phone on the table as Paula quietly crept from the room and closed the door.

"Why didn't you tell me you were in labor?" He moved to the end of the bed.

"I thought I was having false pains, like last time," she said breathlessly. There was a sheen of sweat on her face. "They were irregular and not so bad, and by the time they got regular and bad, it was too late." She fastened her eyes on him. "You're a cop. You're supposed to know how to do this."

She had another contraction, and this one looked bad. The strain on Frannie's face was more than he could stand. Dammit, this had been hard enough in a delivery room full of doctors and nurses who knew what they were doing!

He very carefully lifted the sheet she'd draped over her knees.

"A head," he whispered.

He grabbed the phone and returned to the end of the bed. "I'm going to have some badges and some butts if somebody doesn't get here *now!*"

"Lieutenant Bridger," answered the much too serene 9-1-1 operator. "Nice to talk to you again. Stay cool, sir, it's just a baby. I can talk you through this."

"I don't want you to talk me though this, I want—"

Frannie let out a scream and Mal dropped the phone.

He didn't have a choice. This little girl was coming, and

she was coming now. He climbed into the bed, balancing on his knees, and looked over the sheet to Frannie. "Okay, honey, we're going to have this baby." His voice was relaxed, and for some reason he was suddenly calm.

He'd been in the delivery room twice, but standing aside and watching was nothing to compare to actually delivering a child. He was terrified, he was elated, and the tears that sprang to his eyes surprised him.

"You're doing great," he said gruffly, glancing over the top of the sheet to see Frannie's face.

"So are you," she said breathlessly.

Watching Frannie going through labor had never been easy. She strained and he held his breath. She cringed and he hurt. She fastened her eyes on him and pushed, and he broke into a sweat. He cradled the head of his child as it came into this world.

"One more push," he whispered. "That's all we need."

The child was delivered into his hands, a tiny, fat-faced baby who let out a healthy cry and worked up an unhappy face.

"It's a boy," he whispered.

Frannie grinned. Sweating and breathing hard and looking as if she wanted nothing more than to collapse onto the bed and sleep for a week, she grinned at him. "A little Bridger."

Mal wrapped the baby in a towel and laid him on Frannie's chest, where he let out another hearty squall. Her hands settled shakily over the tiny bundle and she peeked at his face. "He looks a little grumpy," she said, "like his daddy. He looks like he wants to say, 'I was perfectly happy where I was. Why'd you have to go and ruin everything by making me come here?'" She glanced up with a wicked grin. "He looks like he's having a *very* bad day."

Mal smiled at her as he snatched the phone from the floor. "Now what?" he asked.

The operator instructed him, step-by-step, as to what came next. Fortunately, Frannie and the baby had both done remarkably well, and in a matter of minutes he was finished.

Mal hung up the phone and took a chair beside the bed. Frannie turned her head his way and smiled again. "Looks like the doctor missed something in the sonogram."

"Looks that way." He leaned over and kissed her gently. "I love you." The words came easily to him these days.

"I love you too, Bridger," she said breathlessly.

He took the baby from her and peeled back a corner of the towel to study the perfect little face. "I never expected that I'd be the one to deliver you," he said to his son. "I never even expected that you'd be here. Frannie," he glanced up sharply, "we don't have a boy's name picked out."

"Malcolm James Bridger, Junior, of course," she said, and her eyes drifted closed.

"We can call him James," Mal added.

"Or Jimmy."

"Or Jamie."

Frannie barely opened one eye. "Or little Bridger."

Outside, the faint wail of ambulances signaled the tardy arrival of the paramedics. Mal leaned over and kissed Frannie quickly. "He's just a kid. What does he know? It's been a good day."

"The best," she whispered.

*   *   *   *   *

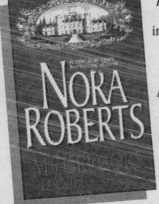
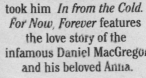
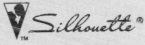

Silhouette Romance proudly presents an all-new, original series...

Six friends dream of marrying their bosses in this delightful new series

Come see how each month, office romances lead to happily-ever-after for six friends.

In January 1999—
THE BOSS AND THE BEAUTY by Donna Clayton

In February 1999—
THE NIGHT BEFORE BABY by Karen Rose Smith

In March 1999—
HUSBAND FROM 9 to 5 by Susan Meier

In April 1999—
THE EXECUTIVE'S BABY by Robin Wells

In May 1999—
THE MARRIAGE MERGER by Vivian Leiber

In June 1999—
I MARRIED THE BOSS by Laura Anthony

Only from

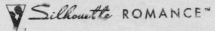
Silhouette ROMANCE™

Available wherever Silhouette books are sold.

Look us up on-line at: http://www.romance.net   SRSLTB1

INTIMATE MOMENTS®

Silhouette®

and

DOREEN ROBERTS

invite you to the wonderful world of

RODEO MEN

A secret father, a passionate protector,
a make-believe groom—these cowboys are
husbands waiting to happen....

HOME IS WHERE THE COWBOY IS
IM #909, February 1999

A FOREVER KIND OF COWBOY
IM #927, May 1999

THE MAVERICK'S BRIDE
IM #945, August 1999

Don't miss a single one!

Available at your favorite retail outlet.

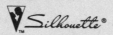

Silhouette®

Coming in May 1999

BABY Fever

by
New York Times Bestselling Author

KASEY MICHAELS

When three sisters hear their biological
clocks ticking, they know it's
time for action.

But who will they get to father their babies?

**Find out how the road to motherhood
leads to love in this brand-new collection.**

Available at your favorite retail outlet.

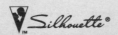

COMING NEXT MONTH

#925 CATTLEMAN'S PROMISE—Marilyn Pappano
Heartbreak Canyon

Guthrie Harris was shocked when Olivia Miles and her twin daughters
showed up on his Oklahoma ranch—with a deed!—and claimed it was *their*
home. But since they had nowhere else to go, the longtime loner let them
stay. And the longer Olivia stuck around, the less Guthrie wanted her to
leave—his home *or* his heart.

#926 CLAY YEAGER'S REDEMPTION—Justine Davis
Trinity Street West

Clay Yeager hadn't meant to trespass on Casey Scott's property—but he
was glad he had. The emotions this ex-cop had kept buried for so long were
back in full force. Then Casey became a stranger's target, and Clay knew
the time had come to protect his woman. He was done with moving on—
he was ready to move in!

#927 A FOREVER KIND OF COWBOY—Doreen Roberts
Rodeo Men

Runaway heiress Lori Ashford had little experience when it came to men.
So when she fell for rugged rodeo rider Cord McVane, what she felt was
something she'd never known existed. But would the brooding cowboy ever
see that the night she'd discovered passion in his arms was just the
beginning—of forever?

#928 THE TOUGH GUY AND THE TODDLER—Diane Pershing
Men in Blue

Detective Dominic D'Annunzio thought nothing could penetrate his
hardened heart—until beautiful but haunted Jordan Carlisle needed his
assistance. But Jordan wasn't just looking for help, she was looking for
miracles. And the closer they came to the truth, the more Dom began
wondering what was in charge of this case—his head or his heart?

#929 HER SECOND CHANCE FAMILY—Christine Scott
Families Are Forever

Maggie Conrad and her son were finally on their own—*and* on the run.
But the small town of Wyndchester offered the perfect hideaway. Then the
new sheriff, Jason Gallagher, moved in next door, and Maggie feared her
secret wouldn't stay that way for long. Could Maggie keep her past hidden
while learning that love *was* better the second time around?

#930 KNIGHT IN A WHITE STETSON—Claire King
Way Out West

Calla Bishop was desperate to save her family's ranch. And as the soon-to-
be-wife of a wealthy businessman, she was about to secure her birthright.
Then she hired Henry Beckett, and it wasn't long before this wrangler had
roped himself one feisty cowgirl. But would Henry's well-kept secret cause
Calla to hand over her beloved ranch—and her guarded heart?